Charles T. Newton, D. E Colnaghi

Travels & Discoveries in the Levant

Volume 2

Charles T. Newton, D. E Colnaghi

Travels & Discoveries in the Levant
Volume 2

ISBN/EAN: 9783337344160

Printed in Europe, USA, Canada, Australia, Japan

Cover: Foto ©Andreas Hilbeck / pixelio.de

More available books at **www.hansebooks.com**

TRAVELS & DISCOVERIES

IN THE LEVANT.

BY

C. T. NEWTON, M.A.

KEEPER OF THE GREEK AND ROMAN ANTIQUITIES, BRITISH MUSEUM.

WITH NUMEROUS ILLUSTRATIONS.

IN TWO VOLUMES.—VOL. II.

DAY & SON, LIMITED,
6, GATE STREET, LONDON, W.C.
1865.

CONTENTS.

LETTER XXX.

PAGE

Recruiting for Land Transport Corps—Visit to Kalloni—
Monasteries there—Byzantine Paintings—Ancient Custom
of sticking Coins on Pictures—Inscription at Ennea
Kamaris; at Daphia—Character of the Plain at Kalloni... 1

XXXI.

Visit to Ayasso and Plumari—*Panegyris* at Ayasso—Votive
Offerings in the Church there—Their conversion *pro bono
publico*—Similar application of Sacred Treasures in Anti-
quity—Miraculous Cures of the Sick attributed to the
Panagia of Ayasso—Village of Plumari—Costume of the
Women—Archbishop of Mytilene—His account of Ancient
Customs in Macedonia—Inscription at Plagia, near Plumari
—Church of Agios Phokas—Promontory Brisa—Hot
Springs at Basilica—Mediæval Fortress near Misagro—
Ancient Customs observed there—District of Hiera—Re-
mains of Ancient City of that Name—Antimony mine ... 6

XXXII.

Taking of Sebastopol—Visit of Colonels Shelley and O'Reilly
—Their Account of the Present State of Asia Minor—
Unedited Coins of Methymna and Eresos—Last Exploit
of the Smyrna Robbers—Vigorous Measures for their Ex-
tirpation taken by Colonel Storks 15

XXXIII.

Visit to Constantinople—The Bosphorus—Illustration of a
Metaphor in Aristophanes, taken from the tunny-fishers—
Collection of Coins of Baron Tecco—Rare Archaic Coin of

PAGE.

Macedonia— Excavation round the Base of the Bronze
Serpent in the Hippodrome—History of the Monument—
Results of the Excavation—Discovery of Inscription on
the Folds of the Serpent — Historical Interest of this
Inscription—Identity of this Monument with the Serpent
dedicated by the Greeks at Delphi—Character of the Composition—Conversion of the Serpent into a Fountain during
the Byzantine Empire—Further Excavations in the Hippodrome—Reliefs round Base of Obelisk of Theodosius—
Destruction of Ancient Monuments at Constantinople, not
exclusively the work of the Turks—Tradition respecting
the Palladium said to have been placed under the Burnt
Column...   21

XXXIV.

Cruise in the Medusa — Rhodes — Marmarice — Ruins of
Ancient Acropolis—Journey to Mughla—Djova, the Ancient Bargasa—Hellenic Remains—Mughla—The Acre-
polis—Probably the site of the Ancient Tarmiani—Return
to Rhodes — Calymnos — Budrum — Second Journey to
Mughla—Guverjilik—Mylasa—Eski Hissar—Lagina—Remains of Temple of Hekate—Frieze—Inscriptions—Bargylia—Return to Budrum   39

XXXV.

Castle at Budrum—Plan of the Fortifications—Tombs at
Kislalik — Various Modes of Interment — Discovery of
Vases, Coins, and other Antiquities—Return to England—
Expedition to Budrum for the purpose of Removing the
Lions from the Castle   58

XXXVI.

Arrival of the Gorgon at Budrum—Excavation in Field of
Mehemet Chiaoux—Discovery of Terra-cotta Figures on
probable site of Temple of Demeter—Excavation of Agia
Marina, probably the site of a Gymnasium—Earthquake
and Explosion at Rhodes.................   68

XXXVII.

PAGE

Discovery of Roman Mosaic Pavements in Field of Hadji Captan—Subjects of these Mosaics—Statue found under them—Bronze Lamp found in Well—Manner of taking up the Mosaics 75

XXXVIII.

Discovery of the Site of the Mausoleum—Correspondence of its Position with the Statement of Vitruvius—Progress of the Excavations—Difficulties in obtaining the Right of Digging—Plan of the Basement of the Mausoleum—Discovery of Torso of Equestrian Figure, Slabs of Frieze, and other sculptures—Staircase—*Alabaston* with name of Xerxes—Removal of Lions from the Castle 84

XXXIX.

Turkish Wrestlers 105

XL.

Further Excavations on Site of Mausoleum—Imam's Field—Discovery of Steps of Pyramid ; Colossal Horse ; Statues—Departure of the Gorgon—Description of the Sculptures from the Mausoleum—Statue of Mausolus—Female Figure —Chariot Group—Wall of *Peribolos*—Architectural Marbles—The *Pteron*—The Pyramid—The Basement—Guichard's Narrative of the Destruction of the Mausoleum by the Knights—The Frieze of the Order—Other Friezes—Remains of Colour on these Marbles—Equestrian Group—Lions 108

XLI.

Discovery of Eastern *Peribolos* Wall—Excavation on Site of Temple of Mars—Description of Halicarnassus by Vitruvius compared with remains *in situ*—The *Agora*—The Palace of Mausolus—His Arsenal—Temple of Venus and Mercury —Fortress of Salmacis—Inscription relating to People of Salmacis—Gymnasium of Apollo and Ptolemy—Walls of Halicarnassus—Ancient Cemeteries—Arrival of Mr. R. P. Pullan 137

XLII.

PAGE

Visit to Branchidæ—The Temple of Apollo—The Sacred
Way—The Avenue of Archaic Seated Statues—Inscription
on Statue of Chares, ruler of Teichioussa—This figure the
earliest example of a Greek Iconic Statue—These Statues
probably the work of Artists who had studied in Egypt—
Connection of Egypt with Asia Minor in the reigns of Psammetichos I. and Amasis—Lion and Sphinx—Dedication on
Back of Lion—Probable Date of these Figures—Inscriptions relating to Temple of Apollo—Dedications made
by Seleukos II. and other Monarchs—Fate of the Sacred
Gens called Branchidæ—Probable Date of the Building
of the Temple — Its *Hieron*—Return of the Supply to
Budrum 147

XLIII.

Establishment at Cnidus—Mehemet Ali, the Aga of Datscha 160

XLIV.

Description of the Site of Cnidus—Triopion—Harbours—
Acropolis—Temples on the Continent — Excavation in
lower Theatre—*Temenos* of Demeter and other Infernal
Deities—Discovery of Statuette of Persephone—Inscription
relating to the Dedication of a Temple to Demeter and
Persephone—Seated Statue of Demeter—Leaden Tablets
inscribed with *Diræ*—Elliptical Chamber—Marble Pigs—
Votive Breasts—Glass—Fictile Lamps—Female Statue,
perhaps Demeter Achæa—Base inscribed with Dedication
to Pluto and other Infernal Deities—General Summary of
the Results of this Excavation—Probable Date of the
Temple—The Sculptures may be of the School of Praxiteles
—Physical Peculiarities of the Site suitable for a Temple
dedicated to the Infernal Deities—Myth of Demeter and
Persephone—*Triopia Sacra* 167

XLV.

Final Excavations on Site of Mausoleum—Eastern *Peribolos*
Wall—Lower Soil within the *Peribolos*—Discovery of
Ancient Tombs — Reasons for believing that the Site
of the Mausoleum was originally a Quarry in which

PAGE

Interments took place—Geological Character of the Hill on the Base of which the Mausoleum stood—Galleries for Drainage—An English Sailor's Account of the Diggings —Departure from Budrum...................................... 200

XLVI.

Discovery of Colossal Lion near Cnidus—Doric Tomb from which he had fallen—Grand Effect of this Lion in the open air—Difficulties in its Embarkation 214

XLVII.

Description of the Doric Tomb—Chamber within it—Vaulting similar to that of the Treasury of Minyas, as described by Pausanias—The Cnidian Monument may commemorate the Naval Victory of Conon—The Lion of Chæroneia— Visit from Pirates—Difficulty in the Transmission of Money in the Levant 221

XLVIII.

Second Visit to Branchidæ—Removal of the Statues from the Sacred Way—Excavations on the Way—Tombs— Archaic Dedication by Sons of Anaximander—Anecdote of the Nicariotes—Return to Cnidus—Departure of Supply 231

XLIX.

Temple of Venus—Reasons for not admitting Leake's Site for the Aphrodisium—Inscription to Artemidoros—His son Theopompos—Discovery of supposed Gymnasium—Inscription relating to Hermes ; to Artemis Iakynthotrophos— Doric *Stoa*—Inscription with name of Theopompos—Discovery of Odeum ; of Temple of Muses—Dedication to Muses ; to Apollo Pythios ; to Athene Nikephoros and Hestia Boulaia—Probable Site of the Demiourgion......... 236

L.

Triopion Promontory—Discovery of Roman Tomb ; Statue ; Sarcophagi—Inscriptions relating to the Senate of Cnidus— Changes in the Constitution of this Body mentioned by Aristotle—The *Demiourgos* of Cnidus 246

LI. PAGE

Eastern Necropolis—Ancient Road—Tombs—Discovery of
Inscription relating to the *Temenos* of Antigonos—An-
cient Christian Church—Inscriptions in the Pavement—
Destruction of Pagan Monuments by the early Christians—
Excavation in large sepulchral *Peribolos*—Recall of the
Expedition 251

LII.

Return of Lieut. Smith—Difficulty of obtaining Money, from
non-arrival of Coquette—Excursions in the Doric Peninsula
—Hellenic Wall near Yasiköi—Ancient Bridge east of
Chesmaköi—Fortress of Kounya Kalessi—Inscription at
Dum Galli—Remains of Acanthus—Scenery in the Doric
Peninsula—Character of the Turkish Peasantry—Curious
Tradition of a Greek Myth 257

LIII.

Visit of H.R.H. Prince Alfred to Cnidus and Budrum in the
Euryalus—Return of the Supply—Departure for Malta—
Discoveries on the Site of Kamiros by Messrs. Salzmann
and Biliotti—Arrival at Malta................................. 264

LIST OF PLATES.

—◆◆◆—

FRONTISPIECE.—Map of Caria.

Plate.   To face Page

1. Plan of Halicarnassus (Budrum)   59

2. Plan of Site of Mausoleum.................................   93

3. Sections of ditto   94

4. Fragment from group of mounted Persian Warrior.
   Photographed by F. BEDFORD, from a Drawing by
   Mrs. C. T. NEWTON.......................................   96

5. Amazon from Frieze of Mausoleum, from a Photograph
   by B. SPACKMAN   96

6. Head of Mausolus, from a Photograph by B. SPACKMAN   111

7. Female head, Mausoleum, from a Photograph by
   B. SPACKMAN   112

8. Statue of Mausolus. Photographed by F. BEDFORD,
   from a Drawing by Mrs. C. T. NEWTON   114

9. Mausolus, side view. Photographed by F. BEDFORD,
   from a Drawing by Mrs. C. T. NEWTON   114

10. Female Figure found under Pyramid steps, Mausoleum.
    Photographed by F. BEDFORD, from a Drawing by
    Mrs. C. T. NEWTON......................................   116

11. Colossal Horse from Chariot group, Mausoleum.
    Photographed by F. BEDFORD, from a Drawing by
    Mrs. C. T. NEWTON......................................   118

Plate.   *To face Page*
' 12. Details of the Order, Mausoleum 123

I 13.⎫
   14. ⎬Frieze of the Order, Mausoleum. Photographed by ⎧ 128
   15.⎭ F. BEDFORD, from a Drawing by Mrs. C. T. NEWTON ⎩ 130

16. Figure from Frieze representing Chariot-race, Mauso-
    leum. Photographed by F. BEDFORD, from a Drawing
    by Mrs. C. T. NEWTON 132

I 17. Lion's Head, Mausoleum. Photographed by F. BED-
    FORD, from a Drawing by Mrs. C. T. NEWTON 136

' 18. Budrum.—Harbour and Castle. Aquatint by W. J.
    ALAIS, from a Photograph by B. SPACKMAN............ 140

⎰ 19. View of Budrum taken from the hill above the
    Theatre. Aquatint by W. J. ALAIS, from a Photo-
    graph by B. SPACKMAN 140

20. Plan and View of Sacred Way, Branchidæ 149

, 21. Plan of Cnidus 168

22. Plan of Temenos of Demeter, Cnidus 192

23. Lion Tomb, Cnidus 223

LIST OF WOODCUTS.

—--◦◦•—

	PAGE
1. Silver Coin of Methymna	19
2. Idem of Eresos	19
3–5. Three Silver Macedonian Dodekadrachms	24
6. Bronze Lamp found in Well, Halicarnassus	78
7. Small Conical object found *ibid.*	79
8. View of Stair and Flanking Wall, Mausoleum	97
9. Bronze Dowel from Great Stone, *ibid.*	98
10. The same, End View	98
11, 12. Head of Colossal Horse, Bronze Bridle	111
13. Chariot-wheel, Mausoleum	118
14. Bronze Cramp from Pyramid Step	121
15–18. Ornaments of Chairs of Statues from Sacred Way, Branchidæ..	150-51
19. Plan of Entrance to Theatre, Cnidus	173
20, 21. Glass Phials from Temenos of Demeter, *ibid.*	182-83
22, 23. Lamps, *identidem*	184-85
24. Stone Spout, *identidem*	191
25. Ivory Elephant from Mausoleum	201
26, 27. Vase in form of Female Head, Iron Dagger, Mausoleum	204
28. Bronze Grating, Mausoleum	207
29. *Lekythos* from Lion Tomb, Cnidus	225

ERRATUM.

Page 81, line 21, *for* "glaze" *read* "glue."

TRAVELS

AND

DISCOVERIES IN THE LEVANT.

LETTER XXX.

MYTILENE, *July* 20, 1855.

SINCE my return from Calymnos I have been
much occupied with enrolling recruits for the Land
Transport Corps, and shipping them off for the
Dardanelles, where they remain at the *dépôt* till
they are organized for service in the Crimea. As I
have to give them each £1 bounty money on their
enlisting, and as they are very ready to desert, I am
never happy till they are shipped off. How such a
motley lot of vagabonds as are now collected at the
Dardanelles will ever be kept together and drilled
into shape is very difficult to imagine. The Alba-
nians, who have enlisted in great numbers, are
already beginning to give a good deal of trouble.
About 200 of them deserted the other day, and
nearly succeeded in sacking the hospital at Renköi.

I went last week to the group of villages called
Kalloni, at the head of the gulf of the same name,
which I have already noticed in the account of my
visit to Ereso (I. pp. 101-2).

B

This district forms one of the three cazas or provinces into which the Turks have divided Mytilene, and is governed by a Mudir, assisted by a Mejlis and Cadi.

In the plain of Kalloni are seven villages lying close together, — Daphia, Keramia, Papiana, Sumaria, Achyrona, Argenna, and Agios Cosmas, or Tzumali.[1] The name of Kalloni is given to the whole group. The most important of them is Achyrona, where the Archbishop of Methymna resides in a large uncomfortable house, with little of the dignity which we should associate with an episcopal dwelling. The diocese of Methymna extends over the northern part of the island. The revenues of the see amount to about £1,300 a year, or one-half that of the see of Mytilene.

The present Archbishop is a good specimen of his class, and received us very hospitably. On riding into his courtyard, I found his secretary, a good-looking young monk, walking up and down, reading a French translation of Locke, of whose philosophy he seemed to have a clearer idea than could have been anticipated, considering the uncivilized society in which he dwells.

At the distance of about a mile and a half from Achyrona are two monasteries, one for monks, the other for nuns, founded by a certain St. Ignatius, about A.D. 1500. That for monks, called "the Monastery of the Meadow," τοῦ λειμῶνος, and dedicated to St. Michael, is pleasantly situated in a little valley surrounded by hills. It is an irregular stone building running round a courtyard. The chambers of the monks are on an upper story, to which stone steps give access, as in a *pyrgo*. Over the entrance gate is a fresco representing St. Michael. Formerly there were a hundred and fifty monks here, but now not above one third of that number. They are governed by an Hegoumenos or Prior, of very unprepossessing and dirty aspect. At 11 a.m., when I first called on him, he was still in bed, and there was about the whole monastery a look of squalid sloth which disgusted me much. There is a small collection of MSS. here, which I had only time to glance at. The books which I opened were chiefly old services of the Greek Church. I noticed a 4to MS. on paper, of the 15th century, entitled Ἀριστοτέλους Φυσικὴ ἀκρόασις, much wormed and in bad condition. It contains the first four books and part of the fifth of the Physics. On a previous visit, Colnaghi noticed a MS. of the New Testament illuminated with a miniature of St. Mark, much injured, but in a bold style. He thought that the age of this MS. might be the 10th or 11th century. On cross-examining the Hegoumenos, I found him very little disposed to give information about the collection of MSS.

The church of the monastery contains some frescoes executed by monks of Mount Athos in the 18th century. Between the nave and the chancel is a richly-carved wooden screen, the work of native artists and of the same period as the frescoes.

The nunnery at Kalloni is a penitentiary, to which ladies who have led naughty lives are banished from Mytilene. All the specimens of the sex, however, who were exhibited to me here were so very old, ugly, and repulsive, that if they had ever done anything wrong, it must have been a very long time ago. They were beguiling the long summer hours with knitting and spinning, by which they maintain themselves. They do not live in common; each nun has her own chamber and a little garden, which she cultivates herself.

Attached to the monastery is a small church elaborately decorated inside with pictures of the Panagia and various saints, in which the old Byzantine style of painting has been handed down with Chinese fidelity from the time of Cimabue. In the porch are some mural paintings with subjects from the Old Testament. Here is also represented the trial of the celebrated heretic Arius before the emperor Constantine at the council of Nicæa. In the church are several scenes from the life of the Virgin, and representations of the different parables in the New Testament. Among these I particularly noticed the picture of the Broad and Narrow Gate, in which a lady dressed in red and green has given her hand to a fantastic devil, and is tripping down the broad path at the head of a goodly company; while a number of monks are creeping with infinite difficulty through the low entrance of a mediæval fortress.

I observed that a picture of the Panagia had a gold Turkish coin stuck like a beauty-spot on the cheek, and from the chain hung a little silver hand with a list of names attached to it. I inquired what all these things meant, and was told that the coins and the hand were votive offerings made by sick people, and the writing was a list of the names of invalids cured by the saint to whose picture the paper was attached. This custom illustrates an expression in a Greek inscription, which contains a list of offerings, *anathemata*, in the temple of Amphiaraos, in Bœotia, and gives direction for the repair of such of them as required it.[2] Among these offerings are mentioned silver ornaments from which coins had fallen off. These coins had probably been attached to votive objects, in the same way as they are to this day at Kalloni.

About half an hour from Achyrona is a bridge called Ennea Kamaris, where is a Byzantine inscription referring to the building of the bridge.[3] In the neighbouring village of Daphia I found an inscription on a step outside a mosque, recording how one Claudius Lucianus, of Alabanda, dedicated a hound to the Artemis of Thermæ.[4] In a garden at Achyrona I noticed the capital of a large Corinthian column.

The plain at the head of the Gulf of Kalloni, now called Campo, is formed by alluvial deposit, and the part of it to the east of the group of the villages is evidently of recent formation, as will be seen by reference to the Admiralty chart, where a lagune is marked. Small rocky eminences rise like islands out of this monotonous level, which is traversed by a raised causeway. This must be that plain of Methymna mentioned by Strabo, for the country immediately round Molivo is rocky and barren. The city of Napé, situated, according to the same author, in this plain, probably occupied the site of one of the small rocky eminences which overlook it.

XXXI.

LAST week, having occasion to go to Plumari, on the southern coast, I took the opportunity of exploring some of the district lying between the gulfs of Olivieri and Kalloni. My first halting-place was Ayasso, where we arrived in the middle of a great festival, or *Panegyris*, celebrated there every year in this month. It was formerly frequented by an immense concourse of people from the neighbouring islands and continent; but the attendance has much diminished of late years.

A great sale of manufactured goods takes place at this festival; so that it serves the purpose of a fair. During its duration, the church is used as an inn, and the women are allowed to sleep there at night. When I entered it on the second day of the *Panegyris*, a multitude of both sexes were lying about on the pavement eating and drinking. Towards the close of the festival the Archbishop arrives, and drives out this *profanum vulgus* from the church, which is then duly purified. At Rhodes, as I have already mentioned in previous letters, more suitable accommodation is provided for the reception of the visitors at the feasts held at Zambika and Kremastò. (See I. p. 184.)

The pilgrims who thus profane the church of Our Lady of Ayasso, have, however, made some atonement by the value of their votive offerings at her shrine. These offerings are allowed to accumulate till they amount to a large sum, when they are converted into money. The priests receive a portion as their emolument, and the rest is expended in some public work for the benefit of the community.

It is by this discreet application of sacred things to secular purposes that the village of Ayasso has been supplied with an excellent aqueduct. A large school at Morea has been built from similar resources.

Such a mode of appropriating the treasures which piety had invested was not unknown to the ancient Greeks; but they regarded such resources as only to be used in cases of extreme emergency, when the safety of the state required it. In the Peloponnesian war, Pericles told the Athenians that the ornaments of the Chryselephantine statue of Pallas Athene, weighing forty talents of pure gold, were so attached as to be removable, if it were necessary, and that the votive objects, deposits, and sacred plate in the temples of Athens amounted to more than five hundred talents. These he reckons among the resources of the state, only to be resorted to in case of need, and if so used, to be replaced on the first return of prosperity.

In a later age, when religious feeling was much weakened among the Greeks, Dionysios the Elder, of Syracuse, had no such pious scruples. He stripped the gods of their golden mantles and wreaths, substituting ordinary ones, such as mortals wear; he took the gold cups out of the very hands of the statues, and having persuaded the women of Syracuse to propitiate Demeter by dedicating to her all their jewels, he took the liberty of borrowing these offerings from the goddess immediately afterwards. These pilferings were far surpassed by the audacious sacrilege of the Phocians, who a few years later sacked the vast treasures stored up at Delphi. It is clear, therefore, that, though the ancients regarded their temples as banks of deposit, the ruler who appropriated these offerings to state uses without due cause was sure to incur the charge of sacrilege. It was as if the Bank of England were to invest their sacred metallic reserve in ordinary commercial speculations.

The Panagia of Ayasso is held in special reverence as possessing the power of miraculously curing the sick or insane, who are brought to the church and left to pass the Saturday night there, the result of which is a perfect cure on the Sunday morning.

This custom seems a relic of the ancient ἐγκοίμησις, or *incubatio*, which I have described in a former letter in my account of the Amphiaraïon. (See I. p. 30.) The church at Ayasso is one of the finest in Mytilene; two rows of seven columns divide the interior into a nave and two aisles. The altar-screen is of polished grey marble; in the panels are portraits of the Panagia and other saints.

From Ayasso I rode along the base of Mount Olympus through a picturesque and beautiful country, full of rushing torrents and park-like glades, shaded by immense chestnut-trees, whose ample verdure shut out the fierce rays of an August sun. The lower ravines were fringed with a rich luxuriant growth of pear and other fruit-trees; the atmosphere was deliciously cool and bracing, like that of the lower levels of the island in November.

As I crossed a high ridge, I saw the coast of Asia Minor stretching far away towards Smyrna and Scio, and behind me a most picturesque background, broken into endless ravines by the intersecting spurs of Mount Olympus. As we descended towards Plumari, the rich forest timber gradually dwindled away into a few scanty pines scattered over a wild and barren district.

The village, or small town, of Plumari, formerly called Potamo, is picturesquely situated on a bold cliff by the mouth of a little river. It contains about four thousand inhabitants, who trade in olive oil and corn. This village has an aspect of stir and activity about it which is rare in Mytilene. The inhabitants are a fine race; but notwithstanding their healthy appearance, leprosy, λώβα, is very prevalent here. The dress of the women is very picturesque. They wear bright scarlet trousers, and jackets embroidered with gold.

I was hospitably entertained here by the Archbishop of Mytilene, who is now making his annual progress through the island to collect his dues. He has lived much in Macedonia, and told me some curious particulars about the peasantry there, who have retained many ancient customs which have nearly disappeared in the Archipelago.

A marriage in Macedonia is in this wise. On the wedding morning, the bride proceeds on horseback

from her home to the bridegroom's house, after
taking leave of her parents, on which occasion a
loaf is cut in half, one portion being left in her
old home, the other taken with her.   Before
quitting her own village, she takes a solemn
farewell of all the inhabitants, old and young,
kissing their hands and asking their pardon, if she
has wronged any of them.   She then sets out on
her journey, conducted by her brothers, or nearest
of kin, one of whom walks on either side, with his
hand on her bridle, and holding out two daggers
crossed to avert all evil influences.   When she
arrives at the bridegroom's house, he entreats her
to dismount, an invitation which she declines by
shaking her head, in token that she has arrived
portionless and that she looks to him for a dowry.
He then offers a lamb ; then, a second lamb ; the
lady still shakes her head ; and so they go on with
a succession of bids and refusals till a satisfactory
bargain is struck.   Then the bride is taken into the
courtyard, still on horseback, and her horse led
round a fire three times to purify her from evil
spirits, a ceremony which recalls the ancient rite of
Amphidromia, a rite in which new-born infants were
carried round a blazing altar.   After this ceremony,
the bride is at length lifted from the saddle either
by the father-in-law or the bridesman and carried
upstairs in the state-room, where she is placed
on the divan in the most honourable place.   In
passing into the house her feet are never allowed to
touch the ground, for fear, probably, of such an
ominous casualty as stumbling.

I next inquired about funerals, and was told that one day when the body of a young girl was lying in a church waiting to be interred, the Archbishop observed a woman slipping a quince into the bosom of the corpse. On questioning her, she confessed that she had secreted this offering in the hopes that the dead girl might convey it to her own son, who had died about three weeks before. The Archbishop was greatly scandalized; and telling the poor woman that such superstitious practices might cause her own death, gave the quince to a child, who ate it with happy unconsciousness that he was robbing the *Manes* of their due.

At every funeral in Macedonia a dole of food, wine, and rakee is distributed to the poor. The house of mourning is not swept out till three days after the burial; the broom used for this purpose is always destroyed. Forty days after the funeral, a lyke wake, τράπεζα, takes place at the tomb itself, to which all the relations and friends are invited. The plates and dishes used in this banquet are always broken on the tomb and left there, being considered unfit for other uses.

On the opening of barrows and graves of the heathen period in Germany, it has been noted that great quantities of potsherds are constantly found outside the tomb itself. These are, doubtless, the fragments of the crockery used in the funeral feast; and in like manner, in my diggings at Calymnos, I frequently found cups or lamps in the soil close to Hellenic graves.[5] When a Greek archbishop is buried in his own diocese, he is placed in the grave seated, with a lamp burning.

I could hear of no antiquities at Potamo; but at the distance of about an hour from this place is a village called Plagia, where I was shown a Greek inscription, excavated near a church called Hypopanti. This is a dedication in elegiac verse of a statue of Hermes, to be placed in a vineyard. The dedicator is one Bacchon. At the same church I was shown a sepulchral tablet representing two draped figures joining hands, inscribed with the name of Antiochos, and another slab on which is sculptured in relief a figure of Artemis-Hekate running with a torch in each hand, and at her side a hound. I was told that about ten years ago there were found near this church about 300 silver coins, which, from the description, I should imagine to have been Roman.

To the west of Plumari is Cape Vurkos, where is a ruined church, Agios Phokas, in the walls of which are large fragments of marble and part of a fluted column. Foundations, probably, of a Genoese tower and the outline of an ancient harbour may still be traced. A mole of squared stone juts out into the sea, and there are foundations built with concrete. A little to the N.E. of this cape a salt river flows into the sea, near the mouth of which are the ruins of a church dedicated to St. Katharine, which contains a few insignificant fragments of ancient architecture.

In a field a little to the south of this church, and nearer the mouth of the river, are squared blocks and fragments of ancient red tile. Between this field and the church are foundations of walls built with mortar, but which do not appear to be antique. To the north of Cape Vurkos is the promontory called Brisa by Stephanus Byzantius, on which was a celebrated temple of Bacchus;[6] and there is a village of the same name in the neighbourhood, near the places marked Gripa and Polichniti in the Admiralty chart. At Basilica, in this district, are ferrugineous hot springs, which mark 80° Réaumur. This great heat would render them useless were it not for a spring of cold water close by, which falls into the same basin. The heat of the mineral water is thus reduced to 32° Réaumur.

From Plumari I returned home by Skopelo. The distance is three hours; the road winds picturesquely along the sides of deep ravines covered with pines. Close to the village of Skopelo is that of Misagro, at the distance of half an hour from which are the ruins of an ancient mediæval fortress, on a hill called, as usual, Palaio Kastro. The walls which run round the crest of the hill are built of rubble, in which I could not discover any ancient squared blocks. The hill on which this castle stands is of grey marble, which has been curiously divided into lozenge-shaped blocks caused by natural fissures.

At Misagro I saw a boy bringing round the μακάρια, or cakes given as dole by the relations after a death. The name of this dole is evidently due to the same euphemism which gave to the dead the name οἱ μάκαρες and οἱ μακαρῖται, "the blessed." The

latter word is still in use among the Greeks. These
cakes are circular in form, like the πλακοῦς in the
funeral banquet, as represented in ancient sepulchral reliefs, and have a little sweetmeat on them.[7]
They are quartered and distributed to people in the
streets on the day of the death and on the next
anniversary. Little round comfits, called *kollyba*,
are given in like manner on the 3rd, 9th, and 40th
days after death, and again after three and six
months successively.[8] While I was in the church
at Misagro, the priests went round to collect their
dues. Those who were too poor to contribute paras
gave beans, the κύαμοι which in ancient Athens were
used as lots in the election of public officers.

The dress of the women at Misagro is very picturesque, with red trousers as at Plumari. I saw
two young girls swinging in a swing, *kounia*, suspended from the branch of a large plane-tree, while
their companions stood by singing a melancholy
ditty. The sight reminded me of the festival called
Αἰώρα, by which the maidens of Athens commemorated the tragic end of Erigone, chanting mournful
songs as they swung, the pastime itself being an
allusion to the manner of her death.[9] It is not,
however, probable that any tradition of the Attic
festival should have survived in Mytilene.

Misagro is one of a group of seven villages lying
close together, and forming one district, called Hiera.
The city of this name mentioned by Pliny, as
having perished before his time,[10] must have
stood here, and has given its name to the gulf.
Near Plakado, one of the seven villages, are some

richly sculptured architectural fragments in white
marble at a tank; and following the course of the
stream by which this tank is supplied, I found more
of the same fragments in the sides of the water-
course. The tank is called Manna. I was told
here by the peasants there were formerly extensive
ruins here, from which the great mosque at
Mytilene was built. Near Misagro is an antimony
mine, now being worked by a French engineer, employed by the owner of the mine, a rich Turk."

XXXII.

MYTILENE, *September* 20, 1855.

THE news of the taking of Sebastopol was a source
of great satisfaction to the small European colony
here; but our rejoicing was not in harmony with
the general sentiments of the Mytileniotes. A salute
of 105 guns was fired from the castle, but the Pasha
declined to illuminate the town, being afraid of pro-
voking a counter-demonstration from the Greeks.
Their mortification was so great at the defeat of the
Russians, that they discontinued their horrible nasal
songs for three days, and on the morning when the
news came, the Archbishop descended from his
throne in the metropolitan church, and sat in the
midst of his assembled flock in token of the general
mourning and self-abasement which beseemed them
on such an occasion. They are beginning to smother
their rage now, and to resume their old fawning

ways. They no longer call their pigs Anglo-Galli,
a name invented since the war to show their scorn
of the allied powers, and they now condescend to
salute the French and English consuls in the streets,
an honour of which for some months they had
thought us unworthy.

Since Colnaghi left me in April my life here has
been singularly dull and monotonous. I have hardly
stirred out of the town of Mytilene all the summer,
having been obliged to stay in my office attending to
the enlistment of Land Transport recruits. I never
speak my native language, I have no amusement
of any kind except the change from one book to
another, which after a while becomes like the turning
of a sick man in his deeply indented bed. I am
weary of Greeks and lies and petitions for the re-
covery of small debts alleged to be due to Ionians.
My droning Hoja comes every morning to give me a
lesson in Turkish; my gorge rises at him as if he
were a dose of castor oil. He heedeth not my dis-
gust, but proceeds to din into my ears the same
weary jargon of words which have as yet no meaning
for me. After studying Turkish writing for many
months, I can just manage, when I get a letter from
the Pasha, to unravel my own name out of a knot
of intricate groups of characters!

In the evening I generally take my book and sit
in a cave on the shore, enjoying the distant view of
Asia Minor and the refreshing plash of the wave.
This cavern is the only place where I can escape
from the many discordant sounds which rend the
Eastern air; horrible Greek songs (was there ever

yet a people so destitute of feeling for music?);
brawling termagants railing at each other in the
street under my window; the yells of neglected
squalid children; the howlings of homeless dogs, a
gaunt band of nomad scavengers; and the screams
of half-starved cats, fierce and rapacious as the
Smyrna brigands.

The other day I detected my servant in the very
act of robbing me. He had opened a secret drawer
in a desk, and had not had time to replace the spring,
when I suddenly entered. Though a Greek, he
completely lost his presence of mind. I have not
seen so livid and hideous a complexion since the day
when Timoleon Pericles Vlastò was detected stealing
coins from the British Museum. This man came to
me from Smyrna with an excellent character. He
had most engaging manners, and was always
thanking me for my goodness to him, and telling
me that I was better than a father to him. I have
little doubt that he would have cut my throat with
the same pleasant smile on his face.

People in England wonder how it is that, after a
long residence in the East, Europeans become so
suspicious, jealous, and generally cantankerous; but
they forget that an Englishman in the Levant is
doomed to pass his life surrounded by people who
may be described by the ever-recurring phrase
applied by Darius to his enemies in the Behistun
inscription, "And he was a liar." The very air we
breathe in Turkey is impregnated with lies.

I had written thus far, when, on a sudden, I saw
at the door of my courtyard the apparition of two very

tall British officers. They spoke that mother tongue
so welcome to my ears after long disuse; their complexions were burnt to a rich brick-red, their beards
long and unkempt, their clothes worn and torn by
many a hard day's ride; there was nothing smart
about them but their long clanking swords and the
still untarnished gold lace on their red foraging caps.
I guessed at once whence they came, and, after the
old Homeric fashion of hospitality, invited them into
my house without knowing their names.

  They had been all over Asia Minor recruiting
for General Beatson's Irregular Turkish Cavalry.
Starting from Amasia, they had made a circuit by
Kaisarea, Angora, Kutaya, Adramyt, and thence
across the Strait to Mytilene. They had been in
districts where travellers were unknown, and where
they were offered ancient coins in handfuls. They
had met with various adventures. Sometimes they
were thwarted by the fanaticism of the priests,
and on those occasions carried matters with a high
hand, putting refractory Mollahs in prison, and doing
all sorts of unheard-of things in the name of the three
allied Governments. Their only credential was a letter
from the Seraskier; but, being always accompanied
by about fifty mounted Bashi Bozouks, they made their
way like Xenophon with his Ten thousand. As their
recruits accumulated, they had sent them on to the
Dardanelles in troops of fifty or sixty at a time, commanded by Turkish officers.

  They told me that in many remote parts of Asia
Minor, the rural population, consisting chiefly of
Kurds, complained greatly of their Turkish rulers,

and expressed themselves ready for any change of government.

Everywhere they found in the minds of the people one ruling idea, that the three Allied Powers, English, French, and Turks, were carrying on the government of the Porte in partnership. The country swarmed with thieves. I wish I had been attached to this expedition. What an opportunity of making archæological discoveries lost for ever! The names of my two guests were Colonel Shelley and Colonel O'Reilly. Both seemed hard as flints, and made of the right stuff for the rough work they will have to encounter. Colonel O'Reilly had been for the last two years in the Turkish service, and both had served in India. They left me for the Dardanelles last night.

I have just sent home to England a batch of coins collected in Mytilene, of which the most remarkable are a coin of Methymna, with the type of Arion on a dolphin, and a coin of Eresos, both silver and unedited.[12]

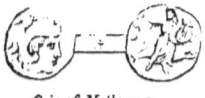

Coin of Methymna.

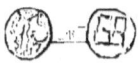

Coin of Eresos.

The Smyrna robbers have at last met with a check. Poor Dr. McCraith going out to visit a patient at Bournabat was seized in open day, carried off to the mountains, and not released till he had paid a ransom of £500, which Mr. Whittall very generously lent him. Colonel Storks, now in charge of the

military hospital at Smyrna, immediately went to
the Pasha, and called upon him to take energetic
measures to root out the brigands. The chief of the
band hearing of this, sent Colonel Storks a threatening message, informing him that he was to be
their next victim, and that the price they intended
to demand for his ransom would be £20,000.
Upon this, Colonel Storks obtained from the Pasha
a force of about 200 soldiers, with whom he pur-
sued the brigands, driving them into the mountains
and cutting off their retreat. A reward was at the
same time offered for the heads of all the more noted
robbers; and the villages which harboured them
were held responsible in every case in which their
complicity could be proved. These energetic
measures have had their effect; after a few days
two cavasses brought in the head of the chief of
the band, whom, as they said, they had been obliged
to kill in self-defence, and brigandage is in a fair
way of being put down in the neighbourhood of
Smyrna, though, as it has been going on there for
the last twenty years, it will be very difficult to
extirpate an evil which has taken such deep root
that it has come to be regarded almost as an
institution.

XXXIII.

THERAPIA, *November 26th*, 1855.

COLNAGHI'S return from England having released me from my long imprisonment at Mytilene, Lord Stratford kindly invited me to pay him a visit here, in order that we might talk over future archæological plans.

I have now been staying at the Embassy for rather more than a month. The change from the dreary isolation of Mytilene to the refined life of Therapia was so great, that at the first aspect of ladies and gentlemen, I felt like Christopher Sly, and thought it was all a dream; and it was not till after several days' practice in talking English, that my long-congealed ideas began to flow and my tongue became unlocked. A most choice and agreeable society is gathered together at this time round the Ambassador's table, and I have seldom enjoyed more intellectual and interesting conversation. It is something, too, in such a momentous crisis, to be so near the head-quarters of a mighty war, and to note its progress, day by day, as telegram after telegram comes in from the Crimea.

I never quite realized the vast scale on which this contest is being carried on, till I stood on the shore of the Bosphorus, and saw the huge ships of war and transports plying up and down these Argonautic straits in ceaseless movement. People talk of watching the tide of life at Charing Cross or on the Thames; but the thoroughfare of the Bosphorus at this time is the grandest in the world. The channel runs so deep near the shore, that it is not an uncommon thing for a ship's bowsprit to find its way through a ground-floor window on to a breakfast-table; and the windows are often broken by salutes.

We have had a succession of charming rides varied by water excursions in the Ambassador's ten-oared caique. The scenery of the Bosphorus has not the severe and sculpturesque grandeur of the Archipelago. The landlocked bays rarely enlivened by a sail; the storm-beaten headlands, and treeless iron-bound coasts; the mountains rising from the long, levelled line of the seaward horizon, and relieved on the deep blue ground of the sky, like metopes on a temple; all these grander features are wanting in the scenery of the Bosphorus, which, in its exquisite finish, reminded me of some of the backgrounds in the early Italian pictures.

Along its well-wooded shores are an endless succession of villas and kiosks, fantastic Castles of Indolence, in which the Turk and the Perote are content to dream life away, watching the caiques gliding by, and only reminded of the flight of the hour by the periodical necessity of replenishing their chibooques and narguilehs.

In the mode of fishing on the Bosphorus, I noticed a curious illustration of an ancient word. A high wooden perch is fixed in the water close to where the nets are laid. A fisherman sits on the top of this perch, watching till the fish have entered, when he gives a signal to his comrades on the shore to draw in the net. Such a sentry is evidently the θυννοσκόπος, or "watcher of tunnies;" and an Athenian audience accustomed to this sight must have appreciated with peculiar zest the metaphor by which Aristophanes describes the demagogue Kleon as sitting on the rocks and watching the shoals of tribute-money coming in like tunny-fish—τοὺς φόρους θυννοσκοπῶν.[13]

Since I have been here, I have seen the collection of Greek coins of Baron Tecco, the Sardinian minister. It is particularly rich in coins of Macedonia and Asia Minor. He possesses a fine specimen of a rare archaic dodekadrachm, in silver, which has been attributed with probability to some early king of Macedonia. On one side of this coin is a bearded figure seated in a car drawn by a single bull; above the bull is a helmet, like that which occurs as the principal type in the early silver coins of the kings of Macedon. Below the bull's body is a lotos flower. On the reverse is what is known to numismatists as a *triquetra*, formed of three human legs conjoined, as on the arms of the Isle of Man. The car is of a very primitive kind, the body being of wickerwork, and the wheel having crosspieces instead of spokes. Mr. Cumberbatch, our Consul-General here, had a coin similar to this (see cut 1), which perished when his house was burnt. In the library of Christ Church, Oxford, is a third specimen (cut 2), in which the adjuncts are different; and I have seen a fourth coin (cut 3), from the collection of M. Gilet, French

Consul at Salonica, in which the type of the reverse
is a helmet instead of a *triquetra*. This curious
early Macedonian dodekadrachm may be compared

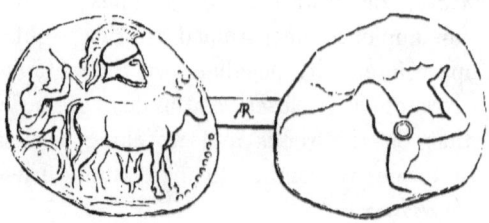

(1.) *From the Collection of Mr. Cumberbatch.*

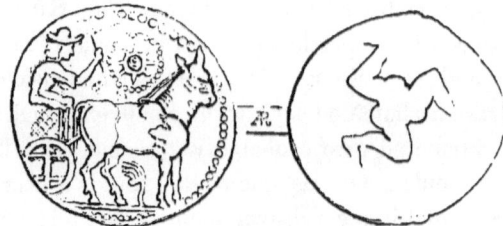

(2.) *From the Collection at Christ Church.*

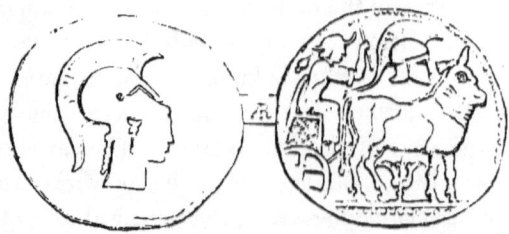

(3.) *From the Collection of M. Gilet.*

with two silver octodrachms, which, from their
inscription, appear to have been struck by Geta, king
of the Edonians, at an early period, and which,
singularly enough, were found in the Tigris.[14] Baron

Tecco has also a silver coin of Heraklea, in Bithynia, with the type of a Victory crouching, a very fine specimen of the art of Asia Minor; and a coin of Cilicia in the same metal, which has on the obverse a female figure seated between two sphinxes, and on the reverse an Athene Nikephoros. This coin is remarkable for finish and preservation. The style is very elaborate and mannered, but has less of the stiffness which generally characterizes Cilician coins, and which is probably due to Persian influence.

Since I began this letter, I have been engaged in an excavation round the base of the famous brazen serpent in the Atmeidan, or Hippodrome. This serpent is a relic dating from remote antiquity, and has a very curious history.

Herodotus states that the golden tripod dedicated to Apollo by the allied Greeks, as a tenth of the Persian spoils at Platæa, was placed on a bronze serpent with three heads which stood near the altar at Delphi. On this monument, as we learn from Thucydides, Pausanias, regent of Sparta, inscribed an arrogant distich, in which he commemorates the victory in his own name, as general in chief, hardly mentioning the allied forces who gained it. This epigram was subsequently erased by the Lacedæmonians, who substituted for it an inscription enumerating the various Hellenic states who had taken a part in repulsing the Persian invaders. The golden tripod perished in the plunder of Delphi by the Phocians; but the bronze serpent on which it stood, not attracting their sacrilegious cupidity, was left *in situ*, and was seen at Delphi by the topographer

Pausanias, when he visited the temple in the second century of the Christian era.

We learn from Zosimus and several other Byzantine writers, that Constantine the Great, when he enriched his new Eastern capital with the spoils of the Greek pagan temples, removed the bronze serpent from Delphi to the Hippodrome at Constantinople, where it has remained ever since, surviving all the sieges, revolutions, and conflagrations which have destroyed so many precious relics of the Byzantine city.

A succession of travellers, from the fifteenth century to our own day, have described the bronze serpent as standing in the Hippodrome; and the testimony in proof of its identity so completely satisfied the sceptical mind of Gibbon, that he declares that "the guardians of the most holy relics would rejoice if they were able to produce such a chain of evidence."

The serpent was triple, being composed of three snakes intertwined. In two views of the Hippodrome taken at the commencement of the sixteenth century, it is represented with the three heads mentioned by Pausanias and Herodotus. It is said that Mahomet II. struck off the under jaw of one of the heads with his mace, and that the three heads were broken off about the end of the seventeenth century by the followers of Count Lisinsky, then Ambassador from the King of Poland at the Porte.[15]

Signor Fossati, the architect who restored St. Sophia, in digging near that church found a bronze

serpent's head without a lower jaw, which is believed
to belong to the Delphic monument, and which is
now preserved in the Museum of St. Irene, in the
Seraglio. (See *ante*, I. p. 44.) The idea of making
the excavation in the Hippodrome was suggested
to me by Lord Napier, who thought that some inscription relative to this monument might be found
on its base. Lord Stratford having obtained for
me a firman enabling me to dig in the Hippodrome,
I proceeded to the spot under the protection of a
guard of cavasses, and accompanied by twelve lusty
Croats, with picks and wooden shovels. On our
way we were met by Admiral Slade, who, seeing an
Englishman surrounded by cavasses, imagined that
he beheld a fellow-countryman about to be carried
off to a Turkish prison, and called out, " Hallo!
what are you going to do with that Frank ? " The
chiaoux, or sergeant, in charge of the party informed
him that I was no prisoner, but only "a wise man
who digs holes in the ground ; " an explanation
which at once re-assured the Admiral.

After three days' digging, I cleared away the
ground which concealed the base of the serpent.
The soil had evidently been disturbed at no very
distant period, and contained no ancient remains,
except very small fragments of marble. After
digging to the depth of rather more than 6 feet, I
came to the base of the serpent, a rough-hewn
stone plinth, evidently of the Byzantine period.[16]
A few feet from this plinth, at the depth of 8 feet
below the surface, was an ancient aqueduct formed
by cylindrical earthen pipes jointed one into the

other, and laid continuously with an oblong block of marble 16 inches long, through which an earthen pipe passed lengthways. This block was pierced on one face at right angles to the channel, probably for ventilating. Close to this aqueduct was a foundation of tiles bound in strong mortar, which appeared to be the remains of a small square tank. Within three-quarters of a yard of the serpent was a marble archway, like that of a *cloaca*, and near it a drain large enough to admit a man's body. The serpent in its present state appears like a hollow twisted Byzantine column, and, being placed in the centre of the tank, has probably been used at some period as a fountain. Both the heads and tails are wanting.

The entire height of this monument from the plinth to the highest spiral is nearly 18 feet. The earth accumulated over the plinth is evidently made soil; and, according to a Turkish historian, the Hippo- drome was raised to its present level at the com- mencement of the seventeenth century, when the mosque of Sultan Achmet was built there.[17]

I am anxiously awaiting the arrival of the Medusa from the Crimea, which Lord Lyons is about to send down the Archipelago, and in which he has kindly offered me a berth during her cruise. We hope to have another look at Budrum.

[In the foregoing letter, I have placed on record the simple facts of the excavation as they appeared to me at the time. I regret that being much hurried at the time in preparations for a cruise in the Medusa, I did not allow sufficient time for the examination of the portion of the serpent which had been uncovered; otherwise, I should probably have had the satisfaction of making the remarkable discovery which was reserved for other archæologists, and to which I only contributed as a humble pioneer.

The portion of the serpent which had been buried in the ground was thickly incrusted with an earthy coating. In January, 1856, Dr. Otto Frick, a German archæologist, hearing that letters had been discovered on the bronze, examined its whole surface minutely in company with Dr. Dethier, director of the Austrian school in Pera. After the incrustation had been removed by acid, a long inscription appeared, following the spirals of the serpent from the base upwards to a little higher than the surface of the soil removed by me. Above this line, long exposure to the air had effaced nearly all traces of the letters. After a labour which lasted some weeks, the inscription was finally deciphered, and a cast in plaster taken of it, from which Dr. Dethier has published a perfect fac-simile in his Memoir on the Bronze Serpent.[18]

The inscription contains exactly what the statements of Thucydides and Herodotus would lead us to expect: the names of those Greek states which took an active part in the defeat of the Persians.

Thirty-one names have been deciphered, and there seem to be traces of three more. The three first names on the list are the Lacedæmonians, Athenians, Corinthians. The remainder are nearly identical with those inscribed on the statue of Zeus at

Olympia, as they are given by Pausanias. This statue, as has been already stated, was dedicated out of the same spoils of Platæa as the offering at Delphi.

It is probable that, though these dedications were intended specially to commemorate the victory of Platæa, the two lists included the names of all the Greek states who took a part in the battles of Thermopylæ and Salamis, except in those which furnished very inconsiderable contingents; and, accordingly, we find that of the thirty-six states mentioned by Herodotus as present in one or other of these three battles, we have certainly thirty-one, and probably thirty-four, on the Delphic monument.

The names of the several states seem to be arranged on the serpent generally, according to their relative importance, and also with some regard to their geographical distribution. The states of continental Greece are enumerated first; then the islanders and outlying colonies on the north and west. In the list at Olympia, as given by Pausanias, the same order is observed, except in five cases. Dr. Frick, in an interesting memoir on the Bronze Serpent, in the " Jahrbücher für Classische Philologie,"[19] has printed both lists in parallel columns.

I have already alluded to the metrical inscription, or epigram, placed by the Spartan regent Pausanias on the Delphic monument, which was afterwards effaced on account of its egotistical and pretentious character. From a comparison of the several passages in ancient authors in which this erasure is mentioned, it may be fairly inferred that the epigram was removed from the same part of the monument on which the list of states was subsequently inscribed, and accordingly, Dr. Dethier states that on the thirteenth coil of the serpent there is a visible depression of the surface, such as would be caused by cutting away an inscription. Dr. Frick, however, does not concur with him in supposing that the epigram was erased from this part of the monument.

As the date of the battle of Platæa was B.C. 479, it may be assumed that the setting up of the tripod took place very shortly afterwards. Dr. Dethier consequently supposes that the present inscription was placed on the serpent B.C. 476. In that case it must be considered one of the earliest specimens of Greek palæography of which the date can be positively fixed, and it is especially interesting because we have several nearly contemporary inscribed monuments with which it may be compared. These are the coins struck by the Messenians on establishing themselves at Zancle, B.C. 494; the Syracusan decadrachm, which there is good ground for supposing to have been struck by Demarete, the wife of Gelon the First, after his victory over the Carthaginians, B.C. 480; the bronze helmet dedicated by Hiero the First at Olympia after his naval victory over the Tuscans, B.C. 474; and the inscription discovered by me at Halicarnassus, which contains the names of Lygdamis and Panyasis, and of which the date is probably about B.C. 445.[20] All these inscriptions exhibit in the forms of the

letters a gradual transition from the more archaic
to the more modern mode of writing, and form
an instructive series for the student of palæography.

The identity of the brazen serpent in the Hippodrome with the Delphic monument is proved, therefore, not only by the chain of external evidence
which so fully satisfied the acute mind of Gibbon,
but also by the historical and palæographical evidence
afforded by the inscription itself.

On the first discovery of this inscription, Professors
E. Curtius and Carl Bötticher were disposed to think
that the bronze in the Hippodrome was a Byzantine
reproduction of the original bronze serpent; and it
has been alleged in support of this view, that all the
ancient writers who notice the Delphic monument
state that the list of states was inscribed on the golden
tripod itself, and not on the serpent which formed its
pedestal. But such perfect accuracy of expression is
seldom observed by ancient authors when they write
of objects so familiar to their own generation that a
description of them in detail would have appeared
superfluous. When tripods, or similar objects, were
dedicated in temples, it was usual to place them on
high columns or bases; whence their name, ἀναθήματα,
"things set up;" so that in the mind of an ancient
Greek, the idea of a base of some kind was implied
in that of an object dedicated; and though, in some
instances, the inscription was graven upon the
anathema itself, it was more usually placed upon the
pedestal.

Hence, the writers who notice the Delphic monument have not thought it worth while to state what they supposed to be known to every one.

Their statement, moreover, if taken literally, is not only contradicted by the recent discovery, but is in itself improbable; for if, as Herodotus and Pausanias state, the tripod stood on the bronze serpent, which we know to have been at least 20 feet high, it seems very improbable that an inscription so interesting to the Hellenic race for all time should have been placed at so great a height above the eye.

Another inaccuracy in former notices of the monument in the Hippodrome should also be noted. Herodotus speaks of it as a single serpent, with three heads; an error in which all the Byzantine writers and most of the travellers who mention it follow him. But it is certain that the bronze is composed of three serpents, so cunningly intertwined together that their bodies appear one spiral column. From the rude drawings made in the seventeenth century, and also from the fragment of a head preserved in the Museum of the Seraglio, it seems certain that the three heads were represented with gaping jaws.

The tripod, of course, rested on the heads. Two imaginary restorations of it are exhibited in Plate IV. of Dr. Dethier's Memoir, of which Fig. 24 B seems the most successful. The eyes of the serpents must have been made either of precious stones, or some vitreous paste, as the fragment of a head in the Museum of the Seraglio has hollow sockets.

Nowhere on the surface of the bronze is there any

trace of scales, and it is evident that the bodies of
the serpents were left smooth, as they are constantly
represented in ancient sculpture in marble, for the
inscription would have been less legible on a. scaly
surface. The entire mass of bronze appears to have
been cast. Dr. Dethier with the most minute examination could not detect any join in the metal;
yet it is not likely that so great a length should have
been cast in one piece.

Of the merits of this monument as a work of art
it is hardly possible now to judge, on account of its
mutilated condition. I must confess that, neither
in the fragment of a head in the Seraglio nor in the
general treatment of the surface in the Hippodrome
bronze, could I recognize that force in the indica-
tion of structure, those refined gradations in the
modelling which characterize Greek art even at so
early a period as the Delphic dedication ; and it was
this want of *style* which led me, on first examining
the serpent, to consider it a Byzantine restoration
from the original,—an opinion which has been
strongly maintained by Professor Curtius, but which
has been condemned by the general voice of German
archæologists.

In criticizing this bronze it must be borne in
mind that in designing it the main object of the
artist was so to compose the coils of his triple serpent
as to suggest the idea of an erect and steadfast
column. The natural form of the reptile was therefore rather adapted than directly imitated. The
treatment was analogous to that of the floral ornaments of Greek architecture, which are rather floral

types than representations of real flowers, imitation
being only carried as far as is compatible with archi-
tectonic conditions.

I have already mentioned that on digging round
the base of the serpent I came to a pavement, which
appeared to be the bottom of a small tank, and which
suggested the idea to me that the serpent had been
used as a fountain. Subsequently to my excavation,
a piece of leaden pipe was discovered inside the
serpent, on which was part of an inscription in
Byzantine Greek, relating to some one who was
præfect, ἔπαρχος, of Constantinople.

Frick thinks that the serpent was probably converted into a fountain in the time of Valens, A.D.
364—378. Dethier supposes that this was done in
the reign of his successor Theodosius, and that the
præfect whose name was inscribed on the pipe may
have been Proclus, under whose direction the obelisk
of the Hippodrome was set up. The discovery
of the pipe shows that the serpent was used as a
fountain, and the tank in front of it was evidently
for the reception of the overflowing water. Bundel-
monte, on his visit to Constantinople in 1422, about
thirty-one years before it was taken by the Turks,
was told that on great festivals water, milk, and wine
flowed from the three mouths of the serpent. This
statement may not have been literally true, but it
shows that at that time the serpent was regarded as
a fountain. The stone base on which the serpent
rests appears to be the cover of a cistern.[21]

After the discovery of the inscription on the bronze
serpent, a larger excavation took place in the Hippo-

drome, at the expense of the British Government, by whom a company of sappers was employed for the purpose, in April, 1856. On this occasion the earth which had accumulated round the base of the obelisk of Theodosius was removed so as more completely to exhibit the sculptures in relief on each side. These sculptures, though rudely executed, are exceedingly curious as memorials of the Byzantine empire in its palmy days.

The obelisk, as we learn from an inscription on its base, was placed in its present position by Theodosius. The operation was directed by Proclus, and was performed in thirty-two days. The relief on the north side of the pedestal is a rude representation of the manner in which this difficult piece of engineering was accomplished. The foot of the obelisk is attached to a wheel. Two gangs of workmen are hauling it by ropes attached to capstans. On the south side of the pedestal are the emperor Theodosius, his empress, Ælia Placidia, and his two sons on a throne, under an alcove supported by two columns. On either side are body-guards and attendants. Below the emperor are two rows of lattices, κιγκλίδες (whence the Latin cancelli, and our chancel and chancellor). Four steps lead up to this lattice, on the lowest of which two figures stand, one of whom appears to be pleading. This scene, therefore, probably represents the emperor presiding in the tribunal, which anciently stood on the Hippodrome.

Below these steps is a semicircular recess or tribune, and below this another lattice with steps, on

which stand officers flinging purses of largess. Below
are two friezes, the uppermost of which represents
the Hippodrome as it appeared after the obelisk had
been set up.

The scene is bounded on either side by the *meta*,
or goals. Next to the *meta* on the left, is a runner,
—a horseman ; then the obelisk of Theodosius,—a
triumphal arch,—a figure kneeling to receive a crown,
—a group of several figures. Next comes a stump,
which appears from its position to be the bronze
serpent, but which is too much decayed to be satis-
factorily made out; then a second obelisk, doubtless
the one which was once covered with bronze plates,
and which still stands in the Hippodrome ; then a
figure standing, — a horseman, — and the *meta*
closing the scene on the right. The lowest frieze
on this side of the pedestal represents a chariot-
race.

On the east side the subject of the sculpture is
the emperor on his throne, surrounded by his court
and presiding over a feast. Below is a band of
music, among which are two kinds of organs, an
instrument originally suggested by the Pan's pipe
or syrinx, and which, according to Athenæus, was
first invented B.C. 200. Below are dancers. On the
west side is another representation of the emperor
on his throne, with his empress, his two sons and
his attendant courtiers. Here he is receiving
foreign ambassadors or tributaries, of whom there
are two groups, kneeling in token of submission.
Those on the left appear from their costume to be
Scythians ; those on the right are clad in sheepskins.

There is in the Hippodrome a second obelisk,
built of blocks of stone, which was once covered
with plates of gilt bronze.   An inscription on its base
records that this obelisk was restored by the Emperor Constantine, son of Romanus II., who reigned
A.D. 1025-8.   The plates of gilt bronze have long
since disappeared.   They were stripped off during
the Latin invasion of Constantinople by the same
Western barbarians who melted down the bronze
statues, masterpieces from the hand of Lysippus, and
converted them into coin to pay their troops with.   If
the bronze serpent escaped a like destiny, its preservation was probably due to the accident that it seems to
have been regarded in the Middle Ages as a talisman.
We are in the habit of ascribing all the destruction
of ancient works of art in the Levant to the Turks,
but it must be remembered that Greek Iconoclasts
and Latin Crusaders have had a good share in
this work.   Before digging in the Hippodrome 1
had an interview with Fuad Pasha, in order to
obtain the necessary permission.   Inquiring whether
there were still any ancient MSS. in the Seraglio,
I expressed my regret that the Turks on taking
Constantinople should have destroyed the precious
libraries which must have existed there.   Fuad
admitted the barbarism of the act, "but," he added,
"did not the Spaniards take Granada about the
same time ? and did they show more regard for the
ancient MSS. and archives which were stored up in
the libraries of the Moors ?   You must not," he said,
"blame the Turks so much as the century when
these barbarous acts were perpetrated."

As the Porte has now allowed the Hippodrome to be completely explored, it is to be hoped that at some future day an opportunity may occur for digging under the foundations of the porphyry column, which stood in the Forum of Constantine, and, having suffered in a conflagration, is now known by the name of the Burnt Column. It is said that under the foundations of this column Constantine deposited the celebrated Palladium, which had been preserved at Rome from time immemorial in the Temple of Vesta.[22] If this tradition be true, this relic would probably be found where Constantine placed it ; and if ever a new Christian empire is founded at Constantinople, the discovery of this relic of old Rome would be an incident worthy of its inauguration.]

XXXIV.

BUDRUM, *January* 30, 1856.

I LEFT Constantinople in the Medusa about six weeks ago, bound for a cruise to the south.

Lord Stratford having promised to apply to the Porte for a firman to enable me to excavate here, we went in the first instance to Rhodes, intending to wait there till the firman arrived. As, however, the weather was very stormy, and Rhodes is an unsafe anchorage in winter, we crossed over to Marmarice on the opposite coast, where is one of the finest harbours in the world, completely land-

locked; well known as the station of the English fleet
both in Sir Sidney Smith's time, and more recently
during the Syrian war.   The village of Marmarice is
a wretched place, built on a low marshy site, with
bad water.   The harbour has been defended by a
small castle built by the Knights, which is now in
ruins.   Marmarice is the site of the ancient Physkos,
of which I could find no remains, except on a hill
about three-quarters of a mile to the north of the
village.   On the summit is a mediæval castle, called
Assarlik, and lower down the hill some remains of
Hellenic walls, by which an ancient *acropolis* has
been defended.

To employ our time while we were waiting for
the firman, I set out with Lieutenant Heath on a
journey along the coast, with the hope of reaching
Budrum by the overland route.   Leaving Marmarice
at 9.15 a.m., we arrived at Djova, at the head of the
gulf of the same name, at 5.30 p.m., hoping to find
a sailing-vessel to take us to Cos.   The anchorage
at Djova is good, but the place is very unhealthy in
summer, and the few inhabitants have a wan, fever-
stricken look, which reminded me of Strabo's
account of the Caunians, whose green complexions
induced an ancient wit to quote on seeing them
Homer's well-known line—

οἵηπερ φύλλων γενεὴ, τοιήδε καὶ ἀνδρῶν.

This place is considered to be the ancient Bargasa.
I noticed here a square niche cut in the side of the
cliff which overhangs the sea, and on the road to
Mughla, at the distance of half an hour's walk from

the harbour is an eminence, on which is an old castle overlooking the marshy plain. This was probably a Greek Acropolis, as on the side looking towards the port is a piece of polygonal masonry, and in the road below traces of Hellenic walls along the edge of the valley. Failing to hire a sailing-vessel at Djova, we rode on to Mughla, a town in the interior, the place of residence of the Caimakam of the district. The journey took us a day. On leaving Djova, we crossed a lofty ridge, from the summit of which a magnificent view opened to the south. The horizon was bounded on the south by the snow-crowned peaks of the Lycian mountains, and in the middle distance could be seen other mountains of the most picturesque forms, and a large salt-water lake, Knjis, distant about eight hours.

On arriving at Mughla we were quartered by the Caimakam on a rich Greek, who received us very hospitably. Our host, who was a scraff, or money-changer, showed us a letter and book from England, which had been sent to him through the British Consul at Smyrna, and which he could not read. To my surprise, the book was the volume of Reports of the Jurors of the Great Exhibition, and the letter a certificate declaring that our host, Constantine Nicola, had been a contributor.

He was much disappointed when he was told that this certificate would not entitle him to British protection, having had a vague hope that a document with so official a look might be converted into a passport.

Mughla is situated in a plain at the foot of a

steep rock, on which has evidently stood an ancient
Acropolis. This rock is distant about twenty
minutes' walk to the north-east of the town. The
top is nearly level, so that, seen from below, the
rock presents the appearance of a truncated cone.
A road from the town winds along the south and
west sides of the base. This road follows the line
of an ancient approach to the Acropolis, as is
shown by the number of square niches and caverns
cut in the rock on each side; these, doubtless,
contained votive offerings.

On arriving at the summit of the rock, I found
a level platform, which has been surrounded by an
Hellenic wall constructed of squared blocks of no
great size without mortar. At the south-west end
of the platform extensive landslips appear to have
taken place, and great fissures occur in the rock,
as if it had been rent asunder in some convulsion of
nature. On this side the wall has been carried
away, but there are marks in the rock where a
bed has been cut for its reception. On the south-
east side the platform terminates in an open precipice, below which is a mountain torrent. On
this side two chambers are cut out of the rock,
in one of which was a window with two steps on
the inside of the sill, but all has been torn and con-
vulsed by earthquakes. This hill fortress commands an extensive view over the plain.

I purchased at Mughla the small gold coin
of Pixodarus, Prince of Caria, which is very
seldom to be met with in the districts over which he
reigned.

I could not hear of any antiquities at Mughla, but Ross discovered here, in the house of a Greek inhabitant, a marble pedestal inscribed with a dedication by Nicolaos, son of Leon, of Rhodes, to Hermes, Herakles, and the κοινόν or community of the Tarmiani. He supposes that this κοινόν was one of the *conventus* noticed by Pliny, and that it was probably attached to the συντέλεια of Cibyra. This inscription having been found at Mughla, Tarmiani is probably the ancient name of this place.[23]

Immediately after our arrival at Mughla the rainy season set in; and the weather looked so unpromising that we gave up our projected visit to Budrum and returned to Marmarice. When we started, the rain fell in such torrents, that, had it not been for a stringent order from the Caimakam, it would have been impossible for us to have induced any suriji to accompany us to Marmarice. The first day of our journey it rained for six hours continuously; but our luggage being well protected by a large mackintosh sheeting, was quite dry.

We found shelter at night in a hut on the summit of a mountain-pass. A splendid fire of logs of pitch-pine soon dried the wet clothes of our poor followers; and we had a very comfortable supper, eked out by a tin of preserved vegetables from the ship. On the evening of the second day we arrived at Marmarice.

The whole route from Marmarice to Mughla is singularly destitute of villages, cultivation, or even animals. The greater part of the road traverses

pine forests and mountain-passes, where the only
signs of man are the black tents of the Turcomans
or their lonely graves scattered about in the glades
of the pine forest. We saw very little game, and
hardly any wild bird but the jay. Now and then
the monotony of our route was relieved by meeting
a long string of camels, with their melodious chime
of bells, conveying the produce of the interior to
the ports of Djova, or Marmarice, along roads fitter
for goats than for beasts of burthen.

The weather having become less threatening, we
returned to Rhodes, and anchored this time in the
open road outside the harbour. Here we attempted
to enjoy Christmas-day; but just in the middle
of the usual merry antics which sailors perform
after dinner on this day, it came on to blow from
the north, and we were obliged to take shelter
under the lee of Cos. Here we spent two days,
and then crossed over to Cape Crio, where we
landed, and passed a day in exploring the ruins of
Cnidus. We made a small excavation in the
theatre near the southern harbour, but without any
result. From Cnidus we went to Calymnos, where
we were very enthusiastically received by a party
of my old workmen, who were in hopes that we
were coming to make excavations on a great scale.
I purchased here a very curious inscription from
the Temple of Apollo, relating to the enfranchise-
ment of slaves by a kind of deed of sale, by which
they were assigned for life to the service of the
god.

I was interested to see that since my visit to Calymnos the inhabitants had made great progress in the making a pier into the deep water of their harbour, alongside of which ships of 200 tons can be safely moored. This pier has been formed by a very simple process. Each Calymniote caique that goes out on a cruise is expected to bring back a certain number of stones for the pier, according to its capacity and opportunities. And so the work goes on by slow and gradual deposits, each native mariner contributing his mite towards it. Such energy in the improvement of natural advantages is rare in the islands on this side of the Archipelago.

Doubtless commerce has in many places been checked by the jealous restrictions imposed on its development by the Turks; but the absence of commercial enterprise in the Archipelago is not wholly to be attributed to this cause, but is due in part to the apathy and helplessness of the islanders themselves, and still more to the want of that probity in their dealings one with another which is the only basis of commercial credit.

From Calymnos we crossed over to this place, where we were not sorry to find ourselves in a secure roadstead. Here we were most kindly received by Salik Bey, a rich Turk, who lives in a large ruinous konak on the shore of the harbour. He is the son of Halil Bey, who was Governor of Budrum when Sir Francis Beaufort visited this place in 1811.

Here I had to take leave of my comfortable quarters on board the Medusa, for Lieut. Heath had now prolonged his cruise to the latest period

named in his instructions, and was obliged to proceed to Malta. Having received no tidings of the
firman for which we had so long waited, I determined to employ the interval till it arrived in a
visit to Mughla, whither I had been requested by
Mr. Campbell to proceed for the purpose of enrolling
a number of recruits for the Land Transport Corps
in the Crimea. The only disagreeable part of this
expedition was the necessity of carrying with me
about 300 Napoleons, to be paid to the recruits as
bounty on my arrival at Mughla.

After leaving Budrum, I arrived after six hours'
travelling at Guverjilik, at the head of the Gulf of
Mendelet, or Mendelia, where we halted for the
night. This is a wretched hamlet, once a village,
but now consisting of about three houses. A Turkish
custom-house is placed here to levy duties on the
pine-timber of the neighbouring forests on its
exportation. There is safe anchorage here, but its
situation is very unhealthy. The sea appears to
be gradually receding from the head of the gulf,
and its extreme shallowness along the shore of
Guverjilik is probably the cause of the miasma
which makes this place very subject to intermittent fever. No good drinking-water is procurable
here.

After leaving Guverjilik, I proceeded to Mylasa,
crossing a plain to the east of the site of the ancient
Bargylia. At the distance of an hour and forty
minutes from Guverjilik, I passed the village of
Wavri-Köi,[24] on an eminence overlooking the plain
about two miles distant on our right. Large herds

of cattle are kept here, as the plain bordering on the salt marsh affords rich pasturage.

Five minutes after passing this village, I noticed a rock on the right-hand side of the road, in which was a small cavern surmounted by a niche 3 feet high by 2 feet 4 inches wide.[25] The road here falls in with the line of a causeway, in which I observed square blocks and part of an ancient cornice.

At two hours and ten minutes' distance from Guverjilik, I noticed a tumulus on the right hand. Here a mountain beyond Mylasa comes in sight. Mylasa is a large Turkish town picturesquely situated in a great plain. This place has been so fully explored by Lebas and other travellers, that I found but few remains which had not been already noticed.

At about ten minutes' distance to the south-west of the town is a field called Guwisch Guza. Here are a number of unfinished columns of grey marble ranging in a line with an old Turkish tomb and a decayed fountain. To the south-west of these columns is a platform which appears to be supported by a wall under the surface. In a hedgerow near these remains are some smaller fluted columns.

In this field I noticed at a well part of a large column on which were the prongs of a trident rudely cut in relief, and some letters of a Greek inscription partly concealed in the wall. Near these remains a portion of the ancient city wall runs east and west for about 117 yards. Towards the south it runs up to the foot of a rocky hill, where it is lost. The masonry is polygonal. A view of this wall is given in the work of Lebas (Itin. Pl. 64).

On the north side of the town is a very beautiful mosque, with a portal composed of three doorways with pointed arches.

. From Mylasa I went to Eski Hissar (Stratonicea), of which the stately Roman ruins have been so often described that I have nothing to add to the notices of former travellers. Halting here for a night, I continued my journey the next day.

At the distance of half an hour from Eski Hissar the road crosses the source of a small river called Buzlik Chai, which was flowing north, and which I was told was a tributary of the Mendere. The water issues from a built passage under ground.

Here are foundations, as if some ancient edifice had stood on this spot. At the distance of one hour from Eski Hissar, we passed on the left the village of Agriköi, which contains about 200 inhabitants. The direction of the road here was due east. Half an hour further on we passed on the right the village of Buzuk, close to the road. From Agriköi for two hours onwards we traversed a rich plain cultivated with Indian corn. The remainder of the route passed over a more barren and mountainous district.

We arrived at Mughla on the fourth day after leaving Budrum. After waiting here five days, I ascertained the fact that no land transport recruits were forthcoming. Either the agent employed at Mughla by Mr. Campbell for their enlistment had deceived him, in the hope of getting hold of the bounty money, or they had been scared away by local influence.

The Turks in the thinly populated parts of Asia Minor feel the drain of their own conscription so much that they secretly discourage all recruiting for their allies in their own district, having very few able-bodied men to spare.

Having disposed of the business on which I was sent, I set out on my return, with the same uncomfortable weight of gold suspended round my waist in a canvas girdle. Though the roads were reported safe, I thought it as well to have with me one of the Pasha's mounted police, or Zapties, who are fairly armed and equipped, and very useful in securing for the British traveller good quarters and food at all the places where he halts on his journey.

My first object on leaving Mughla was to visit Lagina, distant about two hours from Eski Hissar, where, as we learn from Strabo, was a celebrated temple of Hekate. The first night I halted at Agriköi, distant about six hours from Mughla, and came in just at the moment of the wedding of some rich Turkish country gentleman. The Aga's konak whereon I was billeted I found full of grave sententious Turks, many of them agas from the surrounding villages, each with a small wiry Turkish horse, tethered in the Aga's court-yard, a pair of saddle-bags made of carpet, and an attendant cavass. They were very courteous and well-bred specimens of Turkish country gentlemen, and had something of that "landed look" which Sydney Smith attributes to the English squire. One of them, more knowing than

his neighbours, read extracts from a Constantinople
newspaper about three months old, which told of
the fall of Kimburn; the rest smoked in that silent,
meditative manner which accords so well with Turkish
tobacco. They were not lively or intelligent, perhaps, as Greeks might have been; but then they
were at least better bred. They had the good taste
to let the tired stranger alone. They did not poke
their hands into my carpet-bag, nor inquire what the
object of my travelling was, or how much I possessed
a year, or what wages I gave my cavass. They
neither fished for compliments nor bestowed them.
Their hospitality did not oppress by excess of attention and officious meddling. In short, I felt quite
at my ease.

After passing the night at Agriköi, I rode next
morning to Lagina, which is a small secluded village,
where I was quartered in the Oda, or strangers'
room, which Turkish hospitality provides in so many
places for the passing traveller.

On inquiring for ruins, I was taken to a place
about half an hour distant from the village where
I found the remains of the temple mentioned by
Strabo, lying *in situ.* Columns, pieces of frieze and
architrave, and other architectural marbles, were
lying piled up, one over the other, just as they must
have fallen, if, as can hardly be doubted, this temple
was thrown down by an earthquake.

The ruins form an irregular mound, extending
N.W. and S.E. for about 73 paces, and presenting
two principal heaps connected by an intermediate
lower ridge. The heap on the N.W. is formed by

the ruins of a Corinthian temple, peristyle, and octo-style in the fronts. Four columns are still in position on the north-west front ; their diameter, at 6 feet 2½ inches above the base, was 2 feet 10½ inches. Their intercolumniations, measured from centre to centre, are 8 feet ⅓ of an inch. The width of the temple is 59 feet 10¾ inches,[26] and of the cella 26 feet 10 inches. The architrave is 2 feet 3¼ inches high, and a sculptured frieze 3 feet ½ inch high.

On the south-eastern heap are shafts of columns partially fluted, 2 feet 1 inch in diameter, and fragments of Doric architecture, which seem to belong to a smaller edifice adjoining the Corinthian temple.

Of the frieze I found nine slabs, on all of which were groups of standing and seated figures. From the composition and general type of these figures, I should infer that they represent deities. I was unable to recognize the subjects of any of them. On one slab was represented a female seated on a throne, near whom a female figure stands holding in her left hand what may represent a new-born female child, wrapped in swaddling-clothes. Several other figures, male and female, are represented on this slab. It is possible that the subject may be the birth of Hekate herself.[27] Most of these slabs have suffered greatly from the weather. The style of the sculpture is bold and forcible, though somewhat coarse and conventional. The drapery is rather too angular and deficient in flow.

In the south-east heap I found a statue, lying half-buried in the ground. It is engaged at the back

E 2

in a pilaster, and was, therefore, probably an architectural statue. It represents a female figure, draped
to the feet, rather larger than life-size. The style is
somewhat meagre.

The temple is surrounded by a *peribolos* of an
oblong form, its sides being parallel to those of the
temple. On the south-west, the wall of the *peribolos*
may be very distinctly traced. It commences
near the north-west angle, and runs to a gateway,
which is formed of three stones, an architrave
and two jambs, slightly converging towards each
other.[28] On the architrave is an inscription in
several lines, of which I could only make out a few
letters, on account of its height and decayed
condition :—The words [Καῖσ]αρ θεοῦ υἱός may be
distinguished. It therefore probably records the
building or repair of the temple by some Roman
emperor.

On the same side of the *peribolos*, but more to the
west, were steps with a projecting *cyma*, like those
of a theatre, ranged in horizontal rows one above
another.

The north-west boundary of the *peribolos* is
marked by many drums of columns strewn about.
The shafts of these columns were fluted for half their
length. The diameter of the fluted part of the shaft
was 1 foot 9 inches, inclusively of the flutings,
which were so much broken away that their depth
could not be ascertained. The building material
employed in this temple is, throughout, a coarse
white marble.

Among the ruins in all parts of the site I found

inscriptions, containing, for the most part, registers
of the names of priests of Hekate and of benefactors
of the temple.

The following particulars may be gathered from
them. The temple of Hekate probably had a numerous sacerdotal body of both sexes, as mention is
made of the High Priest (ἀρχιερεύς), the priests
(ἱερεῖς), with whom their wives were associated as
priestesses, the officer in charge of the Mysteries
(ὁ ἐπιμελούμενος τῶν μυστηρίων), and the Κλειδοφοροῦσα,
or key-bearing priestess. The office of this latter
priestess is explained by the expression κλειδὸς
πομπή ("the procession of the key"), which occurs
in several inscriptions. This key was one of the
attributes of Hekate Τριοδῖτις, or Trivia, the goddess whose statue was usually placed at the inter-
section of three roads.

Among the Roman sculptures in the British Museum may be seen a statue of this Hekate Trivia,
represented with three bodies looking different ways.
In one of her hands she holds a key.[29]

The priesthoods were probably limited to particular families and with succession in rotation. The
priests, doubtless, had the management of the sacred
lands belonging to the temple, out of the revenues of
which they gave largesses and public entertainments.
On one occasion, certain priests presented to each
citizen two *denarii*, equal to about one shilling and
fourpence. This largess was given in the theatre,
the citizens being called over by name from the
registers (δέλτοι) of their deme, or township.

There appears to have been a great festival in

honour of the goddess every five years, called *Pen-taëteris*. The procession of the key appears to have been an annual festival of great importance, on which occasion gymnastic entertainments were given by the priests. There were also in the course of the year various other festal days sacred to Hekate.

The temple appears to have had a territory (*περι-πόλιον*), which probably contained villages. It is uncertain whether this was an independent district, or whether it was part of the neighbouring canton, or *σύστημα*, of villages, of which the Temple of Zeus Chrysaoreus, near Stratonicea, was the central point.[30] Lagina is described by Stephanus Byzantius as *πολίχνιον Καρίας.*[31]

In the course of the inscriptions, mention is made of the Senate (*boulé*) and popular Assembly (*demos*), and of civil magistrates, such as *Prytanes* and *Ste-phanephori*, in whose name the decrees made by the senate and people were registered.

In a fragment of one of these decrees mention is made of some king whose name has perished, and of two Carian towns, Themessos and Keramos. The former of these cities is evidently the Themissos of Stephanus Byzantius; Keramos was one of the most important towns in the Chrysaorian confederacy of Carian cities.

The site of the temple overlooks a plain to the north-east, and commands an extensive and beautiful view, bounded by mountains. In the village is a mosque almost entirely built of fragments of white marble, among which I noticed an Ionic volute and other architectural fragments. In the road descending from the village to the temple is an abundant spring, which was probably used in the rites of Hekate. At this fountain the water falls into an oblong marble basin, which appears ancient.

I spent five days at Lagina copying inscriptions, and left it reluctantly, feeling sure that there was much more to be discovered on this interesting site, which has been singularly overlooked by travellers, though it lies so near the main route from Mylasa to Mughla.

I returned to Mylasa and thence to Iakly, where there is a Corinthian temple of the Roman period, which has been described by several travellers.

This site, which has been erroneously called La-branda, is probably that of Euromus. Wishing to visit the ruins of the ancient Bargylia, near Guver-jilik, I proceeded from Iakly to Tekrambari, where I halted for the night. Tekrambari is a village on a small eminence, in the midst of marshes, among which, arriving after nightfall, we lost our way, finding the village at last after some difficulty.

Between this place and the sea is a low alluvial plain which has probably filled up the head of the Iassic Gulf. If Tekrambari was ever on the sea-shore, it is very probably the site of the ancient Passala, the port of Miletus, as Lebas supposes.[32]

From Tekrambari I continued my journey to Guverjilik, intending to visit the ruins of Bargylia on my way. In the plain, at the distance of one hour from Tekrambari, is a small eminence on which has stood a Greek temple. On the north side a few blocks remain *in situ*. The columns are of grey

marble, fluted. They have been used as gravestones
in a Turkish cemetery on the spot. I was told that
this place was called Assari. These ruins may be
the same as those described by Texier, iii. p. 144, as
being distant a league from Bargylia, *dans la plaine
de l'autre côté des collines.* He conjectures that the
temple of Artemis Kindyas stood here.

The site of Bargylia is on a peninsula round which
is a shallow salt-lake, which has been an arm of the
sea. As we passed this lake on our way to Guverjilik, seeing the ruins of Bargylia on the opposite
shore, I made an attempt to cross over at a ford,
where my muleteer said the mud would bear our
weight.

We were going along in single file, and had
nearly crossed over the mud, when I heard a loud
shriek behind me, and looking back, saw the bag-
gage-horse sink deep into the slough. We dragged
out the baggage, the state of which I was afraid to
examine till we got into our night quarters at Guverjilik. To my horror, I then found all the impressions
of inscriptions made at Mylasa and Lagina floating
in the tin box in which I carried them, the bibulous
paper on which they were taken being reduced to a
pulpy mass. Remembering that paper will always
dry when let alone, I succeeded by delicate manipu-
lation in saving all the impressions, which retained
the forms of the letters, with very slight diminu-
tion of their sharpness. After sleeping at Guverjilik, I went to Bargylia, distant two hours to the
north. This site, now called Assarlik, is a wild
deserted spot, cut off from the mainland by the sea

and salt-lake. The ancient city stood on rising ground, to the east of which is a dreary waste of muddy marsh, where are now salt-pans, and which in the time of the Romans must have been covered by the sea.

The ruins are all laid down in the Admiralty Chart, No. 1531. Those principally to be noted are as follows : —

A small temple on an eminence, lying north-west and south-east, and overlooking an Odeum on the south-east and a theatre on the east. The line of the foundations appears at intervals. The peristyle seems to have been about 96 feet in length.

The small *Odeum*, or musical theatre, marked in the Chart, measures 49½ feet at the chord of its arc. The distance from the centre of the chord to the centre of the arc, at the lowest step, is 38 feet. There are in all ten rows of steps, which are each 1 foot 5 inches in height.

South-east of the Odeum is the foundation of a Doric portico, lying north-east and south-west. Its length is 50 feet. The position of each column is marked by a circular space cut in the stone. The intercolumniation is 7 feet 9 inches and the columns have a diameter of 1 foot 11 inches. Several pieces of the architrave lying *in situ* have inscriptions relating to the dedication of the portico, called πυλών.

The temple on the shore, marked in the Chart, had very small fluted columns and a few pieces of cornice, and little else. Close to the causeway on the shore, marked in the Chart, I found the in-

scription, No. 496, of Lebas, containing a decree of
the senate and people of Bargylia in honour of one
Exekestos, son of Diodotos, who is styled φιλόκαισαρ,
or friend to some Roman emperor.

We found in a hut at Bargylia six or seven individuals of very forbidding aspect, one of whom was
a Samiote, and another a Bashi Bozouk, who pointed
out my gold watch-chain to his companions, with an
unpleasant chuckle, but made no attempt to extort
money. I was not sorry to get away from such
company, considering that I was then carrying in
my girdle about £240, the money intended as
bounty for the Land Transport recruits. Two or
three of this party were tending sheep and goats;
but I suspect that the rest were hiding from the
pursuit of the Pasha's police.

The peninsula has at present no regular inhabitants. A Turkish village on the site of the ancient
city was, like many small places along this coast,
ruined during the Greek revolution by incursions of
pirates. I returned to Budrum by Guverjilik.

XXXV.

RHODES, *April* 5, 1856.

AFTER my visit to Mughla, finding that the
firman which I had so long expected did not arrive,
I spent some weeks in exploring the antiquities of
Budrum.

Having free access to the Castle there, I

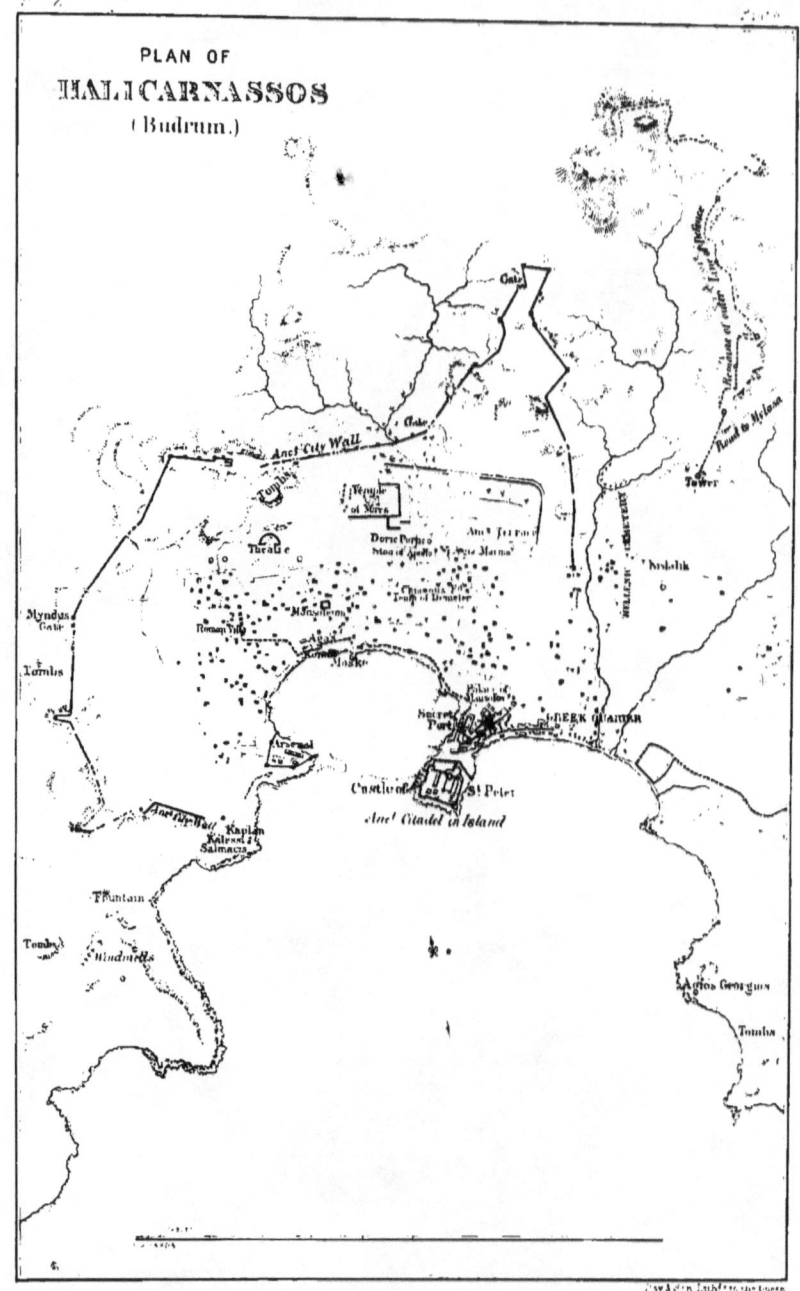

PLAN OF

HALICARNASSOS

(Budrum.)

examined it very carefully, copying all the inscriptions I could find there. It is built on the rocky extremity of the eastern side of the harbour. (*See* Plate 1.) This rock, which is about 400 feet square, was in antiquity the site of an acropolis, and according to Pliny was once an island. Before his time it became united to the mainland by a sandy isthmus. On the site of the old Greek acropolis Philibert De Naillac built the stately castle which still stands, a specimen of the military architecture of the Knights, not less worthy of study than the fortress of Rhodes.

The position of this castle is one of great natural strength as compared with the means of attack known in the 15th century. It is surrounded on three sides by the sea, while on the land side the rocky nature of the soil would have made mining impossible.

The castle is entered from the isthmus by a ramp cut through the western corner of a glacis of unusual size, which forms the outer defence on the north side. Within this ramp is a fosse, which widens as it approaches the sea, having a breadth of 150 feet in the part where the gateway from the ramp opens into it. This end of the fosse is protected by a casemated battery to hinder the landing of troops within the glacis. This battery has a roof of solid masonry, gabled externally to prevent the lodgement of shells. The north side is further strengthened by two towers, connected by a curtain wall and a smaller fosse, running parallel to the larger fosse. On the western side which faces the harbour the castle is defended by a wide rampart, within which is a deep fosse. It is in the sea face of this rampart that the lions' heads from the Mausoleum are placed. On the eastern and southern sides the external line of defence is a curtain-wall, with a strong tower at the south-east corner. The opposite angle on the south-west is protected by a platform, with embrasures for nine guns on the south and eight on the west.

The entrance to the castle is through a series of seven gateways, to the first of which the ramp in the northern glacis leads up. After crossing the northern fosse, the road passes through three more gateways into the sea-rampart of the western fosse, and thence winding through three more gateways finally enters the interior of the fortress at its south-western angle. The seventh and last of these gateways is protected by the platform already noticed. The object of so winding an approach was of course to guard against surprises. The area contained within these external defences is divided into an outer and inner bayle. In the inner bayle, which is the highest ground within the castle, are two lofty square towers, which form the keep. The outer bayle contains the chapel of the Knights.

The two central towers seem to be the earliest part of the fortress, which was probably built by instalments, the lines being gradually extended till they embraced the whole of the rocky platform. It was constructed by Henry Schlegelholt, a German knight, who found in the ruins of the Mausoleum an ample supply of building materials.

The masonry is throughout in admirable preservation. Since the day when the castle was handed over to the Mussulman conqueror, it has undergone very few changes. The long brass guns of the Knights still arm the batteries, and their powder lies caked up in the magazines. The Turks change nothing in their fortresses. There is in this castle a magnificent cistern cut in the rock, full of water. A few years ago a soldier fell into it and was drowned. The Turks, instead of troubling themselves to fish the body out, ceased to use the water of the cistern, regarding it as polluted for ever.

Here, as at Rhodes, the stern monotony of military masonry is constantly relieved by shields and inscriptions sculptured on white marble and let into the walls. Wherever architectural decoration occurs, it is of the same *flamboyant* character as at Rhodes. In the chapel may still be seen a beautifully carved rood-screen, now adapted to Mussulman worship.

In the tower, at the south-east corner, is a room which was probably the refectory of the Knights. Here, sitting in the wide bays of the windows, they beguiled the weariness of garrison life by carving their names and escutcheons on the walls. Many hundred valiant soldiers of the Cross, unmentioned in the glorious annals of the Order, have thus been preserved from utter oblivion, for the inscriptions are as fresh as if cut yesterday. Some of the names are Spanish.

This tower was probably erected by Englishmen, as the arms of Edward IV., and of the different branches of the Plantagenet family, together with

many other English coats, are sculptured in a row
over the door. Scattered about the castle are the
arms of its successive captains, ranging from 1437
to 1522, when the garrison surrendered to the
Turks. Among these is the name of a well-known
English knight, Sir Thomas Sheffield, with the date
1514. The arms of another Englishman, John
Kendal, who was Turcopolier, 1477—1500, may be
seen under the Royal arms, on the tower at the
south-east angle.

The care with which the Knights fortified their
castle at Budrum was justified by the importance of
the position, for without this fortress they would
not have had the complete command of the channel
of Cos, and that island and Calymnos would have
been liable to invasions from the opposite coast of
Asia Minor.

After examining the castle, I explored part of a
district called Kislalik, lying just outside the
eastern wall of the city. The course of the ancient
road to Mylasa may be here distinctly traced by a
row of square basements of tombs, on which modern
Turkish houses are built. These basements generally contain a small vaulted chamber, entered by
two small doorways. They are wholly built or
faced with blocks of grey marble. Several sepulchral inscriptions are built into the walls of the
Turkish houses. Immediately to the north of this
row of houses is a field belonging to a Turk named
Suliman, where I opened a number of tombs of
different kinds. They may be thus classified :—

1. *Hypogœa*, or subterraneous chambers, the largest

about 17 feet square, and containing two stone coffins or *sori*.—These are built of a volcanic tufa, the πώρινος λίθος of the ancients, still called πωρί by the Greeks at Budrum. The roof is constructed of long stone beams laid side by side, over which is a solid pavement of slabs of tufa.

2. Vaulted chambers above ground, built of concrete and rubble, which have been faced with ashlar-work, and are now in ruins.—These and the preceding class had all been rifled.

3. Built tombs in the earth lined with slabs and covered with thick blocks of tufa.—They were generally about 6 feet 5 inches in length. I never found anything in them but bones.

4. Large stone coffins or *sori*, with monolithic lids.—Of these I found two, under a depth of about 3 feet of soil. One had a very massive lid; on lifting which up, I saw at one end of the coffin a vase lying on its side, and a bronze cup of very elegant form. All trace of the body had disappeared except a fine layer of dust, on examining which I found a silver coin of Chios, placed there as the *naulon*. The vase was an *amphora* of a late period with a group of Dionysos, satyrs, and female dancing figures on the obverse, and on the reverse three youths conversing, painted in red on a black ground. At the side of this coffin was a smaller one, containing an *amphora* of the same period, on which was painted a combat between an Amazon and a Greek, in red and opaque white on a black ground, and a small two-handled cup of the kind called *kantharos*, painted black.

5. Tombs in the form of an oblong trough, πύελος, made of baked red clay, with a separate cover.— These troughs were laid in the earth very near the surface. They contained no bones : in several of them I found a silver coin deposited as *naulon*. Several of these coins had on the obverse a lion's head, and on the reverse a trident, and were evidently struck at Halicarnassus, as the same type is found on the copper coins of that city.[33]

6. Graves lined and roofed with flanged tiles.— This class of tomb has been met with in many parts of the Hellenic world.

7. Large πίθοι or jars of baked red clay laid in the earth.—I have already noticed this mode of interment in my account of the tombs in the Troad and at Calymnos.

8. Cinerary urns.—Of these I found one placed in a square hole, each side of which was formed by a wall built of rough stones without mortar. The urn, made of coarse unpainted ware, contained only bones, and was covered with a rough stone.

9. Tombs formed of two slabs placed at an acute angle so as to form a penthouse roof.—Each of these graves was closed by a stone set vertically at each end.

10. Graves built of rubble walls sometimes lined with mortar, and covered with rough flat stones.— These were only a few inches under the surface of the soil. One of these graves had for its cover a Greek *stelé*, the inscription on which is probably as early as the time of Alexander the Great.[34] The rudeness of construction in these graves, the absence

of Hellenic remains in them, and their nearness to
the surface, leads me to suppose that they are of a
very late period, an opinion confirmed by the discovery of the *stelé*. I found nothing in these tombs
but very coarse unglazed pottery, three plain bronze
mirrors, two of which were square, and a few small
objects in the same metal.

Digging in a field separated from that of Suliman
by the road to Mylasa, I found, about two feet
below the surface, a large *diota* of coarse earthen-
ware placed upright in the ground. At the foot of
this vase was a built grave covered with slabs of
hewn stone, lying on which was a bronze *simpulum*
or sacrificial ladle, which must have been left there
with the *diota* after the performance of sepulchral
rites, either at the time of the interment or at some
subsequent period. This grave contained no remains whatever.

Exploring the district to the south of Kislalik, I
found a sepulchral inscription built into the doorway of a house, which had evidently been placed
under a statue surmounting an architectural tomb.
Digging in front of this house, I found several
graves, in one of which were the fragments of a
flageolet (*plagiaulos*), made of bone covered with
bronze; the mouthpiece was still entire. In another
grave was a circular leaden box, about 2 inches
high, and a bronze *spatula*. Another grave on this
site, built of loose stone, contained about two hundred small vials of common unglazed pottery.

On the western side of the city is another cemetery, through which the road leading to Myndus

must have passed. Here are several square basements built of rubble and concrete, with an ashlar
facing. I tried an excavation here, but the soil was
full of springs, and the pottery in the graves had all
decayed in consequence. I opened about seven
graves, mostly clay troughs, but found nothing in
them but the silver coin of Halicarnassus already
described.

After thus partially exploring the tombs, I made
several excavations within the walls of the ancient
city, in places to which I was directed by the Turks.
The only one of these sites which promised much
was a field belonging to an old Turk called Mehemet
Chiaoux, situated near the centre of the town. (*See*
Plate 1.) On digging here, I came to foundations
of the Roman period, within which was a layer of
black earth containing many hundreds of small
terra-cotta figures, averaging from 5 to 8 inches in
height, and coarsely executed. With these were
found a scarabæus of green basalt, a hand from a
female statue in white marble, a long strip of beaten
gold, and the bottom of a small marble *pyxis*.
I should have been glad to pursue this excavation
further; but as the field had been recently sown, I
could not extend my diggings without destroying
the crop. I therefore determined to resume this
excavation on a future visit to Budrum.

I had now exhausted the sum placed at my disposal for excavation by Lord Stratford, the firman
had not arrived, and in the mean time I had received
news from Mytilene which rendered my presence
there desirable. I therefore brought my diggings

at Budrum to a close, and returned to Rhodes,
where I am now waiting for a steamer to convey
me to Mytilene.

[On returning to my post in April, 1856, I found
a despatch from the Foreign Office waiting for me, in
which I was instructed to proceed at once to Rome,
to value the Campana collection, then offered to the
British Government. I remained at Rome till the
autumn of the same year, when I went to England
on leave of absence. I took advantage of this opportunity to submit my views as to further operations
at Budrum to Mr. Panizzi, the principal librarian at
the British Museum, and through him to the Earl of
Clarendon, then her Majesty's Secretary for Foreign
Affairs. I suggested that a firman authorizing the
removal of the lions from the Castle at Budrum
should be obtained from the Porte, and that the
sum of £2,000, and the services of a ship of war for
at least six months, would be necessary to insure the
success of the expedition. I also recommended that
an officer of the Royal Engineers and four Sappers
should accompany the expedition, to direct any difficult engineering operations; and, in order to secure
an accurate record of the excavations, I suggested
that one of the Sappers should be a photographer.

These suggestions were at once carried into effect
by her Majesty's Government, and the small party
of Royal Engineers was further provided with every
kind of stores and appliances from the War Office,
which might be needed in the varied operations of
such an expedition.

The ship appointed by the Admiralty for this
special service was her Majesty's steam-corvette
Gorgon, under the command of Captain Towsey,
with a crew of 150 men. Lieutenant R. M. Smith
was the officer sent in command of the party of
Sappers, who consisted of Corporal William Jenkins,
Corporal B. Spackman, as photographer, and two
Lance-Corporals, one a smith, the other a mason.
The Gorgon arrived at Budrum at the beginning of
November, 1856.]

XXXVI.

BUDRUM, *December* 14, 1856.

AFTER spending a few days at Constantinople on
my way out, I joined the Gorgon at Smyrna, where
I found all the staff of the expedition on board. It
was satisfactory to find that the numerous requisitions for stores which had been sent in by the War
Office and the Admiralty had been carefully attended
to, and that everything which we required for the
expedition had been promptly and punctually supplied. After taking in a large stock of pale ale and
such creature comforts at Smyrna, we resumed our
voyage, and arrived at Budrum at the beginning of
November.

The first thing I had to do on disembarking was
to establish a base of operations on shore, where
our stores might be kept, and where smiths and

carpenters might work. We should have had great
difficulty in finding such a place, had not my old
friend Salik Bey placed his konak at our disposal in
the kindest manner. Here Lieut. Smith and I took
up our quarters, with the four Sappers attached to
the expedition.

The rooms in the konak were windowless and
rat-ridden, with floors made of thin plank, through
which many a loophole let in the north wind from
the street below. However, with the aid of double
tents, pitched in the courtyard, we managed to stow
ourselves away very comfortably.

When we had disembarked our stores, the natives
crowded round us to examine the wonderful tools
and appliances which we had imported from England.
Except at Constantinople and a few great towns
in Turkey, metallurgy is a most neglected art, and
iron a costly article, imported generally from Russia.
Great, therefore, was the astonishment of the Turks
at the sight of our miners' picks, iron spades, crow-
bars, and sledge hammers. Still more did they
admire the wheelbarrows with wrought-iron wheels,
the trucks which trundle over even Turkish roads
with resistless impetus, like the cars of the ancient
Britons ; and the huge tackles and triangles, suggesting to their minds unknown and mysterious
mechanical powers. Everything was *Marafet, Chok
Marafet*. This word is applied to all masterpieces of
mechanical ingenuity, and is the epithet specially
associated with the name of Franks.

The magnitude of our preparations of course led
the native mind to the conclusion that we must have

a superabundance of money, and my old workmen,
all of them Greeks, had the modesty to ask just
double the wages paid for a day's labour at Smyrna.

These pretensions were speedily reduced when a
party of fifty sailors landed with picks and shovels,
and in the course of about six hours did as much
work as a Greek would do in a day and a half.

I then tried the experiment of employing Turks,
and was very well satisfied. When properly treated,
they are most intelligent and docile workmen; not
so handy and expeditious as sailors, but their dogged
perseverance makes up for the slowness of their
movements. They have great strength for carrying
heavy weights on their backs. They do not strike
so heavily with the pick as Englishmen, which is
rather an advantage in excavations where antiquities are found. The poorer Turks of Budrum are
most of them more or less mariners; hence many of
my labourers have a certain familiarity with ropes
and blocks, which makes them very apt and handy
in learning the use of the triangle. Wages vary from
six to eight piasters a day, according to the quality
of the workman.

No sooner were we ready to commence operations
than I was invited by my old friend Mehemet
Chiaoux to resume my diggings in his field. It was
here that the year before I had discovered a great
quantity of small terra-cotta figures. Enlarging the
opening in the ground, I came to a number of foundation-walls, running at right angles to each other, so
as to enclose small rooms or cells. Within these
foundations I continued to find layers of terra-cotta

figures, packed in the soil as if they had been deposited there. Though more than a thousand in all were discovered, the number of varieties of type did not exceed thirty, of which the following were the most remarkable :—

1. A figure either of Persephone or her priestess, holding in her arms the pig (χοῖρος), sacred to that deity.

2. Persephone, draped to the feet, in her right hand a pomegranate fruit, her left resting against her hip.

3. A *Kanephoros*, bearing on her head the *kane*, or sacred basket, used in the worship of Demeter.

4. A *Hydrophoros*, or draped female figure, carrying a water-pitcher (*hydria*) on her head, and in her left hand a *phiale*.

5. Demeter, holding in her left hand two ears of corn.

6. Gaia Kourotrophos, " Earth the nourisher of children," holding in her arms an infant.

7. Cybele seated, in her lap a lion.

8. Aphrodite, draped to the feet, in her right hand a dove.

9. Two varieties of the type of Dionysos, one bearded, the other youthful.

There is no doubt that all these were votive offerings. A few yards to the east of these foundations we discovered a cube of grey marble, inscribed with a dedication to Demeter and Proserpine.[35]

It may be inferred, from the joint evidence of this inscription and the terra-cotta figures, that a temple dedicated to Ceres, and probably to Proserpine, stood

on this site. The foundations among which I found
the terra-cottas appeared to be those of a vaulted
basement. The walls were built chiefly of rubble,
strongly united by grouting; large squared stones,
evidently from some previous Hellenic edifice, were
inserted at intervals. From the circumstance that
so many figures and lamps of the same type were
discovered within these walls, it is probable that this
basement served as a sort of treasury or magazine
where votive offerings were kept. Such vaults, called
by the Romans *favissæ*, were employed for such
purposes in ancient temples.

The field where I made these discoveries being
planted with fig-trees, I could not extend the excavations sufficiently to ascertain the exact site and
extent of the temple which I assume to have stood
here. In the next field to the west I had made a
small excavation the year before, on the site of a
Byzantine church, in the course of which I laid bare
some portions of a large Roman cornice, which may
have belonged to the same Temple of Demeter.

I next explored a field, which Captain Spratt has
marked in the Admiralty Chart as the most probable
site for the Mausoleum.

Here I found Hellenic foundations enclosed within
the precinct of a Byzantine monastery. Within these
foundations were many fragments of Greek tessellated
pavements and painted stucco. The mosaic was of
very fine workmanship, being composed of small
cubes of white, black, and red marble. Occasionally
glass was used. The cubes were beautifully cut and
set in a fine cement. The patterns on these frag-

ments were simple volutes, stripes, and borders. In the volutes the eye or centre of the spiral was formed of *tessellæ*, small by degrees, diminishing in size as they approached the centre of the spiral.

The different colours were used in broad stripes, which appear to have been separately inserted as *emblemata* in the general surface, and then fixed by thin laminæ of lead, which were run into the joints between the colours, and which I found still adhering to them. The patterns on these fragments resemble those found at Herculaneum, and are much simpler and purer in taste than the designs of the later Roman pavements. The fragments of painted stucco found with these mosaics were remarkable for the freshness of the colours and the fineness of the stucco, which was composed of pounded white marble laid on a coarser plaster. The preservation of the surface of these fragments was due to the circumstance that the soil in which they were lying was a fine sand.

A number of architectural mouldings were found, on which were painted borders in green and umber, on a white ground, and some pieces of fluted half-columns, from 4 inches to 6 inches in diameter, in white stucco; also thin slices of marble for lining the walls inside. All these fragments had evidently formed part of the internal decoration of some edifice.

A dreadful catastrophe has just befallen the town of Rhodes. The inhabitants had hardly recovered from the shock of an earthquake, which threw down many private houses and greatly injured the fortifications, when an explosion took place which totally

destroyed the church of St. John, and killed several
hundred people. In the vaults under this church
was a powder magazine, and if the Turks are to be
believed, the explosion was caused in a very singular
manner. The vault of the magazine having been
split open by the earthquake, a flash of lightning
descended through the fissure, and ignited the
powder. Whether the accident was really so caused,
or whether it was rather due to some gross careless-
ness on the part of the officials in charge, who, to
screen themselves from detection, may have invented
the tale about the lightning, it is certain that after
the explosion took place the authorities of the town,
from the Pasha downwards, showed the most utter
helplessness and apathy. The catastrophe occurred
in the evening, about the time when the gates of the
town are closed. As it was known that many persons had been buried under the ruins, the British
consul, Mr. Campbell, immediately sent to the Pasha,
begging him to take immediate steps to rescue those
who might be still alive. The Pasha, with the usual
apathy of a Turkish official, did nothing whatever
that night; and Mr. Campbell, who came at once at
the head of a body of workmen to give assistance, was denied admittance at the land gate, and
forced to pull round on a stormy night from the
Quarantine to the sea gate of the great harbour,
running the risk of getting his boat swamped on
the way.

In consequence of these delays, it was not till
eleven o'clock at night that he reached the scene of
the disaster with his men. Mr. Alfred Biliotti, at

the head of this small party, worked through the night by torchlight as well as he could, and succeeded in disinterring several persons who had been buried alive. Among them was a young Turkish girl newly betrothed, and whose lover had the pleasure of assisting in restoring her to the light of day.

In the morning Mr. Campbell sent again to the Pasha, stating that his small party of workmen were now quite exhausted, and suggesting that as there was a Turkish ship of war in the harbour, part of the crew might be sent on shore to assist in clearing away the ruins. This suggestion was partially carried out, for a large party of sailors and marines were landed soon after, not to dig, but to keep the ground clear with fixed bayonets! The precious hours slipped away in this sort of trifling till the Pasha had been fairly roused up to act vigorously, and by that time the chance of finding persons still alive under the ruins had become quite hopeless.

XXXVII.

Budrum, *December*, 1856.

After exploring the field of Chiaoux, I made an experiment in another field a little to the N.W. of it, belonging to an old Turk called Hadji Captan.

On this site had been found some years ago the torso of a draped female figure of the Roman period,

sent to England when the friezes from the Castle were
removed by Lord Stratford de Redcliffe.[36]

On digging here, I discovered a tessellated pavement at the depth of about three feet below the
surface; following which in various directions, I
laid bare an area extending 119 feet from east to
west, and 89 feet from north to south, and consisting of the floors of a number of rooms. On
the north was a room 62 feet by $25\frac{1}{2}$ feet. At the
west end of this room was a picture of Meleager
and Atalanta hunting. This composition was balanced at the east end by a subject on the same scale
—Dido and Æneas hunting. The details of the
costume of these figures were curious. Between
these two pictures were two circular patterns,
each inscribed in a square. In the square nearest
the west end the angles round the circle were
severally filled up with heads representing the four
seasons.

The names of all the figures represented in this
room were written over them. Round the whole ran
a broad architectural border, formed of the guilloche
plait. In the centre of this room the pavement had
been broken away, and here, lying on the ground, we
found a draped female torso, in two pieces, without
a head. This statue is winged, and the figure is
in rapid motion. It is very hard and wiry in style.
To the west of this room was a smaller apartment,
26 feet by $27\frac{1}{2}$ feet, in the centre of which was a
sunk floor, or *impluvium*, paved with thin slices of
marble, laid on a bed of pounded brick and concrete.
Round this sunk square was a mosaic representing

lions, bulls, goats, and other animals chasing one another.

To the west was a room 10 feet long by 12 feet wide, running east and west, and terminating at the west end in a semicircle. At this end was a group representing a naked female figure, probably Amphitrite, floating amid waves and dolphins. On either side of her is a youthful Triton. The rest of the pavement consisted of geometrical patterns.

At the north side of this room was a narrow room, 14 feet long by 6 feet 3 inches wide. In the pavement were three female busts, each set in a circular frame. These busts, as appears from the inscriptions round them, severally represent the cities of Halicarnassus, Alexandria, and Berytus. The combination may have typified a commercial alliance between these three cities. The costume of these busts is of a very late period, and the drawing very coarse. The pavement in this room was too much decayed to be taken up.

To the south of these pavements were others on a lower level. The principal of these pavements consisted of two distinct parts. On the north was an oblong passage, 51 feet long by 15 feet wide, containing three compartments, surrounded by a border of medallions. These compartments contained severally a figure of Dionysos with a panther; a Satyr pursuing a Nymph or Mænad; and a Nereid seated on a Hippocamp. In the medallions were birds and other animals. South of this passage was a rectangular space, 30 feet by 26 feet.

In this area were the following pictures : — On
the east, a scene in a vineyard, in which Pan
is represented with Eros. A lion, a panther,
a greyhound, and birds are introduced into this
scene. In the centre of the area were two pictures—Europa standing by the Bull, and a water-
nymph.

To the east of this again was a dog pursuing a
hare. The whole was surrounded by a border of
medallions containing birds.

In the N.W. corner of this room the pattern had
been cut away for the insertion of a well, which we
found closed up. A sailor was let down, and
descended into about three feet of water, at the
bottom of which was a deposit of black mud.

Bronze Lamp found in well.

We baled out the water, and were rewarded for
our trouble by finding in the sediment at the

bottom a white marble bust of the Roman period, the portrait of some unknown individual; and a small bronze lamp. We also found here the remains of a wooden bucket, bound with brass

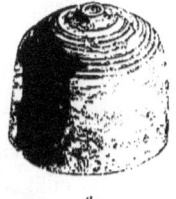 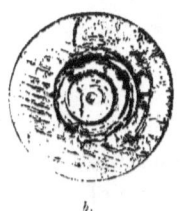

a.   b.

hoops, and a small conical object (cuts *a*, *b*), made of ebony, apparently used in some game like draughts.

The shaft of this well was cut out of the solid rock; the mouth was square, with a groove into which the cover of the well fitted. At the depth of 14 feet 8 inches the shaft was traversed by a gallery cut in the rock. This gallery was 6 feet high, and ran 27 feet to the N.E., and $14\frac{1}{2}$ feet to the S.W. of the well. At the N.E. end it terminated in a small arched opening, leading upwards, evidently intended to receive the surface drainage conveyed in earthen pipes through the soil. On the west and south sides the room was separated by party walls from a passage.

The passage on the west side was $51\frac{1}{2}$ feet in length by 10 feet in width. The pavement was divided into nine rectangular compartments, containing geometrical patterns, ivy-leaves, birds, flowers, and dolphins.

In the centre division was the following inscription, within a laurel wreath :—

ΥΓΙΑ

ΖΟΗ

ΧΑΡΑ

ΕΙΡΗΝΗ

ΕΥΘΥΜΙΑ

ΕΛΠΙΣ

" Health, Life, Joy, Peace, Cheerfulness, Hope," in black, on a white ground—a very pleasant inscription for the eyes of the ancient owner of this villa to rest on as he paced up and down this corridor.[37]

The passage on the south side was in length 64 feet by 14½ feet wide. The design is the counterpart of the passage on the north side of this room, already described. In one compartment a few letters of an inscription in black on a white ground, still remained.

In some places the pavement was laid on an artificial level, composed of drums of columns and ruins of former edifices. In other places the rubble bed of the pavement rested on the earth. Where the rock was very near the surface, the rubble bed was omitted, the rock being used as its substitute. The tessellæ were chiefly of marble; brick was, however, used in the red colour, and in one picture green glass was employed. The cubes were irregularly cut, and not set with the precision and neatness which characterize the earlier Hellenic mosaic.

When we first laid bare this pavement, the patterns were nearly concealed by calcareous incrustation, deposited from the cement of the pavement, as it had decomposed and oozed through the tessellæ. On removing this deposit by water and hard scrubbing, the colours of the patterns gradually came out, and though the drawing of the figures was throughout very rude and coarse, the effect of the whole design, as a piece of colour, was exceedingly rich and harmonious.

Before attempting to take up any of the floors, I had nearly the whole copied by photography, in the following manner :—The photographic lens was placed on a portable stage above the pavement, so as to take a vertical view of a small portion of it, and was shifted from point to point till views of the whole design had been obtained. Notes of the different colours were then made on the photographs. Exact plans of the patterns in each room were also made by Lieut. Smith. After all this had been done, I tried to take up some of the best of the floors.

The usual mode of taking up mosaic pavement is to glaze canvas on the upper surface, and to lay a bed of plaster of Paris upon this. When the bond of the tessellæ has been thus strengthened by this applied surface, the pavement can be safely detached from the ground on which it rests. This is usually done by driving a gallery in the earth below, and then cutting away the lower and heavier part of the bed of the pavement. This bed commonly consists of three strata,—a coarse rubble foundation, a layer of mortar, and a layer of fine cement, in which the tessellæ themselves are fixed. When the bed is in a sound state, and can be got at from below, nearly the whole thickness of its lower layers may be detached with safety. The pavement may then be taken up in large squares, and being held together partly by its original cement and partly by the canvas and plaster of Paris applied to its upper surface, will bear transport if carefully packed. The pavement in Hadji Captan's field being laid on the native rock instead of upon earth, it was found impossible to cut it away from below. It was, moreover, in many places, in a very unsound state. However, I succeeded in taking up one entire room, by dividing it into very small squares, and then lifting them up by a gentle application of leverage at the sides. This room was the one terminating in an apse, in which was the picture of Amphitrite surrounded by dolphins.

On the north side the area which we uncovered was bounded by a wall built of squared blocks, which, it may be assumed, was the outer wall, as we could find no trace of foundations or pavement to the north of it. On the south we carried our excavations only as far as the pavement extended, but we could meet with no boundary-wall on this side. On the east our excavations were arrested by a Turkish cemetery, and on the west by the house of the proprietor of the field, and we were therefore unable to ascertain how far the tessellated pavement extended in either of these directions, or what was the original form and purpose of the building to which it belonged.

It is most probable, however, that a Roman villa once stood on this site. Several large pieces of cornice of a calcareous stone, covered with stucco, were found lying on the pavement, as if they had fallen from the roof; and in the courtyard of Hadji Captan was the base of a Roman column. The walls of the several apartments had been lined with a thin veneer of marble, portions of which were still remaining *in situ* between the wall and the pavement. From the character of the inscriptions in the pavements it is probable that the villa was of the second century of our era. It appeared to have been constructed out of the materials of an earlier building on the same site, and its own plan seems to have been altered in several places after erection.

Hadji Captan, the proprietor of this field, was a jovial old Turk, who took the greatest interest in our diggings. He greatly marvelled at the sight of the strange pictures which had lain concealed under the soil of his field for so many centuries; but when the photographer went to work, and we showed Hadji Captan his own portrait on the glass, and seated beside him another greybeard, his most familiar friend, he began to think that we were magicians. So constant was his interest in the diggings, that he remained watching us in all weathers, till at last the poor old man caught a cold from standing too long on the wet soil, and died. The doctor of the Gorgon attended him, and his life perhaps might have been saved, but for the utter incapacity of his wife to prepare nourishing food. In the sick room the wife of the Mussulman is a poor helpless creature, and the rigid etiquette prescribed by Turkish manners almost prohibits her from taking her natural place at the bedside of her husband.

I visited Hadji Captan a few hours before his death. The room was crowded with silent grey-bearded Turks, solemnly waiting for the moment when their old friend would have to take leave of them for ever. But the wife was concealed in an inner room, taking no part whatever in the scene.

Hadji Captan was buried in the cemetery of his own field, and our sailors, shocked at the shallowness of the Turkish graves, made a neat little mound over it. Let us hope that his bones may rest in peace, undisturbed by the jackal and the wild dog, who often seek their food in the cemeteries of Turkish villages, and the traces of whose recent ravages shock the European traveller, reminding him of the old legend of the Ghouls.

XXXVIII.

AFTER months of anxiety and weary labour I am at length able to say that the main object of the expedition is fulfilled, for the site of the Mausoleum is no longer a matter of uncertainty. The manner of its discovery was thus. In the centre of the town of Budrum, just above the konak of Salik Bey (*see* Plate 1), is, or rather was, a site distinguished by nothing very particular, except the fact that in several places pieces of large Ionic columns

of the finest Parian marble were still lying about
on the surface. Examining the site more closely,
the practised eye might observe a certain artificial
irregularity of ground, such as is the case where
ruins have been thrown about and afterwards
buried under the natural accumulation of the soil.
The site was covered with houses and little plots
of ground divided by modern stone walls. In
several places were drums of fluted columns about
3 feet 6 inches in diameter, and of the purest white
marble, and on a close inspection of the walls of
the houses and gardens, I perceived that here
and there fragments of Ionic architecture of great
beauty were built into the masonry. I then recognized this as the spot noticed by Professor Donald-
son when he visited Budrum many years ago. He,
too, was struck with the beauty of the architectural
fragments lying about here, and his description of
these remains led me, in my memoir on the Man-
soleum in 1847, to place its site conjecturally on
this very spot. This suggestion was not adopted
by either of the distinguished topographers Captain
Spratt or Professor Ross, who subsequently visited
Budrum. The latter rejected my theory with the
somewhat contemptuous remark that such notions
showed how useless it was for any one to write
about the topography of a place without personally
visiting it.[35] Notwithstanding these adverse opinions,
I was more than ever confirmed in my original
view on visiting the site itself. I argued thus:—
We know from Vitruvius that the Mausoleum stood
in the centre of the town half-way between the

harbour and the heights above. There is every
reason to believe that it was an Ionic building of
Parian marble. After a long and laborious survey
of every part of the modern town of Budrum, I
find no other architectural remains of such beauty
and interest as in this one spot, the central position
of which corresponds exactly with the site as marked
out by Vitruvius.

I decided therefore on digging here. The ground
was divided into a number of little plots, each with
a separate owner. After a great deal of trouble, I
obtained leave from one of them to dig a little
strip of ground, the one half of his field.

It was on the 1st of January in this year that I
first broke ground on this memorable site. After
a few spadefuls had been thrown up, I examined
the character of the soil. It was a loose black
mould, full of small splinters of fine white marble
and rubble. The whole appearance of this soil,
and the absence of stratification in it, suggested the
notion that it was a recent accumulation, such as
might have taken place in the 400 years which
have elapsed since the building of the castle of
Budrum by the Knights. The fragments of
marble were evidently from some Ionic building.
I collected them with the greatest care. After
a short time a mutilated leg turned up : this was
evidently from a frieze. I began to have vague
hopes. More bits of sculpture appeared,—always
legs and scraps of frieze, till at last I got a
piece of foot with the moulding of the frieze still
remaining. I at once recognized this to be the

moulding of the frieze from the Castle, which Lord
Stratford obtained for the British Museum in 1846.

About the same time that I made this discovery,
I happened to be examining a wall near where I
was digging, and found that a battered fragment
of a marble lion formed one of the foundation-
stones. From that day I had no doubt that the
site of the Mausoleum was found.

Strange as it may seem to you, the moment of
making this great discovery was not at all one of
great joy and exultation. I cast a wistful eye on the
site covered with houses and plots of garden land,
each belonging to a separate proprietor, and asked
myself how will it be possible to buy all these
people out. The presence of a ship of war, too,
made the process of negotiation all the more difficult, for there was no concealing from the officers
and sailors the fact that the site of the Mausoleum
had been discovered; and the intelligence could
hardly be communicated to a whole ship's company
as a profound secret. Fortunately, at that time, no
one attached to the expedition, except myself, could
speak three words of Turkish; still the proprietors
of the houses very soon got an inkling that the
Consul had found something very wonderful—the
konak of some Padischah who lived 2,000 years
ago. They regulated their tactics accordingly.

After I had dug for some few days on the little
strip of soil which had been assigned to me, the
proprietor of the field observed to me, that, having
now gratified my curiosity, and ascertained that
there was nothing, he concluded that I would with-

draw my workmen. I begged for a few days more delay, which was granted with extreme reluctance.

I then made the discovery that the field where I had noticed the fragment of lion was Vakouf, that is to say, land held in trust for charitable purposes, and that my good friend Salik Bey was Vakoufji, or trustee. Nothing was easier than to persuade this kind and hospitable gentleman to allow me to dig in this Vakouf field. I took down the whole wall in which I had noticed the fragment of lion, and found in it five or six drums of Ionic columns of fine Parian marble, a lion's leg, and a quantity of wrought marble from a Greek building.

I then got permission to dig a piece of land a little to the north of this, belonging to a third proprietor.

After removing the Vakouf wall, I dug down, and found a vertical ledge of native rock, running north and south. From the character of the cutting, I saw that the rock had been prepared for the reception of a wall; and from the regularity of the chiselling, there could be no doubt that this was Greek work. Following the cutting downwards, I came, at the depth of about 12 feet, to what I at first took to be a pavement composed of slabs of green stone, 4 feet square and 1 foot thick, strongly held together by iron cramps. This pavement extended eastward further than I could trace it, for my progress was barred at the distance of about 20 feet by a small house, in which dwelt an old Turk with his wife. In the narrow strip of soil between the vertical cutting and this house I found a drum from the base of an Ionic column

turned upside down, several fragments of bases of
columns, and a marble beam with a richly ornamented soffit, which had formed one side of the
lacunar of a ceiling. On the soffit a blue pigment
was still adhering in large thick flakes. The colour
was equal to ultramarine in intensity. Near this
beam were two portions of the bodies of lions, corresponding in style and scale to those in the Castle.
Though I did not then know that the vertical cutting
running north and south was the western margin of
the basement of the Mausoleum, and that the slabs
which I took for pavement were the lowest courses
of the foundations, it was to be presumed, from the
abundance of large architectural marbles, intermixed
with sculpture, that I was within the precinct of the
tomb itself. As I advanced eastward from the vertical cutting, these remains became more plentiful.
We dug on to within about two feet of the small
house already mentioned, and found that it stood
on a mass of these *debris*. It was evident that
this house must be bought; but how this could
be managed was not so clear, for I knew from
long experience how difficult it is to deal with
an Oriental. I therefore called in to my aid my old
friend Mehemet Chiaoux, who had so kindly allowed
me to dig in his field, and empowered him to
conduct the negotiation. His first attempts were
not very successful, for the old Turk whose
house stood in my way had a termagant wife, who
objected strongly to our proceedings. One day when
we were engaged in an experiment how near to the
foundations we could venture to dig without under-

mining the house, a long gaunt arm was suddenly
thrust through the shutters from within, and a discordant female voice screeched out some unpleasant
Turkish imprecations on our heads.

Mehemet Chiaoux, who happened to be standing
close to the window, with his back to the house, beat
a hasty retreat, with a very discomposed and uncomfortable expression of countenance. It was only after
some days that he told me that the old lady had
taken this opportunity of dropping some burning
cinders down his back, between his shirt and his skin.

Old Suliman, the husband of this formidable dame,
was a trembling decrepit old man, who, though he
had been a famous wrestler in his day, and could still
tell tales of the prowess of his youth, stood in bodily
fear of his wife. In a weak moment he allowed us
to dig in his garden: we soon came to a young fig-
tree, which it was absolutely necessary to remove.
While we were bargaining for the price of this tree,
down it came suddenly, having been maliciously undermined by my workmen. Poor old Suliman got a
beating that day, and our stalwart sapper, Corporal
Jenkins, standing on the edge of a trench, was suddenly upset into it ignominiously by a well-aimed
blow from a chopping-block, hurled at his head from
the window. We paid no attention to these little
interruptions, but continued to dig on, till having at
length worked all round Suliman's house, and left it
standing like an island in a sea of rubble, I thought
the time was come for a definite offer. After much
parleying, the price was fixed at £20. I waited on
old Suliman in his own house, with the money in

my hand, and found myself in the awful presence of
Mrs. Suliman, who looked like the first cousin of the
Eumenides. The wrinkles on her mahogany face
were such as Juvenal describes :—

> "Quales, umbriferos ubi pandit Tabraca saltus,
>   In vetula scalpit jam mater simia bucca."

The poor old man gazed wistfully on this treasure, as if he had never seen as much money
in his life. "It is not enough!" said the stern old
hag. I immediately swept up my little heap of gold
and withdrew. This prompt measure had more
effect than hours of parleying, and I got the house
two days afterwards.

The additional space thus obtained was very
soon dug over, and I was at a loss how to proceed. About this time we had made the discovery
of several galleries cut out of the solid rock, to
which an entrance led from the vertical cutting
which I had first discovered. The big Corporal was
delighted at the discovery of these subterraneous
passages, which brought some of his mining knowledge to bear, and in his eagerness to trace them
out, nearly got suffocated with the foul air they contained. One day, on probing the roof of a gallery
where the rock had been replaced by masonry, he detected a soft place, and his crowbar suddenly finding
its way upwards, lifted up the hearthstone of a grave
sententious Turk, who was sitting quietly smoking
his chibouque in his own house.

The astonishment of this respectable gentleman
at being so invaded was great; but he took the in-

trusion very good humouredly, having a secret desire
to sell me his house. Continuing to pursue these
galleries, the Corporal found that they ramified in
various directions, with shafts at intervals, through
which he took the liberty of poking his way upwards
to get fresh air, emerging sometimes in a garden and
sometimes in a courtyard, much to the terror of the
elder ladies and the diversion of the young ones.
The fact was, the galleries ran under almost every
house on the site. By slow degrees we cleared out
the earth with which they were blocked up, in which
we found great quantities of fragments of pottery,
but nothing more.

While this was going on underground, I continued
to advance eastward from the spot where I had first
broken ground, buying the land, yard by yard, till
I was almost wearied out at the petty delays which
stood between me and my hopes. I continued to
find the same courses of foundation-slabs in various
places. It was evident that they extended over a
very large area, and I could not but conclude that this
area was no other than that of the basement of
the tomb itself. As Pliny states that the Mausoleum
was 411 feet in circumference, and that it was
of an oblong form, I calculated that one side must
have been rather more than 100 feet in length.
As the vertical cutting on the west terminated to
the south in a return where the rock was broken
away, I assumed this to be the S.W. angle of the
building, and measuring off 100 feet from this point
in a direction due north, looked about for some
trace of the corresponding or N.W. angle. Such a

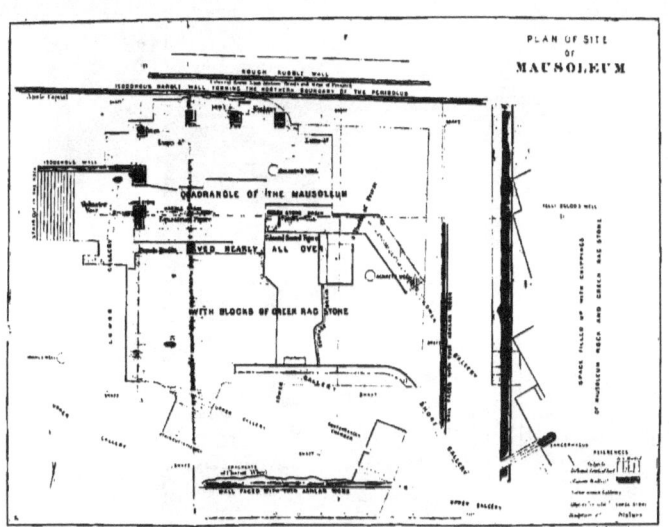

PLAN OF SITE
OF
MAUSOLEUM

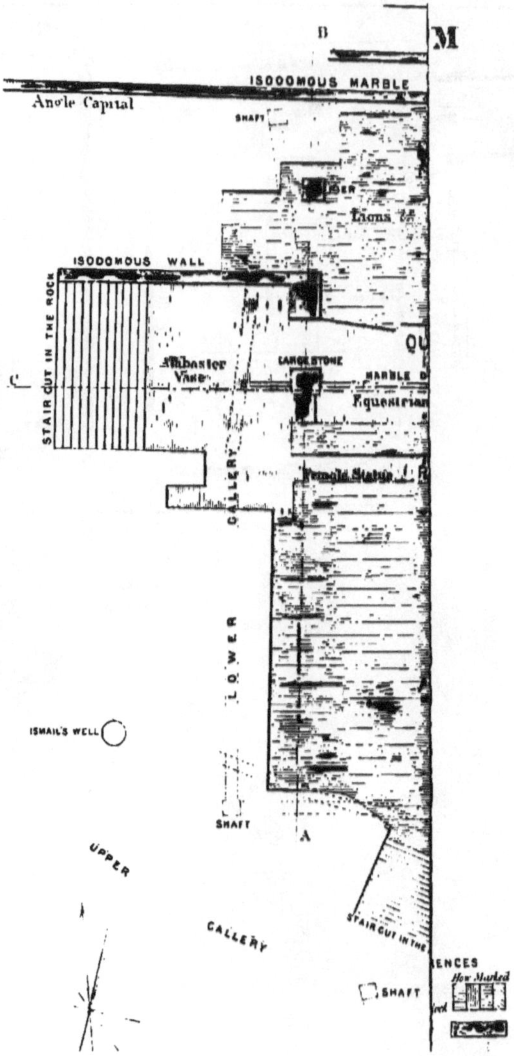

M

B

ISODOMOUS MARBLE

Angle Capital

SHAFT

ER

Lions

ISODOMOUS WALL

QU

Alabaster
Vase

LARGE STONE

MARBLE D

STAIR CUT IN THE ROCK

Equestrian

GALLERY

Female Statue

LOWER

ISMAIL'S WELL

UPPER

SHAFT

A

GALLERY

STAIR CUT IN THE

ENCES

How Marked

SHAFT

return seemed to be indicated by the form of the ground a few feet beyond. I therefore obtained from the proprietor a small slice of his field, and dug here. To my great joy I came upon a most distinct angle cut in the rock, and going deeper, found within this angle the same fragments of architecture, lions, and other sculpture, as in the places already explored. This angle was 108 feet[39] distant from the return to the south. I now saw more clearly in what direction the foundations were to be looked for, and what was the original form of the building. Knowing from Pliny that it was a little longer from east to west than from north to south, I measured off a probable length for this side, and went on probing the ground till at length I hit upon the S.E. angle at the distance of 126[40] feet from the S.W. angle. Three houses in a row stood on this line, which after various delays I succeeded in purchasing.

There remained only the N.E. angle to be found to complete the plan of the foundations. This could, of course, be fixed accurately by measurement to a particular spot, which happened to be in a public road where my digging was unopposed. Having now traced out the plan of the building, I proceeded to buy up and demolish everything which stood in my way—houses, garden walls, fig-trees, almond-trees, were all swept away before my band of workmen.

On clearing the entire site, I made the following discoveries :—The whole area anciently occupied by the Mausoleum is a parallelogram, 469 feet in cir-

cumference. The bed of the foundations within
this quadrangle is cut out of the solid rock to
depths varying from 2 feet to 16 feet below the
surface of the field, but always in horizontal levels.
(*See* the Plan and Sections, Plates 2, 3.)

In this bed the foundations are laid, consisting
throughout of slabs of green stone 4 feet square
and 1 foot thick, bound together by iron cramps.
In the shallow part of the quadrangle these slabs
have been removed; in the deeper levels they still
remain, sometimes to the number of several courses.
(*See* Plates 2, 3.)

The whole of the quadrangular area was strewn
with drums of columns, fragments of architecture,
sculpture, and rubble. The manner in which these
were lying about showed that when the Knights of
St. John removed the remains of the Mausoleum to
build their castle, the foundation-courses were up-
rooted all but in the very deepest parts; and as a
portion of the basement was cleared to the lowest
courses, the heaviest masses of marble were pitched
down into the holes thus formed, so as to be out of
the way of the workmen.

The following are the most important objects which
we have yet discovered :—

1. The torso of an equestrian figure of colossal
size, and in a very fine style (Plate 4). The body
of the horse and the right side of the rider from the
waist to the ancle have been preserved. On the
left side the hind-quarters of the horse and legs of
the man have been broken away piecemeal, by
blows of a sledge-hammer. We found some of the

SITE OF MAUSOLEUM
SECTIONS

ON A·B

ON C·D

ON E·F

SCALE OF FEET

pieces thus broken away in a garden-wall close to
the spot where the torso was lying.

2. The torso of a seated male figure, from the
waist to the knees. This figure is draped. The
back is left flat, showing that the statue originally
stood in a niche or against a wall. This torso
is much mutilated. The drapery is very finely
composed.

3. Part of the chest of a draped figure, probably female. This and the preceding torso are of
colossal size.

4. For a long time after I had begun the excavations, only very small fragments of the frieze
were found; till at length, having nearly cleared out
the whole quadrangle, I had almost given up the
hope of meeting with an entire slab. However,
after obtaining possession of the line of houses on
the eastern side, I came suddenly one day on an
entire slab of frieze lying on its face. On turning
it over, a most beautiful figure of a mounted Amazon
presented itself; the surface of the marble being in
very fine condition (Plate 5). One general expression of wonder and admiration burst forth from
the lips of my Turkish workmen when they beheld
the "kiz," or "girl," as they called this figure.
It was the first time that they had fairly recognized
likeness in anything which I had discovered.

Very near this piece of frieze I found another,
6 feet long; and soon after, two more of the same
length. Three of these slabs were lying under
the foundations of the houses, with their faces
downwards. Considering the height from which

they must have fallen, it is wonderful that they escaped with so little injury.

All four belong to the same series as the slabs of frieze removed from the Castle in 1846. From the circumstance that they were all found on the eastern side of the quadrangle, it is probable that they originally decorated that side of the Mausoleum; and in that case these four slabs must certainly have been the work of Scopas, whose sculptures, Pliny tells us, were on the eastern front.

As he was unquestionably the most renowned of the four artists employed, it was perhaps on that account that the front was assigned to him ; because, so far as we know of the arrangement of Greek temples, the eastern end was always considered more sacred than the western, which was often an *opisthodomos*.

5. An immense number of architectural fragments have been found, out of which nearly the entire order may be reconstructed. On comparing the details of the architecture with those of the Temple of Athene at Priene, published in the Ionian Antiquities of the Dilettanti Society, I found a most remarkable resemblance throughout.

We know from an inscription that the Priene temple was finished by Alexander the Great, after he had conquered Asia Minor. It may therefore have been commenced about the time when the Mausoleum was built, and was probably the work of the same architect, Pythios.[41]

In the Mausoleum, in the temple at Priene, and that at Branchidæ, we have three most interesting

examples of the Asiatic Ionic, which, in richness of
ornament and delicacy of execution, may justly
challenge comparison with the Attic variety of the
Ionic order, as we see it in the Erechtheum.

On the west side of the quadrangular cutting,
near the S.W. corner, I discovered a flight of steps,
twelve in number, and 30 feet wide, terminating

on a level with the lowest course of the foundations.
At the distance of 26 feet to the east of the foot
of these steps was an immense block weighing
about ten tons. This block rested on two slabs of
white marble, and, on being turned over by the aid
of two screwjacks, it was found to have been carefully adjusted to the slabs below in the following
manner. In the great stone bronze dowels were
fixed, corresponding in position with bronze sockets let into the marble slabs. The accompanying
cuts, *a*, *b*, give the perspective view and section of

one of these dowels within a bronze collar, which
was fixed in the great stone with lead. Doubtless
it was intended by the architect that on lowering
this stone the dowels should drop out of their collars
into the sockets below; but, whether through accident or *fraud*, they appear to have remained in the

collars instead of descending into the holes to which they had been fitted. This may be seen by examining the ends of these dowels, which are united all round the edge to the collars by a strong patina. Perhaps the workmen employed on this operation purposely contrived that it should be incomplete, with the same motive as actuated the builder of the treasury of the Egyptian king Rhampsinitus, respecting which Herodotus gives such an amusing anecdote.[12]

On each side of the great stone was a rerebate, or return, affording a groove into which the stones of the adjacent wall fitted. It was evident, therefore, that the great stone had been lowered into its place like a portcullis, and then wedged in by stones on each side. Between this great stone and the foot of the stair I found several alabaster jars, such as the ancients used for unguents, and which were called *alabasta*. Near the jars were found some bones of oxen, and two or three small terra-cottas, among which was a female head of exquisite beauty.

From the peculiar manner in which the great stone was fitted into its place, and its position relatively to the staircase, I am inclined to think that it originally closed the entrance into the sepulchre, having been lowered into its place after the body of Mausolus had been deposited in its last resting-place. This opinion is confirmed by the discovery of the alabaster jars between the foot of the stair and the great stone; for we know that such vases were deposited at the entrance to tombs by mourners, after libations to the dead had been made from them. This may be seen on Greek vases, on which

the visit of Electra to the tomb of Agamemnon
and other sepulchral subjects are represented.

On examining one of the *alabasta* I found on it to
my great surprise an inscription in cuneiform and
hieroglyphic characters.   On a copy of this inscription being sent to London, it was at once recognized
by Mr. Birch and Sir Henry Rawlinson as identical
with one which occurs on a similar *alabaston* found
in Greece, and now in the Bibliothèque at Paris.
Both the hieroglyphic and cuneiform inscriptions
recite the name and titles of Xerxes.   Perhaps this
jar was an heirloom preserved in the family of
Hekatomnos from the time of Xerxes, and offered
as a precious gift by Artemisia to the *manes* of her
departed lord.   A third *alabaston* bearing the
name of Xerxes, together with fragments of three
more, was found by Mr. Loftus in excavations at
Susa ; and in the Treasury of St. Mark at Venice
is a porphyry vase, inscribed in like manner with
the name and title of Artaxerxes.   The custom of
inscribing the name of the reigning monarch on
alabasta was probably borrowed from Egypt, where
such vases have been found inscribed with the name
of Pharaoh Neco, who reigned B.C. 609, and with
those of other monarchs of the 26th dynasty.[43]

While we were making these discoveries on the
site of the Mausoleum, we were anxiously waiting
for the firman empowering me to take possession of
the lions which I had discovered in the Castle last
year.   Unavoidable delays prevented the granting of
this document ; and in the mean time the Commandant of the Castle suddenly received orders from

the Turkish Minister of War to remove the lions from
the walls and send them to Constantinople. He lost
no time in putting this order in execution, and before
many days had elapsed two of the finest lions were
extracted from the walls. It was not a pleasant sight
for us to see this operation performed under our
very eyes, after we had brought spars for scaffolding
and all manner of means and appliances for the
express purpose ; however I gulped down my mortification as well as I could, and despatched two
letters, one by sea, the other by a swift overland
runner, to Smyrna, to apprise Lord Stratford that
the Turkish Minister of War was trying to steal a
march on us. My messenger sped on night and day;
and the Commandant pushed on with his work no
less expeditiously. Two more lions were soon dug
out of the walls. The extraction of two of my eye-
teeth could not have given me so great a pang.
When the Commandant had removed four lions, he
paid a formal visit to my diggings, accompanied by
all the principal Turks in Budrum.

"You have found nothing but little fragments I
see," he said, with an air of triumph. At that time
we were digging up small fragments of lions' tails,
with an occasional leg or hind-quarter, but no heads.
I endured his civil impertinence for about a quarter
of an hour, till at last my inward chafing found vent
in a strong expression or two in English, addressed
to Captain Towsey. The Turks did not understand
what I had said ; but guessed from the expression
of my countenance what was passing in my mind,
and withdrew with many ironical compliments. That

same day, the lions having been duly swathed in raw sheepskins, were placed on board a caique to be sent over to Cos, where they were to be transhipped by steamer to Constantinople. I had a photograph made of two of them, and took a last fond look at these precious remains of the school of Scopas. The caique, as the Commandant informed me, was to sail that night, and I went to bed sick at heart. It was the end of a great hope.

At 4 a.m. the next morning I was suddenly roused from my sleep by the voice of a midshipman from the Gorgon. " The Swallow is come in from Constantinople, and the officer of the watch thinks that the firman is on board." I had had so many disappointments about the firman, that I received this news with sceptical indifference, and doggedly fell asleep again. At 6 a.m. another messenger from the Gorgon woke me up. " The captain wants to see you immediately." I hurried on board, and found Towsey pacing the quarter-deck impatiently, his gig alongside, ready manned.

" Why have you been so long?" he said, " the firman is come."

" Of what use is the firman now?" I answered, very sulkily; " the lions are gone."

" The caique is still in the harbour," he said, " waiting for a fair wind to come out, and we are yet in time."

I jumped into the boat without a word more : a few vigorous strokes brought us into the harbour. The captain of the caique was drawing in his little mooring lines in a lazy, sleepy sort of way.

On the pier-head stood the doctor of the Quarantine, an Italian, who took great interest in our diggings.

"Don't let that caique go," I cried out; "I have a firman for the lions."

"It is all right," he replied; "I have his papers still, and he cannot leave without my signature."

We walked straight into the Castle, and asked to see the Commandant. Very much astonished he was at so early a visit from the Captain of the ship of war and the Consul. He had evidently just emerged from his *gorgan*, and his *narguileh* was hardly lit. We had boarded him with that indecent haste with which mad Englishmen occasionally invade the *kieff* of an Oriental when any real emergency occurs, without waiting for the due interchange of compliments. After hastily wishing him good morning, I put the firman into his hand with that air of cool satisfaction with which a whist-player trumps an ace on the first round. Turks are seldom astonished; but my friend the Commandant was really discomposed. He read the firman through several times. The document was duly signed and sealed; the wording of this writ of *habeas corpus* was so precise that there was no evading it. The lions were to be delivered to me whether still in the walls or already embarked. Suddenly a bright thought struck the Commandant.

"The firman," quoth he, "makes mention of lions, *aslanlar*; but the animals in the walls of the Castle are leopards, *caplanlar*."

"Come, come, *dostum*, my friend," I said, "as-lanlar or caplanlar, you know very well what are the beasts meant by the firman, and where to find them. I claim those beasts, and no others."

"But," said the Commandant, suddenly shifting the ground of his objections, "who is to pay me for the expenses I have incurred? The allowance made to me by the Porte is so small that the outlay for removing the lions has been made in a great measure out of my own pocket."

"Make your mind quite easy on that subject," I said; "I am ordered to pay all the expenses incurred."

"And the caique, who is to pay that?"

"I pay the caique too."

The lions were forthwith handed over to me, and the Commandant reimbursed.

In consideration of the trouble he had had, and the courteous and obliging manner in which he had behaved, I presented him with a handsome gratuity over and above his expenses. He was so touched with my generosity, that he let me take a leopard's head not specified in the firman. This was set in a battlement over the gateway leading into the Castle, and probably came from the Mausoleum. It is on a smaller scale than the lions, and much decayed, but in a good style.

In the narrative of our excavations at the Mausoleum I have already noticed the discovery of the hind-quarters of lions. We have found about seven of these hind-quarters; and from their perfect correspondence in style and scale with the heads from the Castle, I have great hopes that some of them may, on their arrival at the British Museum, be readjusted, after having been severed for so many centuries. The surface of some of the portions which have been lying in the ground is in the finest condition, retaining in one instance the original dim-red colour with which the marble had been painted.

The heads from the Castle have suffered a good deal from exposure to the sea spray and to rain.

XXXIX.

Budrum, *May 5, 1857.*

THE other day I went with Captain Towsey to see the wrestlers at a Turkish wedding—I have often heard of this exhibition, but never had the oppor-tunity of seeing it before. It took place about nine o'clock at night—the Captain came from the Gorgon in his gig, burning two blue lights, one at each bow. The effect was fine and astonished the Turks. We were received on the quay with great honour, and marched along to the wrestling-ground, preceded by a band of Turkish music and by brandished pine torches. We entered a large garden, where I beheld a scene which transported me suddenly into the ancient world. I thought I was looking on the funeral games of Patroclus or Hector. On the ground all around the arena were seated the male part of the Mussulman population of Budrum. This constituted the pit. Above—on garden-walls, at windows, and on house-tops, were rows upon rows of veiled ladies, piled up on the roofs and detached against the blue sky; the whole scene was lit up by the moon and stars—but such stars! and by two immense braziers filled with blazing pine torches.

The wrestlers were introduced by an old man, who held in his hand a white wand, not unlike the *Paidotribes*, who is always represented in attendance in the pictures of athletic contests on Greek vases. This old gentleman ushered in each pair with a short or long speech according to their merits, and stood by as bottle-holder.

The men were stripped all but a girdle round the loins. The first combatant who entered the arena knelt on one knee till his antagonist arrived; both were then placed side by side in an amicable manner by the old herald, who then retired on one side watching to enforce fair play. The two athletes generally walked round the arena two or three times, as a panther does in a cage, each intent on his antagonist's movements. Then turning face to face, they went to work, first stooping to get some dust from the ground on their hands, and then slapping their thighs. The wrestling was very different from our English wrestling. The combatants leant so far forward that tripping up and close hugging were very difficult. The main object was to get a good grip of the antagonist round the waist, and to get his head under the chest. Seeing the struggle continue on the ground after a pair of wrestlers had closed and fallen, I was rather puzzled to know what constituted victory, till I perceived that the adversary must be thrown on the *back*—no other fall counts. Tremendous were the struggles on the ground—the supple limbs of the wrestlers glistening with oil interlaced and writhed, producing many a *symplegma*, like that famous group in the Tribune at Florence. Wonderful was the rapidity and dexterity of the manœuvres employed. In the heat of the struggle the pair would roll over and over out of the ring into the crowd of spectators, deranging carpets and upsetting lighted chibouques —and little recking the burning ashes amongst which they rolled.

All this time the old herald would pour water down their thirsty throats, while they lay panting on the ground. Suddenly the better wrestler, flinging with one mighty effort his antagonist on his back, would break from his grasp, and stand erect amid the shouts of the spectators. Then the defeated hero arose from mother earth—each lifted his antagonist up in the air once in turn, in token of amity, and then with arms fraternally interlaced round their waists, they walked all round the ring, receiving the largess of the spectators, who took the keenest interest in the contest. The ladies were mute, but not unconscious witnesses. I dare say they were not bad critics of physical perfection, according to their way of regarding it.

The earlier pairs of wrestlers rather disappointed me as to form, but those reserved for the close of the spectacle were the finest men I have ever seen— upwards of six feet high, supple and agile as leopards, and in admirable condition. He who would appreciate the wonderful beauty of the form of man, as distinguished from that of all other animals,

should study these Turkish wrestlers in Asia Minor.
I have seen nothing so truly classical in the Levant.

The wedding lasted several days, during which a
series of feasts were kept up with the rude and
lavish hospitality which is customary among the
Turks on such occasions.

The cost of such a wedding, at Budrum, I heard
reckoned at about £100. An amusing incident occurred
in the course of the entertainments. A baboon had
been hired to play antics; but some doubts having
arisen in the mind of the Cadi whether such an
exhibition were perfectly orthodox according to the
Koran, the animal was not permitted to appear in
public for several days, during which the Cadi con-
sulted his books, finally disposing of his conscientious
scruples by ordering the baboon to be clothed in a
pair of breeches, after which he was allowed to
perform his part in the entertainment.

XL.

BUDRUM, *June* 25, 1857.

ON the north side of the Mausoleum, the line of
cutting which marks the limit of the Quadrangle is
not continuous, as on the three other sides, but
a few feet from the N.W. angle a break occurs
in the rock, extending for 59 feet, after which the
cutting is resumed. This space, where the rock
has failed has been filled in with earth, and the
line of the Quadrangle is marked by three piers,

carelessly built, of blocks of native rock, and placed there apparently to give greater solidity to the soil here filled in. (*See* Plates 3, 4.)

Digging on beyond this line, I was stopped by a modern wall of loose rubble, running in front of a Turkish house, and marking the boundary of a fresh property. As this wall was full of fragments of the Mausoleum, I asked the permission of the owner of the house to take it down and to dig a little further north in front of his house. This worthy man, an Imam, looked at me with a wistful expression, and said, " They tell me you are a man who, when once you get your foot into a field, contrive to get your whole body in after it." However, after a little hesitation, he gave me leave to dig a strip six feet wide inside his boundary wall, which we demolished forthwith. Built into its base was the tail of a colossal horse in white marble. Digging below the foundations of this rubble wall, I came to an ancient wall, built of large blocks of white marble beautifully jointed, rather more than six feet in height. On the top of this wall was a lion resting, apparently as he had fallen. His legs and tail were broken off, but the body was in the finest condition, and the head intact : the tongue, when first discovered, was painted bright red.

Behind this wall to the north was a mass of large marble slabs, lying piled one over the other in the earth. After removing the uppermost of these, we saw underneath them the folds of a draped torso. We got this out safely, though the operation was a perilous one, on account of the weight of the superincumbent slabs. Then appeared a male head broken in three pieces, another draped torso, and a singular mass of marble with a piece of bronze attached, which, after some study, I perceived to be the half of the head of a colossal horse. I at once assumed as certain that I had got upon the track of the famous *quadriga*, which, as Pliny tells us, surmounted the Mausoleum, crowning the Pyramid. The result proved that I was right. We dug on, getting out every instant fragments of statues and of lions, till at last we came to the hinder half of an enormous horse, cut off behind the shoulder by a joint, and measuring upwards of six feet from the root of his tail to this joint. Half of this great mass of marble lay in the strip of ground where I had leave to dig, and half in the undug portion of the field beyond, where I had no right to encroach. I expected that the Imam would have taken this opportunity to exact a heavy fine for further trespass on his domain, but fortunately I had to deal in this instance with a liberally minded man, who disdained to take petty advantages; so we had full permission to clear the ground all round the great horse, so as to plant our triangle over his body. After being duly hauled out, he was placed on a sledge and dragged to the shore by 80 Turkish workmen. On the walls and house-tops as we went along sat the veiled ladies of Budrum. They had never seen anything so big before, and the sight overcame the reserve imposed on them by Turkish etiquette. The ladies of Troy gazing at the wooden horse as he entered at the breach, could not have been more astonished.

We dug on, and about 12 feet to the east of the place where the big horse was lying, I found the other half of a similar horse's body, broken off at the ears. After this we found one of his hoofs placed on a massive base. In the same strip of ground was a head, probably of Apollo, broken into three pieces, and another lion.

Having made such remarkable discoveries in this little strip of ground, I at once purchased the Imam's house, and one adjoining it on the east. The price of the two was at least three times their intrinsic value ; but the ground was so promising that I thought the sum asked not unreasonable. After demolishing the house to the east of the Imam's, I found in front of it the other half of the horse's head with the bronze bit still in the mouth, and

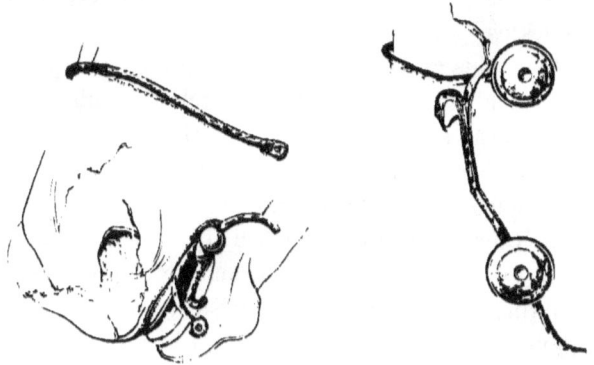

part of a male colossal head, which from the general type of the features is evidently a portrait treated in an ideal manner, and probably that of Mausolus himself (Plate 6). Close to this was part of a bearded head, split off in like manner, so that three quarters of the face have been preserved. It is of heroic size; the portion of the face which remains is in the finest condition.

Under the Imam's house I found a draped torso, and built into the chimney a colossal female head, with a veil falling from the back of the head. The surface of this head was nearly destroyed by fire.

Pursuing the line of marble wall to the west of the Imam's house, I came to a colossal female head (Plate 7) lying in the earth, about two feet north of the wall. Round the face is a triple row of curls symmetrically arranged, each curl forming a perfect volute. This head is remarkable for the largeness and simplicity of treatment, and the pathos of the expression. The cast of features, though ideal, does not recall any of the known types of goddesses.

When this great discovery of sculptures took place we had almost exhausted our stock of timber for making cases, and the hold of the Gorgon was already nearly full. But the resources of a ship of war are manifold. Though we had no more packing-cases, Captain Towsey supplied me with a number of empty casks, in which many hundred fragments of sculpture and architecture were safely stowed, each fragment being separately enveloped in a piece of old hammock or bread-bag to prevent friction. In this way we disposed of all except the very large marbles. The draped torsoes, found in the Imam's field, being very liable to injury from the deep undercutting of the folds, were carefully padded with tow, and then

swathed in a covering of old hammocks, then tightly corded, so as to resemble mummies, and in this condition they were stowed one on the other in the bread-room. The two portions of colossal horses were too large to get into the hold at all, and were therefore fixed on the upper deck, being protected from the weather by a covering of canvas. In this way we managed to stow in the Gorgon 218 packages of various kinds.

We had just time to accomplish this when the Supply arrived, which Lord Clarendon had, with timely forethought, sent to our assistance, as soon as he received news of our recent discoveries.

By this arrangement the Gorgon was released from further attendance on the expedition, and is now on her way to England with her precious cargo. She left us yesterday, and I took leave of my friend Captain Towsey with real regret, for all through my many troubles and difficulties here, he has been my mainstay and sheet anchor, superintending all the operations in which his men were concerned with ceaseless vigilance, and taking a thorough interest in the enterprise from its commencement. When I think that for months past we have had a party of fifty sailors from the ship constantly on shore, and that during all this time they have been on excellent terms with the inhabitants of Budrum, I cannot but appreciate the tact and discretion of a commander who kept his men so well in hand; and who by skilful and timely interposition checked all quarrels and grievances before they ripened into serious causes of misunderstanding.

The Supply is a steam store-ship, very much more suited for this special service than the Gorgon, as her hatchways are much larger, and the capacity of her hold such that, as her commander, Mr. Balliston, assures me, no number of Mausoleums would fill it. She has a crew of forty men. I have received a most kind and encouraging letter from Lord Clarendon, authorizing me to spare no expenditure that may be requisite for the completion of my work.

[It may not be out of place here to give some description of the sculptures and architectural marbles sent home in the Gorgon, which, of course, could not be properly studied and appreciated till the many broken parts had been rejoined at the British Museum. Of these the most remarkable is the colossal statue generally considered to be that of Mausolus himself (Plates 8, 9), which has been put together from sixty-five separate fragments, all of which were found behind the marble wall (see *ante*, p. 110). It will be seen that the head (Plate 6) belongs to this figure. It is evidently a portrait, though treated in an ideal manner. The cast of features resembles, so far as I know, no other type to be met with in Hellenic art. The hair springing upwards from the forehead falls in thick waves on each side of the face; and a fragment recently identified shows that it must have descended nearly to the shoulders;[*] the beard is short and close; the face square and massive, with proportions somewhat shorter and broader than

M A :

those usually observed in Greek art; the eyes, deep-
set under overhanging brows, have a full and majestic gaze; the mouth is well formed, with a set
calm about the lips, indicating decision of character
and the habit of command. The form is that of a
man in the prime of life.

This figure is draped in an ample mantle, under
which is a *chiton*. As both arms are wanting from
the shoulders, the original action can only be matter
of conjecture; but as the left shoulder is a little
raised, and the folds of the drapery drawn towards
it on the back, I am inclined to think that the left
hand was slightly advanced, resting on a sceptre.

The drapery is grandly composed, and the majestic
aspect of the figure accords very well with the
description which Mausolus is made to give of
himself in one of Lucian's Dialogues.[45] " I was,"
he says, addressing Diogenes, "a tall handsome
man, and formidable in war." The height of this
statue is 9 feet $9\frac{1}{2}$ inches without its plinth.

Intermixed with the sixty-five fragments of the
statue of Mausolus were found in the Imam's field
the fragments of a female figure on the same colossal
scale, of which a view is given, Plate 10. The head
of this figure has been identified since my work on
the Budrum expedition was published. It is unfor-
tunately so mutilated that very little is left of the
features. Round the forehead the hair is arranged
in a formal row of curls, rather smaller than those
of the head described *ante*, p. 112. (*See* Plate 7.)
The back of the head is covered with a mantle or
peplos, which is wound round the body in rich folds,

ı 2

and gathered in beneath the left arm. The under garment is a *chiton* reaching to the feet, having sleeves fastened on the arm with studs. The fulness of form and the slight droop of the bosom indicate mature age.

In this statue and that of Mausolus great skill has been shown in the treatment of the drapery, in which a general breadth and grandeur of effect is combined with extraordinary refinement and delicacy of execution. Each fold is traced home to its origin and wrought to its full depth; a master hand has passed over the whole surface, leaving no sign of that slurred and careless treatment which characterizes the specious and meretricious art of a later period. One foot of this statue has been preserved, and is an exquisite specimen of sculpture, the more valuable because, in the few statues from the best Greek schools which we possess, the extremities are generally wanting.

I suppose this figure to have been a goddess standing by the side of Mausolus in the *quadriga*, and acting as his charioteer, just as in the group dedicated by the Cyrenæans at Delphi, their King Battus was represented in a chariot driven by the nymph Cyrene, while Libya was personified crowning him.[46] In like manner, when Pisistratus re-entered Athens after his expulsion, he imposed on the religious feelings of his countrymen by appearing in a chariot driven by a woman named Phye, of remarkable stature, whom he had the audacity to dress up in the panoply and costume of Athene, and who personated the goddess so well that the Athenians, if Herodotus is to be believed, were

completely deceived. If Mausolus and the female figure stood in the *quadriga* on the summit of the pyramid, the chariot group probably represented Mausolus himself, conducted to heaven by the deity whose special protection he had enjoyed in life, and who therefore would act as charioteer. It is thus that on a number of Greek fictile vases the introduction of Herakles to Olympus is represented by a chariot group, in which the hero stands in a *quadriga* driven by his tutelary goddess Athene, and accompanied by Hermes and other deities. The *quadriga* was probably regarded in ancient art as the symbol of *apotheosis*, from its use in the most solemn processions, religious and triumphal.[47]

On examining the fragments of horses from the *quadriga*, it was found that the two pieces of head could be fitted on to the anterior half of a horse, mentioned *ante*, p. 111 (*see* Plate 11); the larger fragment, however, proved to be the hinder half of another horse. From the action of the shoulder and hind quarter, as well as from the fact that two fore hoofs were found attached to fragments of the base of the *quadriga*, it may be inferred that all the horses were in a standing position. Perhaps the fore feet of one or two in the group may have been represented pawing the ground.

Consummate knowledge of form is shown in these few fragments of the colossal group which surmounted the pyramid, and which are the more valuable because there are few extant remains of ancient sculpture of which the author and date can be so positively identified. We know from Pliny that this group was executed by Pythis or Pythios, who is probably identical with the Phiteus mentioned by Vitruvius as one of the two architects of the tomb.[48]

Of the *quadriga* itself the only portions found were some fragments of the wheel. The accompanying cut shows the form of this wheel as restored by Mr. Pullan, the pieces found being indicated by darker lines. From this restoration we obtain for the diameter of the wheel 7 feet 7 inches, a dimension of great value in determining the entire height of the *quadriga*.

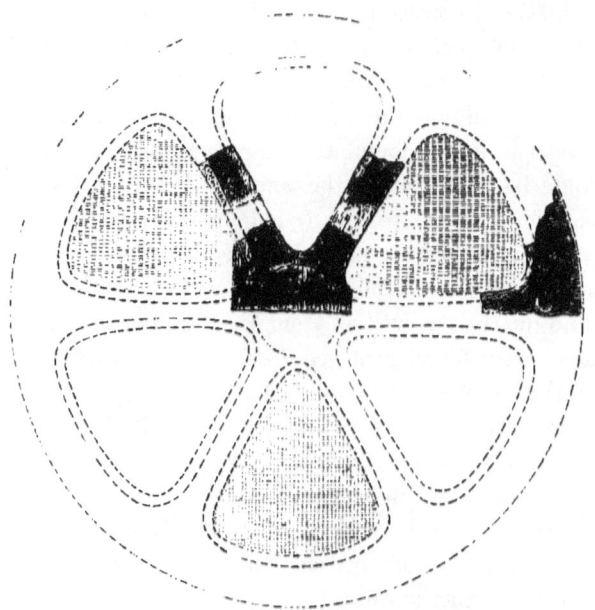

I have already mentioned that, intermixed with the sculptures behind the marble wall, were found a number of blocks, also of white marble.

After extracting all the fragments of statues from this mass of ruins, we examined the blocks of marble, and on measuring them it was found that they were of an uniform thickness of 1 foot ¼ of an inch, averaging 4 feet in length;[49] and that on their upper surface they had certain lines and projections, and on their lower surface certain grooves, which showed them very clearly to have been steps of the pyramid, jointed one into the other with great nicety, as was first demonstrated by Lieut. Smith, in a letter written at Budrum, June 1, 1857, and printed in the "Papers respecting the Excavations at Budrum," 1858. From forty to fifty of these steps were measured; the width of the treads was uniformly either 1 foot 9 inches or 1 foot 5 inches, the only exceptions being the case of the corner steps, which had on one side a tread of 1 foot 9 inches, and on the return or adjacent side the smaller dimension, showing that the pyramid was of an oblong form.

Assuming that Pliny is correct in his statement that the number of pyramid steps was twenty-four, Lieut. Smith multiplied by this number the depth of the steps, and thus obtained the total height of the pyramid. Again, multiplying the tread 1 foot 9 inches by the same number 24, he found the lateral spread of the pyramid on each side to be 42 feet, and repeating the same process with the narrower tread, he obtained as the lateral spread of the pyramid on each end 34 feet. It is obvious that if these spreads are doubled, the dimensions of the base of the pyramid will be ascertained, provided

that the length and breadth of the platform on the
top of the pyramid can be ascertained.

The discovery of the remains of the chariot group
enabled Lieut. Smith to calculate approximately the
dimensions of this platform as 24 feet by 18.

He thus obtained 108 feet as the length of the
base of the pyramid, and 86 feet as its width; viz.
(twice the lateral spread) 42 feet + 24 feet = 108
feet for the length, and (twice the lateral spread)
34 feet + 18 feet = 86 feet.

These dimensions are, however, to be regarded as
only approximative, because the remains of the
chariot group furnish no sufficient data by which we
may determine the size of the platform on the apex,
nor is it certain that all the twenty-four steps had
treads of the same width. Thus in Mr. Pullan's
restoration of the Mausoleum this platform is
made 25 feet 6 inches in length by 20 feet 5 inches
in width; while Mr. Fergusson, with the same evidence before him, prefers a smaller area of 20 Greek
feet by 16.[50]

It has been already mentioned that the steps of
the pyramid were found lying piled up intermixed
with fragments of colossal horses and statues.

In the sides of many of the steps copper cramps
were still fixed, and were generally bent, as if they
had been wrenched from their places. One of these,
broken at one end, is represented in the accompanying cut. The fact that so great a quantity
of wrought copper was found with these marbles,
shows that they never can have been disturbed
since their first fall, for such valuable metal would

never have escaped the cupidity of the Middle Ages, had it been exposed to view.

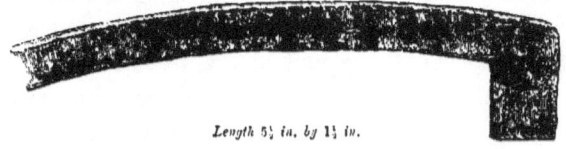

Length 5½ in. by 1½ in.

Another proof that these marbles were lying where they originally fell, is to be found in the fact that the edges of all the fractures were quite fresh, which would have been impossible had they ever been turned over, like the marbles previously discovered in the quadrangle. It is evident, therefore, that this part of the site had never been explored by the Knights when they built the castle.

I have already stated that the strip of ground where these marbles were discovered was immediately to the north of a marble wall. This wall was composed of three courses, the lowest of which was principally built of blue marble, the two upper courses being of white marble of a fine quality. The joints were fitted with extreme care, and the whole work exhibited that sense of proportion and nicety of execution which are the characteristics of Hellenic masonry in its best period. The height of this wall was rather more than 6 feet; it may have been carried two courses higher. In one place a stone of the upper course was driven inward (*see* Plate 6 of my History of the Budrum Expedition), as if some violent shock had dislocated the upper part of the wall, many blocks of which were found lying intermixed with the marble steps and sculpture behind it.

It is probable that an earthquake was the force which rent asunder the pyramid, hurling a portion of the chariot group and of the steps on which it rested over the marble wall, and carrying away the coping of the wall with it in its fall. This must have taken place some time before the occupation of Budrum by the Knights, when the Mausoleum is described as in ruins, and subsequently, on the other hand, to the 12th century, when Eustathius wrote, " It was and *is* a wonder." He would hardly have used the present tense unless the pyramid had been still erect.

The marble wall, as I shall show subsequently, was that of the *peribolus* or sacred precinct round the tomb. The preservation of so great a mass of marble in this particular spot may be accounted for by the configuration of the ground. It will be seen by a comparison of the sections of the ground at AB and EF (Plate 3), with the plan of the environs of the Mausoleum (Plate 2 of my History of the Expedition), that to the north of the marble wall the native rock slopes upwards till it meets the steep side of a conical hill to the north of the road. In the rainy season a considerable volume of water descends from this hill to the sea, and was anciently conducted into cisterns by subterraneous channels; but these ducts having been blocked up after the decay of the ancient city, the water must have lodged against the marble wall till it had deposited a silt sufficient to fill up the narrow strip

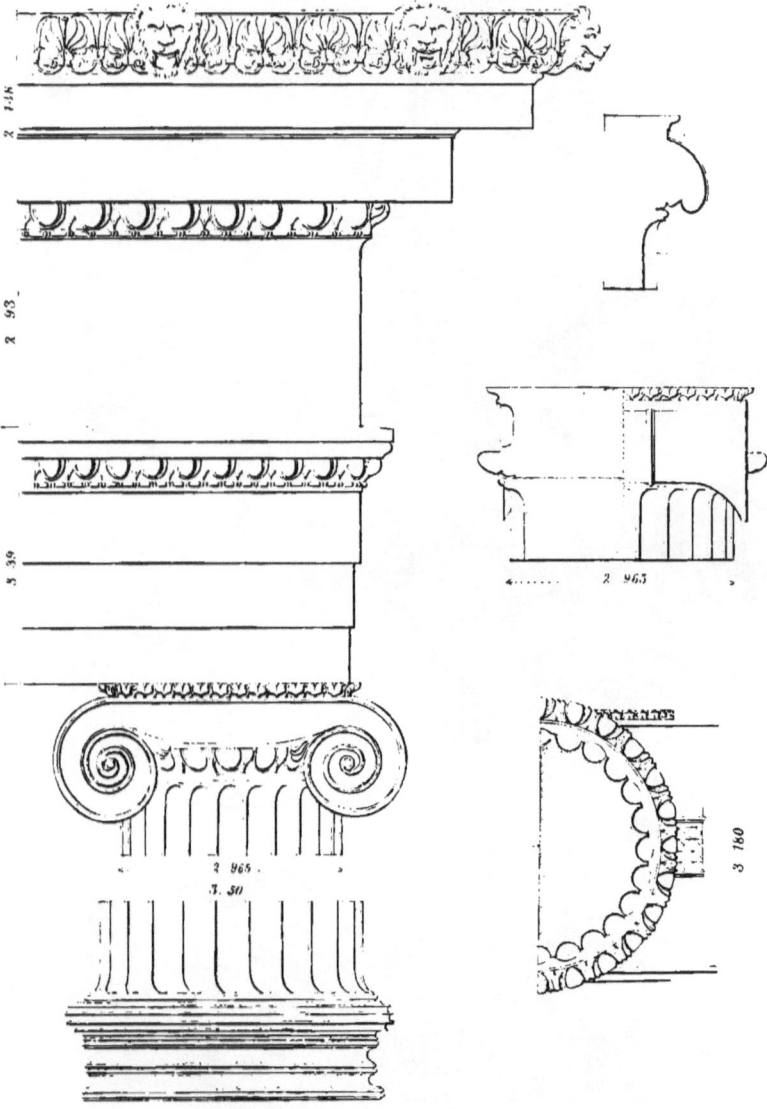

of ground to the north of it, and thus must have gradually obliterated all trace of the wall itself.

The architectural marbles sent home in the Gorgon consisted of portions of the cornice, frieze, and architrave, several capitals and bases, together with two drums from a column.

These data enabled Mr. Pullan subsequently to reconstruct the Order, as is shown in Plate 12.

A transverse beam, an oblong slab which had formed one side of a *lacunar*, and a number of other architectural marbles, were also found, all of which are engraved in my History of the Budrum Expedition, Plates 25—29.

Nearly all the enriched mouldings are worked on detached pieces of marble, which were let into ledges cut on the upper edges of the fascias, for the ornament of which they were designed.

All the ornaments are finished with an exquisite delicacy. This is particularly seen in the cornice, where every leaf in the floral ornaments is wrought with that labour of love which distinguishes Greek architecture in its best age, but which ceases to be its characteristic after the time of Alexander the Great.

All the architectural members of the Mausoleum were painted. The colours were pure red and blue; the pigments employed were probably vermilion and silicate of copper, a cake of which was found in the tombs at Camirus by Messrs. Salzmann and Biliotti. The ground of the ornaments in the Mausoleum was painted blue, the mouldings picked out with red. On many of the smaller mouldings preserved in the British Museum colour may yet be seen.

The greater part of the architectural marbles discovered evidently belong to the *Pteron*, which, as Pliny states, consisted of thirty-six columns surrounding the tomb itself. The height of this *Pteron*, according to Pliny, was 25 cubits (equal to $37\frac{1}{2}$ English feet). The height of the order, as constructed by Mr. Pullan from existing remains, is 37 feet $2\frac{1}{2}$ inches.

The pyramid which surmounted the *Pteron* was, if a somewhat obscure passage in Pliny has been rightly understood, equal to it in height. Twenty-four pyramidal steps, such as were discovered *in situ*, would give a height of 24 feet 6 inches for the pyramid. If we suppose that its apex was surmounted by a pedestal some 13 feet high, on which the *quadriga* rested—as Mr. Fergusson has, with great probability, suggested—the united height of the pyramid and pedestal would be about $37\frac{1}{2}$ feet, and would thus equal the height of the *Pteron*, as Pliny states; and when he says that the pyramid tapered off *in metæ cacumen*, to a point like that of a *meta* or goal, he may have meant to indicate the pedestal as a distinct feature by these words. If we assume that the figure of Mausolus stood in the *quadriga* on a base a little above the axle of the wheel, the height of the chariot group may be calculated at about 14 feet.

The sum of these measurements is as follows :—

Pteron	$37\frac{1}{2}$ feet.
Pyramid and pedestal	$37\frac{1}{2}$ „
Chariot group	14 „

89 feet.

But Pliny states that the entire height of the monument was 140 feet. We must therefore suppose that the *Pteron* stood on a basement 51 feet in height.

Such a high basement or *podium* is a very common feature in architectural tombs, both Greek and Roman, as may be seen by the examples given in Plate XXXI. of my History of Discoveries at Budrum, and by the remains still existing on the Appian Way; and it was within or below the solid masonry of such basements that the sepulchral chamber was usually placed, the upper part of the monument being usually a small temple or *heroön*, in which the dead were worshipped. In the Mausoleum, the basement was evidently built of the blocks of green stone, of which I found the lowest courses still *in situ*, and must have been faced externally with marble slabs, the monotony of the plain courses being broken by one or more belts of frieze.

The disappearance of this marble casing may be accounted for by the fact that this part of the building would have been the first to suffer in the Middle Ages, and would have been stripped off piecemeal, not only in the endeavour to force an entrance into the sepulchral chamber within, but for the sake of the metal cramps by which the slabs must have been attached.

After this marble casing had been torn off, one or more of the corners of the basement would then probably have been attacked, and thus the angle columns of the *Pteron* would have been so under-

mined as no longer to resist the shock of earthquakes. Their fall would bring down the whole
colonnade and superincumbent pyramid; and when
the Knights first came to Budrum, these ruins must
have been lying in a great heap upon and around
the basement.

This is, I think, evident from the well-known
narrative of Guichard, published in 1581. He states
that in 1522, when the Knights were repairing the
Castle of St. Peter, "they looked about for stones
wherewith to make lime, and found in the middle of
a level field near the Port of Budrum, certain steps
of white marble raised in the form of a terrace
(*perron*).

"They therefore removed these marble steps, and,
after having destroyed the little masonry remaining
above ground, proceeded to dig lower in quest of
more. In a short time they perceived that the
deeper they went, the more the structure was enlarged at the base, supplying them not only with
stone for making lime, but also for building. After
four or five days, having laid bare a great space one
afternoon, they saw an opening as into a cellar.
Taking a candle, they let themselves down through
this opening, and found that it led into a fine large
square apartment, ornamented all round with columns
of marble, with their bases, capitals, architrave,
frieze, and cornice engraved and sculptured in relief.
The space between the columns was lined with slabs
and bands of marble, ornamented with mouldings
and sculpture, in harmony with the rest of the
work, and inserted in the white ground of the wall

where battle-scenes were represented sculptured in relief.

Having at first admired these works and entertained their fancy with the singularity of the sculpture, they pulled it to pieces and broke up the whole of it, applying it to the same purpose as the rest. Besides this apartment, they found afterwards a very low door which led into another apartment serving as an antechamber, where was a sepulchre with its vase and helmet (*tymbre*) of white marble, very beautiful, and of marvellous lustre.

This sepulchre, for want of time, they did not open, the retreat having already sounded. The day after, when they returned, they found the tomb opened and the earth all round strewn with fragments of cloth of gold, and spangles of the same metal, which made them suppose that the pirates who hovered along this coast, having some inkling of what had been discovered, had visited the place during the night and removed the lid of the sepulchre."

Guichard gives this curious narrative on the authority of d'Alechamps, the learned editor of Pliny, who heard the story from the lips of the Commander de la Tourette, a Lyonese knight present at Budrum when this discovery took place.

It would seem from this account that the *perron* which the Knights began by destroying, was the stylobate on which the columns of the *Pteron* rested, on removing which they came to the solid core of the basement, built of green stone. On entering the Castle of St. Peter, we recognize on every side the materials taken by the Knights. Many of the walls

are entirely built of green stone, and all the jambs
and architraves of doors are of fine white marble
similar to that of the *Pteron*.

It should be observed, however, that the destruction of the ruins of the Mausoleum by the Knights
did not commence, as Guichard's narrative would
imply, at so late a date as 1522, but must have
been going on since Schlegelholt began to build the
Castle about the year 1402.

Of the frieze of the Order the British Museum
possesses in all sixteen slabs, twelve of which,
as has already been stated, were removed from
the Castle.[51] (Plates 13, 15.)   One other slab of
the frieze is still preserved in the Villa di Negro
at Genoa, to which place it was probably transported from Budrum by one of the Knights of
St. John some time in the 15th or early in the
16th century.   A fragment containing part of a
figure of an Amazon is to be seen in the Museum of
the Seraglio, at Constantinople, where I noticed it in
1852.   (See *ante*, I. p. 43.)   How it found its way
there I have not been able to ascertain.   It may have
been dug up at Budrum and sent to Constantinople
as a present to some pasha, or it may have been
taken out of the walls of the Castle at Cos, also
built by the Knights; for I was told in that island
that the late Sultan Mahmoud on his visit to Cos,
seeing some reliefs built into the walls of the
Castle, ordered them to be sent to Constantinople.

The subject throughout the sixteen slabs in the
British Museum is a combat between Greeks and
Amazons.   These slabs, however, cannot be

arranged in regular sequence, but are taken from various parts of the series ; nor have we any evidence as to the side of the building which they occupied, except in the case of those found by me (see *ante*, p. 95), which are probably from the eastern side. These four are evidently by the same artist, and are in far better preservation than those from the Castle.

Three of these four slabs were found to form a continuous subject (*see* the upper row in Plate 13, where by an oversight the order of these three plates has been transposed, the slab on the right being in the place where the slab on the left should have been).

On the slab engraved Plate 14 the principal figure is a mounted Amazon, whose horse is rearing, as if about to strike with his fore legs a Greek warrior in front of him. The rider has turned round so as to face the horse's tail, and is drawing her bow after the Parthian fashion at an enemy behind her. The Greek in front of her is engaged with an Amazon, who pressing eagerly forward and, laying hold of her adversary's shield with her left hand, has her right drawn back to deal him a blow with a battle-axe. The Greek has his body thrown very far back, resting his weight on the right knee, and trying to cover himself with his buckler. His right has been broken off, but probably held a spear.

Throughout the sixteen slabs the artist has maintained a skilful contrast of nude and draped, of male and female forms. In the composition the groups are less intricate than in the frieze of the Parthenon or that of the temple of Apollo at Phigalia, and are arranged so as to balance each other by a peculiar antithesis of oblique parallel lines. The relief is very salient, the limbs being frequently sculptured in the round with occasional bold foreshortenings. The outlines are marked with extreme force, a channel being worked in the marble round each figure, and deep under-cutting used wherever it would contribute to the effect.

This frieze is distinguished by the wonderful animation and energy which pervades the whole composition.

A happy boldness of invention is shown in the incidents which represent the varied fortunes of a combat in which neither side can claim a decisive victory. A consummate technical knowledge is applied throughout to render the expression of each figure and group as intense as possible, and proportions are boldly exaggerated to produce more striking effects. Tried by the standard of the school of Phidias, and viewed simply as a composition in relief, without regard to its place as a subordinate architectural member, the frieze may perhaps be considered a little strained and overwrought in style. It may be thought that such intensity in the action needs the contrast of forms expressive of repose, such as we see introduced so skilfully in the metopes of the Parthenon and the Phigalian frieze; and the whole composition, if compared with similar subjects as treated by Phidias, seems less ethical and more pathetic. Moreover, among the Amazons on this frieze forms occur which some would regard as

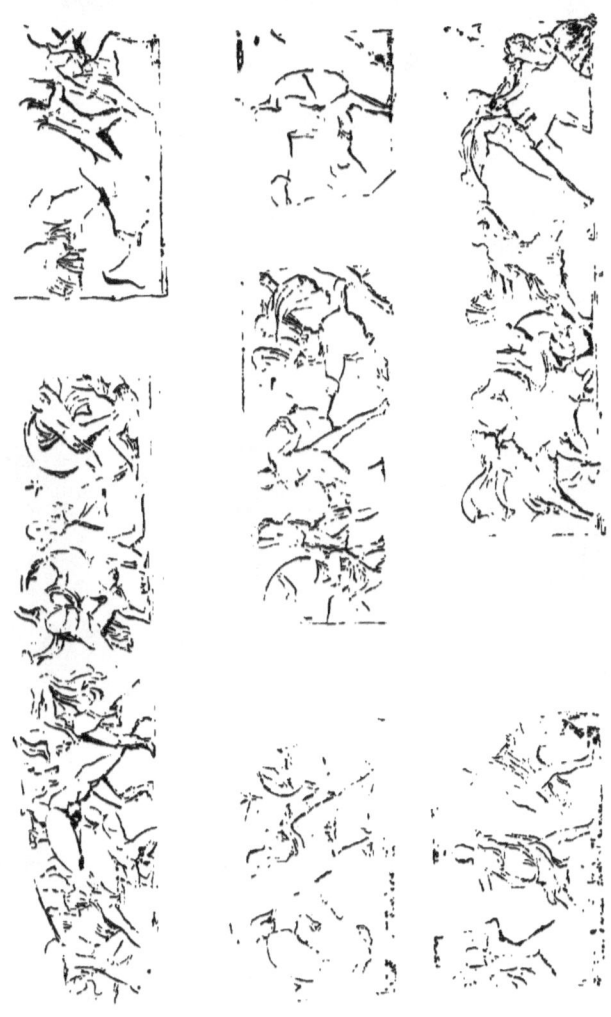

too voluptuous for so heroic a type ; and we may here detect the first germs of that sensual element which gained such an ascendancy in the later schools of art, but of which we have no trace in the works of Phidias.

In making these criticisms on the frieze of the Mausoleum, it must not be forgotten that the slabs which we possess do not form a continuous composition, but are for the most part fragments of very extended groups balanced one against the other with extreme subtlety. We must also bear in mind that as the Mausoleum stood on a lofty basement, the frieze would be placed at a much greater height than this member usually occupied in a Greek temple. Distance would thus tone down and harmonize much that appears strained and exaggerated when seen, as the frieze now is, on the level of the eye and at the distance of only a few feet.

Considering the perfect taste and keeping shown in every part of the design of the Mausoleum, so far as we know it, and the entire absence of exaggeration in the sculptures in the round, it is difficult to believe that so important a feature as the frieze of the Order would have been designed in a style not in harmony with the rest.

It has been already noted that the whole frieze was coloured. From the examination of a number of fragments on their first disinterment, I ascertained that the ground of the relief, like that of the architectural ornaments, was a blue equal in intensity to ultramarine, the flesh a dun red, and the drapery and armour picked out with vermilion, and perhaps other colours.

K 2

The bridles, as on the frieze of the Parthenon, were of metal, for the attachment of which the heads of several of the horses are pierced.

This variety of tint must have greatly contributed to the distinctness and animation of the composition, and to unite the several groups in one great harmony, if, as we may fairly assume, the artists of the Mausoleum had as fine a sense of proportion in colour as they had in form.

While this is passing through the press, my attention has been called to a passage in Mr. Westmacott's Handbook of Sculpture, p. 156, in which he has thought fit to call in question the accuracy of my statement as to the colour observed on the sculptures of the Mausoleum. I therefore beg leave to refer the reader to the documents which I have printed at the end of this volume[52] in corroboration of my official reports on the subject.

Among the many fragments of sculptured reliefs found on the site of the Mausoleum, were some from a frieze which has evidently represented a combat between Greeks and Centaurs. All the fragments of this frieze found on the site are much corroded, as if they had been exposed to weather. The material is white marble, coarse in grain, the relief very salient. I think it not improbable that this frieze ornamented the basement of the tomb.

There were also upwards of a hundred fragments of a third frieze, representing a chariot-race, the charioteers being all female. In this frieze the heads and extremities are for the most part not detached, as in the frieze of the Order, but relieved on the

ENTER A MARIE BACE
MAUSOLEUM

ground. In some cases the treatment is very flat,
as in the frieze of the Parthenon. The execution
is highly wrought, and the material a finer marble
than that employed in the other friezes. On one
of the pieces the blue colour of the ground
may still be traced under an aqueous deposit.
The most interesting fragment of this frieze is
that engraved Plate 16, representing a female
charioteer standing in a *quadriga*, and draped in
a *chiton* reaching to the feet. Her body is thrown
forward, and her countenance and whole attitude
are expressive of the eagerness of the contest. The
features are finished almost with the delicacy of a
gem.

This frieze has a flat ogee moulding at the foot, on
the under side of which the enriched ornament usual
in this moulding has been painted. Faint traces of
the blue ground and of the leaves of this ornament
still remain on the marble. This ornament was evidently designed to be seen from below, and the
whole frieze was evidently meant for nearer inspection and less exposure to the weather, than the two
friezes already described.

Of the sculptures in the round which decorated
the Mausoleum we possess many fragments besides
the remains from the chariot group already noticed.

The most remarkable of these fragments is from
the equestrian group discovered within the quadrangle (see *ante*, p. 94, Plate 4). This group has
been cruelly mutilated. Of the horse nothing remains
but the body cut off at the shoulders; of the rider,
only the body from the waist to the hips, the left

hand and wrist, and the right thigh and leg. This figure wears the close-fitting trowsers called *anaxy-rides*, over which falls a tunic with sleeves, girt at the waist and reaching half-way down the thighs.

The horse is in a rearing attitude, as is shown by the bend of the body, and by the action of the shoulder and arm. In the present mutilated state of this group the action of the rider cannot be made out with certainty; but it seems probable that this figure was represented striking downwards with a spear at a prostrate foe. Thus the group may have originally commemorated the triumph of an Asiatic warrior over one of his enemies.

The upper jaw and nose of a horse found near this torso may have belonged to it. In that case the mouth of the horse must have been represented open, and his nostrils distended with rage, as would be characteristic of a horse in the excitement of battle.

Notwithstanding the great mutilation which this torso has received, it may be considered one of the finest examples of ancient sculptures which has survived the wreck of time. The body of the horse is a masterpiece of modelling; the rearing movement affects the whole frame, and the solid and unwieldy mass of marble seems to bend and spring before our eyes, as if all the latent energy of the animal were suddenly called forth and concentrated in one forward movement. Equal skill is shown in the representation of the rider. Nothing can be more perfect than his seat. The right leg and thigh seems to grow to the horse's side; the manner in which the waist yields to the movement of the rearing

horse is admirably expressed by the composition of
the drapery; the position of the bridle hand is carefully studied; the elbow is fixed, the wrist flexible,
the thumb firmly bent over the reins.

The other sculptures found on the site of the
Mausoleum consist of heads, torsoes, and limbs from
statues, and fragments of lions. These remains
show that the statues differed much in scale, ranging
from colossal proportions to life-size. The arms
and legs are mostly naked, the long sleeves to the
chiton or the *endromides* occur only as the exception.
The muscles are in no instance in violent action,
and the composition of the drapery is inconsistent
with rapid movement. None of the fragments
appear to have been broken off from groups. It is
to be inferred, therefore, that the statues which
decorated the Mausoleum were for the most part
isolated and standing in attitudes of repose.

The lions must have been a marked feature in the
sculptural decoration of the tomb. From the evidence of the fragments which we possess, it may be
calculated that there were at least twenty of these
animals, and probably many more have entirely
disappeared.

Their proportions are evidently adjusted to more
than one scale. The largest measure 4 feet 6 inches
from the point of the shoulder to the hind quarter,
while others are about three inches narrower in the
same part. Their height cannot be exactly fixed,
but it probably did not much exceed five feet.

From the examination of the numerous fragments
of legs and paws, and also from the action of the

shoulders and hind quarters, there can hardly be a
doubt that all the lions were represented standing
like sentinels. Their heads, which seem to have
been all placed nearly on the same level, are turned
with a vigilant look in different directions, as if they
were guarding the approaches to the tomb. Their
expression and attitudes are beautifully varied. In
some the countenance has an angry look, in others
the natural savageness of the animal seems tempered
with a certain earnestness and pathos in the expression which is very peculiar. The frame of these
lions is square and compact; the limbs wiry and
muscular. The mane is short and close, and the
hind quarters do not exhibit that falling off and
disproportion which is so remarkable in the African
lion of the present day. In comparing the lions of
the Mausoleum with nature, it must be borne in
mind that many deviations from the life may have
been made by the sculptors in order to adapt the
forms of these animals to the architectural design of
which they formed a part.

On comparing these lions one with another, it will
be seen that their sculpture is of very unequal merit.
The finest of all the heads is one found in a garden
wall to the north of the Mausoleum, and engraved
Plate 17. This is remarkable for the rich and
flowing lines of the composition. In the sculpture
of the mouth and nose a masterly discrimination of
surface is shown, and the execution, though highly
elaborate, is free and bold, the artist never losing
sight of the general effect. In two other lions, both
of which were found on the north side, the details of

the anatomy are rendered in a somewhat conventional and meagre manner. It is possible that the less carefully executed lions were intended to be seen at a greater distance than the others; but I am disposed to consider them as works from which, for some reason or other, the master hand was withheld.

Great knowledge and skill of execution are shown in the sculpture of the paws, which are beautifully varied in action. The sculptors of the Mausoleum were well aware how much of the general expression and mood of all the feline species may be indicated by so slight a sign as a protruded or retracted claw.

From patches of colour which were visible on two of these lions on their first disinterment, it is probable that they were all painted a tawny red. The marble in which they are sculptured appears to be Pentelic; it is evidently of a choice quality, for much of the surface is as fresh as the day when it left the chisel.]

XLI.

BUDRUM, *September* 30, 1857.

SINCE the date of my last letter we have continued to explore the site of the Mausoleum, extending the excavations on the north and east sides.

The marble wall behind which so much sculpture was found has been traced for 337 feet on the north

side, and its return has been met with on the
eastern side. There can therefore be no doubt that
it is the wall of the *peribolos* or sacred precinct
round the tomb, of which the entire circuit, according to Hyginus, was 1,340 feet.

Considerable progress has also been made in
clearing out the subterraneous galleries round the
Mausoleum. We continue to find torsoes and other
remains of sculpture and architecture in the upper
soil; but in proportion as the excavations are extended to a greater distance from the quadrangular
area on which the Mausoleum stood, the ground
yields less and less of these remains.

I reserve a more detailed account of our operations till a future letter, when the results can be
more clearly stated.

While exploring the site of the Mausoleum, I have
not been indifferent to the general topography of
Halicarnassus, and with this view a small party of
sailors from the Gorgon, under the command of
Mr. Royce, was employed to examine a fine platform which overlooks the Mausoleum, and which,
from its extent, commanding position, and the mas-
siveness of the terrace wall which bounds it, was
mistaken by Mr. W. J. Hamilton and Dr. Ludwig
Ross for the site of the Mausoleum itself.

In the centre of this platform the outlines of an
oblong edifice were indicated by ridges, and close to
these ridges were several drums of Ionic columns of
fine white marble, and 4 feet in diameter.

On excavating here, Mr. Royce laid bare the foundations of an oblong edifice, 46 feet in width, and

probably not less than 100 feet in length. The
marble superstructure had almost entirely disappeared, but a few small fragments of mouldings
were found, which prove that the edifice which stood
on this site was of the Ionic order. The mouldings
were very similar in design and workmanship to
those found on the site of the Mausoleum, and, like
those, bore traces of red and blue colour. It is
probable, therefore, that the edifice to which they
belong was executed in the same century as the
Mausoleum, and we can hardly doubt that here
stood the Temple of Mars, mentioned by Vitruvius
in a passage to which I have already referred, *ante*,
p. 84, and in which he gives the following description of the topography of Halicarnassus :—" Mausolus perceiving that Halicarnassus was a place
naturally fortified, favourable for trade, and with a
convenient harbour, made it his royal residence.
As the form of the site was curved like a theatre,
on the lowest ground near the port was placed the
forum. Along the curve, about halfway up its
height, was made a broad street, which may be
likened to the *præcinctio* of a theatre. In the
centre of this street stood the Mausoleum, constructed with such marvellous works that it is
considered one of the Seven Wonders of the world.
In the centre of the citadel above was the Temple
of Mars, containing a colossal acrolithic statue
from the hand of Leochares or (according to
others) Timotheus. On the summit of the right-
hand extremity of the curve was the Temple of
Venus and Mercury, close to the fountain Salmacis.

Now in like manner as on the right hand was this
Temple of Venus and Mercury and the above-named
fountain, so on the left horn, or extremity of the
curve, stood the royal palace, which King Mausolus
placed so as to suit his own designs : for from it
can be seen, on the right hand, the *forum*, the harbour, and the whole circuit of the walls ; on the left
a secret port, so concealed under the walls that no
one could spy or ascertain what was going on there ;
that the king from his own palace might, without
the knowledge of any one, direct all that was necessary for his fleet and army."

On comparing this description with the Plan,
Plate 1, and with the view of Budrum, Plates 18, 19,
it will be seen that the shore of the harbour bends
round in a curve, terminating in two headlands or
horns, on one of which stands the Turkish arsenal,
on the other the Castle of St. Peter. Around this
curved shore the area of the ancient city is still
defined by its walls, which may be traced in unbroken continuity all round, except where they
approach the seashore on the eastern side, enclosing
a narrow strip of rich soil, studded with flat-roofed
houses, where the Turkish peasant cultivates his
little plot of ground, dwelling under the shade of his
own fig-tree, and enjoying a climate perhaps the
most genial in the Levant.

This fertile strip of shore is hemmed in on the
north by a high range of hills, the natural defence
of the site.

It has been already stated (*ante*, p. 84) that the
site of the Mausoleum corresponds exactly with the

position assigned to it by Vitruvius, *i.e.*, "the centre of the curve, halfway up the height." The platform where I place his Temple of Mars over-looks the Mausoleum, lying to the north-east of it, and is the only spot in the whole range of the northern heights where I could discover any trace of the site of a temple.

Vitruvius describes the Temple of Mars as placed *in summa arce media*. On reference to the Plan, it will be seen that the platform marked "Temple of Mars" lies a little to the south of the wall of the ancient city, at a point where the hill makes a dip between two fortified heights, the two most elevated points in the whole line of circumvallation. Of these strongholds or *arces* the one on the west is a conical hill of tufaceous rock, thrown up by volcanic agency to the height of 520 feet above the sea; while that on the east juts out into a long salient angle to the north-east, rising above the town in precipitous crags of nummulite limestone. A temple lying between two such fortified heights may be fairly described as placed *in summa arce media*—in the midst of or between the two highest points in the northern wall of Halicarnassus.

I have already remarked that the architectural fragments found on this platform indicate that the temple which stood here was probably built at the same period as the Mausoleum. This is the more probable inasmuch as the acrolithic statue in the Temple of Mars was attributed either to Leochares or Timotheus, both of whom were employed by Artemisia on the decoration of her husband's tomb.

Though Vitruvius does not say that the Temple
of Mars was built by Mausolus, it may, I think, be
inferred from his description, that an edifice occupying such a conspicuous and central position was
part of the original plan of the city, and it is probable that, in accordance with a practice which has
prevailed in India down to a recent period, the
tomb of the Carian prince was commenced in his
lifetime.[53]

Two of the three central points mentioned by
Vitruvius being thus fixed, we must look for the
site of his *agora* on the shore, in the ground now
occupied by the konak, harem, and gardens of Salik
Bey. In this ground an Ionic base, resembling those
of the Mausoleum, but only three feet in diameter,
the drum of an Ionic column on the same scale,
and many ancient marbles have been dug up.

On the left horn of the harbour Vitruvius places
the palace of Mausolus; on the right the Temple of
Venus and Mercury, close to the fountain Salmacis.
The position of the palace was such that on the left
it overlooked a little secret port attached to the
arsenal of Mausolus; on the right it commanded
the *agora*, the harbour, and the entire circuit of the
walls. The position of the secret port was first laid
down by Captain Spratt, in the Admiralty Chart,
No. 1606. He was the first to notice the foundations of its mole, which are still visible in the
harbour at the side of the isthmus. The position of
this port being fixed, it follows, if the description of
Vitruvius is literally exact, that the palace of Mausolus must have been somewhere on the rising

ground to the east of the harbour, for no other
position would have the secret port on the left, and
at the same time command a view of the fortified
heights above. We can hardly doubt that in the
time of Mausolus the rocky platform on which the
Castle now stands was an island, and that here was
one of the two citadels mentioned by Arrian in the
account of the siege of Halicarnassus by Alexander
the Great. The arsenal of Mausolus must have
extended over the low ground on the isthmus now
occupied by the Greek quarter. This arsenal, like
those of Rhodes and Carthage, and the port itself,
were jealously screened from view by high walls.
It was here that the princes of Caria prepared
naval and military operations in secrecy, and it was
out of this port that Artemisia issued when she surprised the Rhodians by a dexterous manœuvre.[54]
The canal by which she passed through the isthmus
now probably forms the northern fosse of the Castle.

By reference to the Plan of Budrum (Plate 1), it
will be seen that the site of the palace of Mausolus
was chosen with much judgment for military purposes.
To the east his position was covered by the city
wall; in front of him were his arsenal and fleet; and
behind him the strong citadel into which he could
retreat if necessary, and which was doubtless connected with the mainland by a drawbridge.

Of the Temple of Venus and Mercury which
adorned the western horn, no vestige remains on
the shore opposite to the peninsula. The most
conspicuous feature on this side of the bay is the
steep rock of Caplan Calessy, on the summit of

which is a platform included in the line of the walls where Captain Spratt has with much probability placed the citadel called Salmacis by Arrian. It is to be presumed that this fortress was near the fountain of the same name, which according to Vitruvius was close to the Temple of Venus and Mercury; but after a careful survey of the ground I have been unable to discover any fountain corresponding with the position assigned to that of Salmacis.[55] From an inscription which I have discovered at Budrum, in which a decree is made out in the joint names of the Halicarnassians and Salmacians, it may be inferred that the latter people were of Carian or Lelegian race, and that they originally dwelt on the rocky promontory of Caplan Calessy, the opposite horn of the harbour, then an island, having been occupied by the Doric settlers. The name of Salmacis was retained for the citadel on Caplan Calessy after the separate existence of the native town had been merged in that of Halicarnassus.[56]

After fixing these points in the topography, the account of the taking of Halicarnassus by Alexander the Great becomes quite clear. According to Arrian, he entered the city in the night, and, looking down from the heights which he occupied, saw the two citadels, Salmacis and the fortress in the island, still occupied by the Persians. It was natural that he should have first secured his position in the highest part of the city, taking possession of the fort on the conical hill, and the rocky salient near the Mylasa gate already noticed, and that he should have then descended to the shore.

A little to the south of the Temple of Mars is a

row of Doric columns thirty in number, half buried in the soil. These columns still support their entablature, and are evidently part of a portico or *stoa*. Digging down to the base of these shafts, we found on their north side coarse tessellated pavement of the Roman period. Immediately to the south of this row of columns are a number of vaults built of rubble and concrete, which are partially visible above the soil. Two inscriptions which I found a little to the east of the *peribolos* of the Mausoleum relate to a *stoa* dedicated to Apollo and one of the Egyptian Ptolemies, probably Philadelphus or Energetes; and it is not improbable that the row of Doric columns still standing may be part of this *stoa*. The date of this colonnade would thus range from B.C. 300 to 200. Another inscription found by me in the Castle mentions a *gymnasium* built by one of the Ptolemies, which may have been the site of Agia Marina, where Captain Spratt placed the Mausoleum. (See *ante*, p. 72.)

On the base of the conical hill above the Mausoleum is a fine theatre. The walls of the ancient city have been already noticed.

The plan of these fortifications was probably designed by Mausolus, though, as Arrian states that Alexander razed Halicarnassus to the ground, the walls now existing may be the work of a later period. The lines are well chosen in reference to the natural capabilities of the site for defence, and every point of vantage ground seems turned to the best account. The greater part of the masonry is polygonal, and the material trachyte and limestone. On the west side the masonry is isodomous, and the builders have availed themselves of the native tufaceous rock, easily quarried from the conical hill at the foot of which stands the Mausoleum. The gate on the west side leading to Myndus must, from the lowness of the level, have been one of the weakest parts in the whole circumvallation. Hence this gate has been fortified with three towers still standing, one of which is set obliquely to the wall, in order more completely to command the approach.[57] It was on this side that Alexander sought to find a weak place in the wall, and here he probably directed his real attack, while he threatened the opposite side.

The ancient cemeteries outside this gate, and that of Mylasa on the eastern side, have been already noticed, *ante*, pp. 62-4. Many tombs may also be seen on the conical hill inside the walls ; for here, as in other Greek cities, though extramural interment seems to have been the general practice, it was not enforced by penalties as in the early laws of Rome.

Our party has been recently augmented by the arrival of Mr. R. P. Pullan, an architect sent out by Lord Clarendon to make drawings and plans of the Mausoleum and of other ancient remains.

XLII.

Budrum, *November 28th*, 1857.

On the 20th of October last the Supply left Budrum for Malta, to obtain a fresh stock of provisions. I took advantage of this opportunity to visit the site of the celebrated Temple of Apollo at Branchidæ near Miletus. The Supply having conveyed me as far as Calymnos, I crossed over from that island to Kara-köi, a small harbour lying south of Cape Monodendro, in a Greek ship which my old friend Antonio Maillé the sponge-merchant very obligingly lent me. I took with me Corporal Spackman with his photographic apparatus, and three Turks provided with picks and shovels. Kara-köi is about three miles distant from Branchidæ, now called Geronta (pronounced Yoronda by the Turks). Two giant columns supporting a piece of architrave, and a third unfinished column are all that remain standing of the Temple of Apollo, of which the mighty ruins lie as they originally fell, piled up like shattered icebergs. One piece of architrave which I measured was 18 feet long. The site being on a slight eminence, no earth has accumulated on these ruins, and the general structure of the temple may be easily made out from the architectural members thrown about pell-mell on the ground. The Order is Ionic, very similar in its details to the Mausoleum, but not so delicately executed, and probably of a

(II.) L 2 *

later period. I found no sculpture but part of a frieze
of gryphons, which seemed rather coarse, and very
inferior to the sculptures of the Mausoleum.

The marbles of this temple having been measured
and delineated in the Ionian Antiquities of the
Dilettanti Society, I did not devote much time to
them, the principal object of my visit being the
examination of the ground all round the temple,
and more especially the Sacred Way leading up
to it.

The ruins are encompassed by a wretched Greek
village, which has grown up since the Greek revolution, and bears a very bad reputation as an asylum
and rendezvous of pirates and brigands. All around
this village is an undulating plain, deserted and
melancholy in its aspect, with a rich but neglected
soil, and bounded on the land side by fine mountain
lines. On the north-west this plain descends by
easy slopes and ridges to the sea. It was from this
side that a Sacred Way led up to the Temple from
the Port Panormus, the position of which is marked
in the Admiralty Chart.

On reference to the Plan (Plate 20), it will be
seen that this Way, commencing at a short distance
from the Temple of Apollo, may be traced for a
length of about 580 yards in a north-west direction
towards the ancient port. Throughout this length
the line of the Way has been bounded by basements,
statues, and stone coffins or *sori*, many of which
objects still remain in position on the south-west
side of the Way. At the distance of rather more
than 300 yards from the Temple the line of the

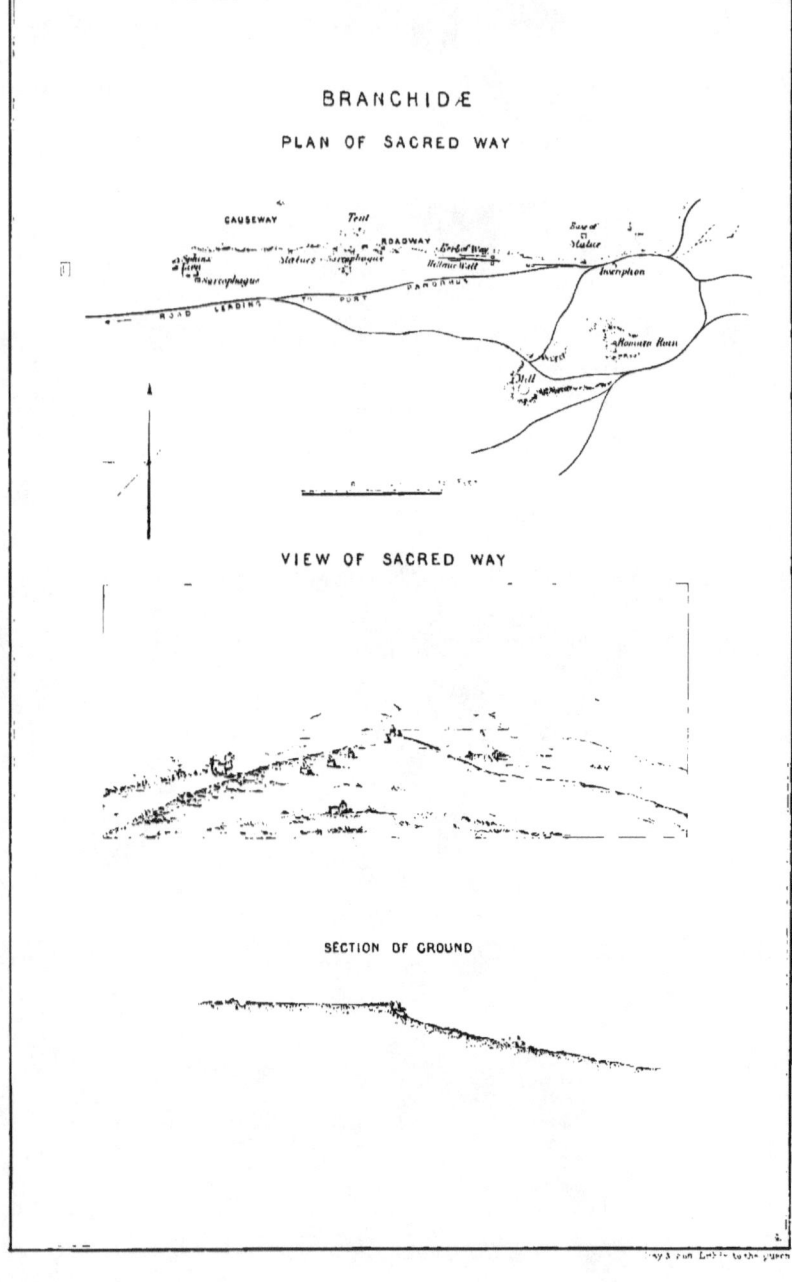

BRANCHIDÆ

PLAN OF SACRED WAY

VIEW OF SACRED WAY

SECTION OF GROUND

Way is marked by a ridge running to the north-west, and deepening as it advances. The ground to the south of this ridge is for some distance a level platform or terrace. North of the ridge the ground sinks, forming a hollow.

This feature of the ground is shown in the Section and the accompanying View, taken from the south-eastern end of the Way. (Plate 20.)

Along the ridge may be traced a continuous line of wall, in front of which a number of statues are placed at intervals. The statues I found partially buried in the soil. In some cases only the base of the neck was visible; in others the soil did not rise higher than the lap of the figure. Clearing away the earth, I took photographs of them all.

The figures are seated in chairs, their hands resting on their knees. Their original height must have averaged rather more than five feet, but the heads are now broken away.

They are all draped in a *chiton* or tunic reaching to the feet, over which is a mantle. The tunic fits close to the body and has sleeves, down the side of which runs a seam, ornamented in the case of two of these figures with the Mæander pattern, now nearly effaced.

The chairs are evidently imitated from the chairs in wood, and are therefore curious as examples of the furniture of a very early period. Two of them are ornamented in front with a pair of pilasters, the capital of which formed a bracket, projecting at the end of the arm of the chair about three inches.

The accompanying cuts show the form of these

pilasters, which are similar to those represented on
early Greek vases, and the ornaments on which
seem to be intended for a double lotos-flower. In

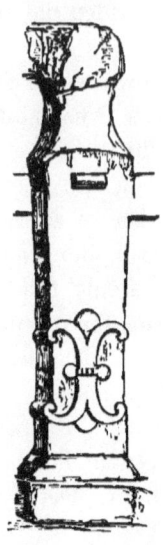 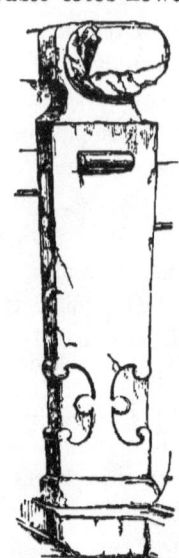

a.   *a.*

several of the statues the cushion on which the
figure is seated is shown under the arm of the chair.
The sides of these cushions are ornamented with
the Mæander and zigzag patterns. (*See* cuts *b, b.*)

To my great surprise and satisfaction I found on
one of these chairs an inscription in two lines, containing these words: "I am Chares, son of Klesis,
ruler of Teichioussa; an offering to Apollo." I
learnt from this brief record that the headless statue
seated before me had been dedicated to the great
deity of Branchidæ by the ruler of a petty town
within the territory of Miletus, and that it represented Chares himself, for the most ancient Greek

dedicatory inscriptions are usually written in the
first person, the object dedicated being supposed to
tell its own tale.

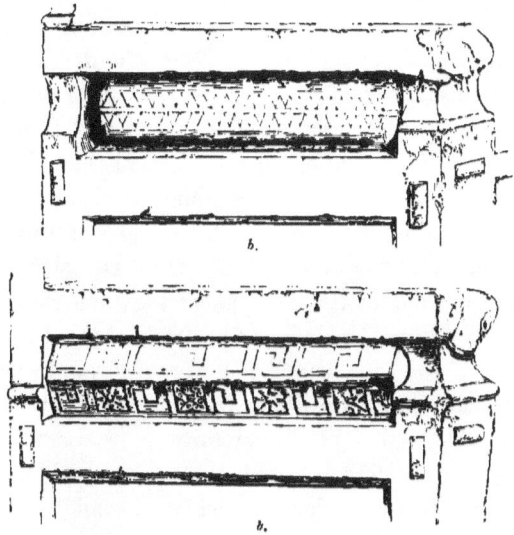

These primitive records addressing all future
generations of men with a quaint simplicity affect
the mind more than the elaborate and pompous
phrases with which the inscriptions of the Roman
period seek to immortalize obscure individuals.
Chares, son of Klesis, whose name by this singular
discovery has been revealed to us, is unmentioned
in Greek history. Concerning the place over which
he ruled we only know that it was within the territory of Miletus, and on the Iassic Gulf, and that
it was rated among the tributaries of Athens at the
time of the Peloponnesian war. Lebas conjectures
that Teichioussa may have been at Kara-köi, the

bay where I landed, because two inscriptions found
there mention "the deme of the Teichiessians;"
but it is very probable that these inscriptions were
brought from Branchidæ.[58]

The inscription on the chair is written in the
manner called by the Greeks *Boustrophedon*, that is
to say, alternately, from right to left and from left
to right, the first line running down the front of
the chair, the second along the adjacent side. From
the character of the palæography and for other
reasons I should imagine that the date of this inscription might be about B.C. 520. The statue is
therefore probably the most ancient extant example
in Greek art of the εἰκών, or portrait statue, though
several of the early Greek sculptors are said to have
made such Iconic statues. We may assume that in
these early attempts at portraiture no exact ren-
dering of the features and expression could have
been accomplished, though such works might serve
to record the general character and proportions
of the figure; the person represented must have
been identified by the inscription or by distinctive
symbols very much more than by the work of
the sculptor. These early Iconic statues, it must
be remembered, were intended to be dedicated
in some temple; it was not till a much later
period that portraits were executed for private
individuals.[59]

On another of these statues I discovered part of
the name of the sculptor who made it, inscribed on
the arm of the chair. This name, of which the
termination only remains, may have been Hermo-

demos, or Eurudemos : then follow the words, "made me," *i.e.* "the statue."

These figures, eight in number, were placed in a line running from south-east to north-west at the side of the ancient Way. They all rested on the bare earth, but must originally have been set up on pedestals. At the side of the one inscribed with the name of Chares was discovered the foundation of a square basement. At the back of two or three figures in the centre of the row, and running parallel to them, was a foundation wall of concrete and rubble, apparently of Byzantine construction.

All the eight figures with one exception were male. Digging to the north-east of the row, I discovered two more statues lying half concealed in the soil. Of these one was a female figure, of which the head has been broken away. The other still retains its head, though the features are utterly defaced. This also appears to be a female figure; the hair flows in long tresses. Both these figures are similar in attitude and costume to those already described.

In the type and attitude of all these statues and in the composition of the drapery there is much which reminds us of Egyptian sculpture. The arms are placed close to the sides, the palms of the hands resting on the knees; the shoulders very broad; the folds of the drapery are expressed by parallel stripes and channellings, arranged in a formal composition of vertical and oblique lines. At first sight the sculpture appears ruder than it really is; for the main points in the anatomy are

indicated, however slightly, without that accumulation and exaggeration of details so general in Assy-
rian and early Greek art. This subdued treatment
of the anatomy gives breadth and repose to these
figures, and suggests the idea that they were executed by artists who had studied in Egypt.

There is nothing à priori improbable in such an
assumption. We know that a connection between
Asia Minor and Egypt had been established in the
reign of Psammetichos I., who maintained a large force
of Ionian and Carian mercenaries. The importance of
the trade between Egypt and the Greek colonies of
the west coast of Asia Minor led to the establishment of an Hellenic factory at Naukratis in the
reign of Amasis ; the costly dedications made to
Hellenic deities by Neco at Branchidæ and by
Amasis at Lindos are further evidences of the
friendly relations which those monarchs maintained
with the Asiatic Greeks. Moreover, if the well-
known tradition preserved by Diodorus is to be
believed, the Samian sculptors, Theodoros and his
brother Telekles studied in Egypt, and thence de-
rived a canon of proportions which enabled them,
though living in separate places, to work at the
same statue, half of which, executed by Theodoros
at Samos, was found to tally with the other half
made by Telekles at Ephesos. It has been somewhat the fashion among recent writers on Greek
art to dismiss this story as mere legend ;[60] but I see
no reason for doubting that it embodies the general
fact that certain Greek sculptors of Asia Minor
studied the principles of their art in Egypt as

early as the seventh, or, perhaps, the eighth century B.C.

The statues at Branchidæ seem to me to present precisely the characteristics which might be expected in the works of a school of sculptors thus educated; for while the predominant impression which these works produce on the mind at first sight is their resemblance to Egyptian sculptures, we may detect in them certain peculiarities in the general treatment, and in the details of the costume and ornaments, which prove them to be the work of Hellenic artists.

At the distance of 118 paces to the north-west of the row of statues, I found a female sphinx lying above ground, greatly mutilated, and a lion nearly buried in the soil, both of white marble. The lion, which is couching, is rudely sculptured, but with a certain normal grandeur of conception. The repose of the folded fore paws is very characteristic of the animal. His head is broken off; along his back is an inscription in five lines, many of the letters of which are nearly obliterated by long exposure to the weather. After studying this inscription for about ten days in every variety of light, I succeeded in reading most of the words.

The inscription is a dedication of certain statues, as a tenth to Apollo. The names of the dedicators, five in number, are given. It is probable that these persons were citizens of Miletus, not only on account of the vicinity of this city, but because two of the names in this inscription, Thales and Hegesander, are known to have been borne by Milesians. It is interesting to compare the palæography of this dedication with that of the rock-cut inscription at Aboo-Simbul, in Nubia, placed there by the Greek mercenaries who served with Psammetichos, king of Egypt. It is not certain whether the king named in this Nubian inscription is Psammetichos I., who reigned from B.C. 664 to B.C. 610, or Psammetichos II., whose date is B.C. 595 to 589. But as either the one or the other of these two monarchs is certainly referred to in this inscription, it may be assigned to a date ranging from Olympiad 40 to 48; and in the forms of the letters and mode of writing it presents so striking a resemblance with the dedication on the Branchidæ lion, that this latter inscription can hardly be attributed to a later date than Olympiad 60.

The dedication by Chares on the statue is certainly less ancient, and its date may be about B.C. 520. At any rate, it cannot be later than the date of the destruction of the Temple of Apollo at Branchidæ, which, whether it was the act of Darius Hystaspes, or of Xerxes, certainly took place before the close of the Persian war.[61]

In the wall of a house near the Sacred Way is the fragment of another dedication made by Histiæos. This may be the celebrated Milesian who brought about the Ionian revolt. The letters are of the same period as in the dedication by Chares.

When Sir William Gell visited Branchidæ early in this century, he found on the Sacred Way the lower part of a seated figure, on the side of the chair of which was a dedication by one Hermesianax of

certain objects, probably statues. This has now
disappeared. There can hardly be a doubt that all
these statues were originally arranged so as to form
an avenue along the Sacred Way leading from the
Port Panormos to the Temple of Apollo. Could
these old headless figures speak, they might tell us
something more interesting than the bare fact of
their dedication inscribed on the marble ; for
through this very avenue may have passed the
envoys sent by Crœsus to consult the most famous
of Asiatic oracles ; and the sacrilegious Persian band
which plundered and burnt the first temple at
Branchidæ, and carried off the statue of the god
to Susiana, must have seen these very figures, and
may have spared them as too insignificant for the
vengeance of the Great King.

After examining the Sacred Way, I spent a few
days in copying inscriptions in the village of Geronta
and its environs. Some of these, which are given in
Böckh's great work, have now disappeared ; but in
the walls of the churches and houses are numbers
which have never been published. From these documents some curious information is to be gathered
respecting the Temple of Apollo, the offerings dedicated there, and the functions of its ministers,
who originally formed a Sacred *Gens*, all of whom
claimed descent from Branchos, the mythic founder
of the temple. The most interesting of these inscriptions is a letter from Seleukos II., king of Syria,
giving a list of gold and silver *anathemata* dedicated
for the use of the temple by that monarch and his
brother, Antiochos Hierax. In this document the

weight of each object is carefully registered. Among
the articles enumerated are drinking-cups fashioned
in those fantastic forms of which Athenæus has
industriously collected the names, and some few
specimens of which have been discovered in the
celebrated Royal Tomb near Kertch.

In other inscriptions given by Böckh are recorded
similar costly dedications by Prusias II., king of
Bithynia, and by envoys from one of the Egyptian
Ptolemies; and in an inscription found by me is
mention of the sending of an envoy sent to the
court of Ptolemy son of Auletes at Alexandria, and
of his bringing back a large quantity of ivory and
a door, probably, of silver.[62]   Perhaps under the
mighty pile of ruins on the site of this temple some
relic of these sumptuous offerings may still remain.

Most of the inscriptions relate to the priests of
the Temple of Apollo, and of other temples at
Branchidæ.   The προφήτης, whose office must have
been not to prophesy, but to announce the oracle, is
constantly mentioned.

The sacred *gens* who claimed descent from Branchos, the mythic founder of the temple, and formed
its original hierarchy, were transplanted by Xerxes,
together with the statue of the god, to Susiana,
where their descendants were found by Alexander
the Great, who, with a strange and unaccountable
fanaticism, is said to have put them to death in
punishment of the apostasy of their forefathers. We
have no information how the hierarchy thus cut off was
renewed; but it is evident from the inscriptions that
the later priesthood formed a distinct *gens*, in which

the same offices, though not, perhaps, hereditary, were filled by successive generations. The second temple at Branchidæ was probably begun soon after the Persian war. Its architects were Paionios and Daphnis, whose date we have no exact means of determining.[63] Judging from the character of the architecture, which, as I have already remarked, seems of rather a later date than the Mausoleum, I should think it probable that the building of this temple was continued as late as the time of Seleucus Nicator, who restored to it the colossal bronze statue of Apollo by Kanachos, which had been carried off to Susa by Xerxes after his defeat in Greece.

The *Hieron* of the Temple of Apollo was a precinct of great extent, and contained according to Strabo a large village, in which, no doubt, were accommodated the many strangers who came to consult the oracle.[64] Within the same precinct were celebrated public games, styled in inscriptions the Great Didymeia. It is possible that the modern name of this place, Geronta or Yoronda, may be a corruption of the word Ἱερόν.

My further researches at Geronta were cut short by a sharp attack of intermittent fever, for which the place has a bad reputation at this season. Having a good supply of quinine with me, I soon got well enough to undertake the journey back to Budrum. Crossing the Gulf of Mendeliah, we landed at the narrowest part of the isthmus, whence I pushed on to Budrum on foot with one of my attendant Turks, leaving Corporal Spackman in charge of the baggage till horses could be sent

to him.   I arrived here about two hours after the
Supply had come in from Malta.   Our meeting was
a very merry one, and I rejoiced to find that all my
requisitions for stores had been carefully attended
to by the Admiral Superintendent and War-office
at Malta, and that we are in a condition to commence a new campaign, well furnished with timber,
iron, rope, trucks, and everything we are likely
to run short of.   As we intend to try our luck at
Cnidus this winter, and the situation is too much
exposed for life under canvas, I made requisition for
eight Crimean huts, which have been sent in the
Supply, bound with hoop iron into many compact bundles of planks, and all ready to be
put together.   We hope to establish ourselves
at Cnidus early in next month.   Smith will
remain in charge of the Budrum diggings, with
Corporal Jenkins as his adjutant, and the Supply
will make Budrum her permanent winter anchorage,
visiting Cnidus every month to see how we are
getting on, and thus forming a floating base of
operations for both of the parties on shore.

XLIII.

ON the 10th of this month I was conveyed from
Budrum to this place in the Supply, with a select
party, consisting of Mr. R. P. Pullan, the architect attached to the expedition; the carpenter of

the Supply ; a sergeant and six marines, who
are assigned to the party as a guard, and two
sappers,—one a photographer, the other a mason.
We landed in the teeth of a bitter north wind.
The anchorage is not very safe, and the harbour very shallow, with no pier. However, we
managed to get on shore the timbers of six of
our huts before the Supply was forced to leave
us to take shelter in the snug bay of Budrum.
Having chosen a site for an encampment within the
peribolos of a temple, on the shore near the isthmus
(*see* Plan of Cnidus, Plate 21), we proceeded to put
one of our huts together. After living for a year
in the old rat-ridden konak at Budrum, it is real
enjoyment to have a night's rest unbroken by
disturbances from four-footed visitors.

We are surrounding our little encampment with a
wall, and intend to keep a strict watch at night; for
though I do not think an attack of pirates likely, still
it might occur if we were careless. There are many
islands within one or two days' sail of Cape Crio,
which could muster thirty or forty armed ruffians
for such an enterprise; and in my short experience
of Turkey I have known whole towns surprised and
plundered by bands not more numerous, for want of
a sentry at night.

There is something very attractive in this place—
the delicious freshness of the air, the beauty of
the scenery, the stir and activity of our little
colony in the midst of such loneliness and ruin,
are a pleasant change after the monotony of our
life for the last twelve months. The sea-view here

is much more lively than at Budrum, as we have a
glimpse of all that passes up and down on the great
highway between the Dardanelles and Rhodes. The
French and Austrian steamers going to and fro with
letters, almost within hail of us, are a cheerful sight,
one of the pleasantest that can gladden the heart of
an exile. The other day I had the satisfaction of
cutting out my own letters from a caique going up
with them to Budrum, but driven in here by contrary
winds.

I have lately had a visit from a remarkable
character, who rules this peninsula like an ancient
τύραννος. His name is Mehemet Ali—he is Aga
of a place called Datscha, halfway between Cape
Crio and Djova, and near the site of the ancient
Acanthus. Smith paid him a visit in the autumn,
when we purchased some timber of him. He is
an Aga, and can trace his descent from Dere
Beys for several generations. He lives in patriarchal fashion, with four harems, flocks, herds,
bee-hives, fig-trees, and gardens innumerable. His
progeny is so numerous that he is the putative
father of half the children in his village—all these,
the offspring of concubines, run about in rags,
while the rights of inheritance are reserved for the
two recognized sons, both children of a beautiful
Circassian, a present from Halil Pasha, the late
brother-in-law of the Sultan, in exchange for a landed
estate in Cos.

Mehemet Ali, though he possesses four harems and
much wealth, is not, like most rich Turks, devoured
by indolence. He is a shrewd, hard-headed man of

business, who ought to have been a Scotchman. He drives an active trade with Smyrna, selling the produce of his territory to the great English merchant Mr. Whittall, of whose friendship he is justly proud. His activity both of mind and body is most remarkable for an Oriental. He employs all his leisure in reading, shoe-making, and gun-making—Smith saw some very fair locks manufactured by him. He is very fond of history, of which he has got glimpses here and there, through the study of Turkish chronicles, which, like the old Monkish annals, begin with Creation and go down through Greek and Roman annals to contemporary times, huddling everything in one confused narrative. Yesterday he rather astonished me by talking about Iskander, son of Philip (Alexander the Great), Plato, Aristotle, and Bokrat (Hippokrates), all of whom he conceived to have lived in the same generation, and to have been on very intimate terms. He had that restless inquisitiveness about general knowledge which characterizes the Greek often, but rarely the Turk. I had just received the Illustrated London News, with coloured prints of Delhi and other Indian cities. I gave him these—he asked the name of each city, and, taking out his reed pen from his girdle, wrote it on the top of the picture, adding a descriptive title, which embodied such scanty information about the place as I was able to give him.

I asked him if he had ever been to Stamboul? "Never since my father's death!" he said; "then they stripped me of all my possessions, declaring that my father had left no heir."

M 2

" Could such a wrong be committed now ?" I said.
" No," he said, "not since the Tanzimat; property
cannot be openly confiscated, though doubtless much
injustice may be committed through the corruption
of Pashas and Cadis."

The rural life of Mehemet Ali has given his manners a certain homeliness which was to me rather
refreshing, after the *fade* compliments and vapid
remarks which generally issue from the lips of
official Turks.

It seemed to me as if for the first time I had the
opportunity of studying a real Turkish country gentleman, full of shrewd observation and mother wit,
which he exercised in a good-natured and very
amusing way on his suite. These consist of a Cadi,
a grey-headed Imam, the head man of a neighbouring village, and a sort of nondescript Greek, who
played the part of *souffredouleur* or toady. He was
always making one of these his butt—the Greek, of
course, got the worst of it. He imitated the manner
in which they make the sign of the cross, and the
genuflections to the Panagia. " Let us make a Mussulman of Demetri," he said ; "I am sure he wishes
it in his heart—to-morrow we will perform the usual
rite." Poor Demetri simpered and looked amiable.
I wonder what private end he was serving by eating
so much dirt.

Mehemet Ali usually travels about his small
peninsular kingdom accompanied by his Cadi,
Imam, and other cabinet ministers, all mounted
on small mountain horses : then come three or
four peasant attendants, with long guns, some

few of which are detonators of French manufac-
ture; the rest the old flint-and-steel. They shoot
partridges as they go along, and when they come to
the coast, Mehemet Ali takes from the hand of an
attendant a long reed fishing-rod with tackle manufactured at Trieste, and angles for a dinner. As for
other provisions, the villages *en route* are bound to
provide them.

Mehemet Ali has one very great merit—he is perfectly aware that an Englishman must *eat*. In the
present destitution of the Turkish provinces, a party
of hungry Englishmen are regarded by the natives as
a nuisance, only less than that of the locusts. The
difficulties of victualling our small messes at Budrum
have required incessant trouble, much of which
naturally falls upon me. I had not been two days
encamped here before a messenger arrived with ten
fowls dangling from his horse's crupper, Mehemet
Ali's first present to the colony. When he arrived
himself, there came a sheep, a good supply of eggs,
honey, and figs. This morning we had a long and
most interesting conversation on the subject of bul-
locks and vegetables, a question of the greatest
importance, as our small party cannot live for ever
on salt meat. Now you may, perhaps, ask why does
Mehemet Ali show so much friendship for me? He
has two very good reasons. First, he wants stone
from Cnidus to build a mosque with, which he hopes
to obtain more easily through our excavations; and
secondly, he confided to me this morning that he has
certain enemies at Mughla, who must be put down by
the intervention of the Pasha of Smyrna. "I dare not

complain of the wrong that has been done me, except through a Consul—they would crush me!" There is no grade of society in Turkey in which the habit of inviting foreign intervention does not prevail. I never refuse to help people if they have any real case—such good offices give much indirect influence and enable me to work the expedition far more economically and efficiently. I wonder how many days I might have waited for eggs and mutton if Mehemet Ali had not had a grievance at Mughla!

On first visiting him in the morning I found him reading the Koran, a ceremony with which he always begins the day. He showed me the book with great pride—it was rather a handsome manuscript. Forgetting that I was in the presence of a Mussulman, I put out my hand to take hold of the volume, when it glided suddenly into its leather case, narrowly escaping pollution from the touch of Giaour. The old fanaticism is not quite dead yet, though they do condescend to ask for British protection.

Before taking leave of me, Mehemet Ali paid a visit to the carpenters. He watched their work with a keen interest. "I, too, am a carpenter!" he said, taking up a saw. I offered him a printed plan of the hut—he declined it. "I have already got the construction here!" he said, pointing to his forehead. Perhaps if he had had the chance, this obscure Aga might have been a Peter the Great for his country, and might have introduced the useful arts. When Smith was staying with him, he gave him the dimensions of the dome of the mosque he was about to build, and asked him how many stones of a given size he would require for it. After some little trouble Smith solved the problem, and then found that Mehemet Ali had calculated it in his head correctly by some rule of thumb.

It is time to wind up this description of my nearest neighbour at Cnidus. Perhaps I have dwelt too long on so insignificant a personage, but I thought the phenomenon of such a man in such a place worth noting, and the more so because few travellers have visited the secluded and barbarous district where he exercises patriarchal sway.

XLIV.

Ruins of Cnidus, *March* 10, 1858.

The winter here since our arrival has been one of extraordinary severity, and from time to time a Crimean north wind sweeping with relentless fury over the naked promontory where we are encamped, split the half-inch planking of our huts, and penetrated the very marrow of our bones. We have no stoves, and the nights have been so cold, that I have sometimes felt tempted to take refuge in the tent where our little flock of sheep are folded to protect them from the jackals, who howl round our encampment all night. This year the wolves have been driven by hunger to the very end of this peninsula, and have devoured two horses within two hours' distance of this place. The anchorage here

is very dangerous in winter, and the Supply can
only pay us flying visits, seldom venturing to remain more than an hour or two off so stormy a
coast.

Notwithstanding these little difficulties, we have
managed to put up our huts, to drill into tolerable
efficiency a number of native workmen sufficient for
our present operations, and to construct a pier in
the southern harbour, which was absolutely necessary to enable us to embark and disembark
heavy cases.

Before giving an account of the excavations in
which we have been engaged here, it may be as well
to give a general sketch of the topography of the
ancient city. (*See* Plate 21.)

Cnidus, like Mytilene, Myndus, and many other
Hellenic cities, was originally built on an island so
close to the mainland as to form two harbours,
connected by a narrow strait such as the Greeks
called an Euripos.

This island, the ancient Triopion, is a lofty rock,
rising abruptly from a low isthmus, by which it is now
united to the western extremity of the Doric Cher-
sonese. Projecting far beyond the adjacent coast
of Asia Minor, this bold headland, now called Cape
Crio, forms a well-known seamark for the navigators
of the Archipelago, and in bad weather small craft
find great difficulty in doubling it. Hence, from the
earliest period of Phœnician and Hellenic navigation, wind-bound mariners must have constantly
taken refuge behind the headland, which, offering to
the sea outside a line of sheer precipices, descends

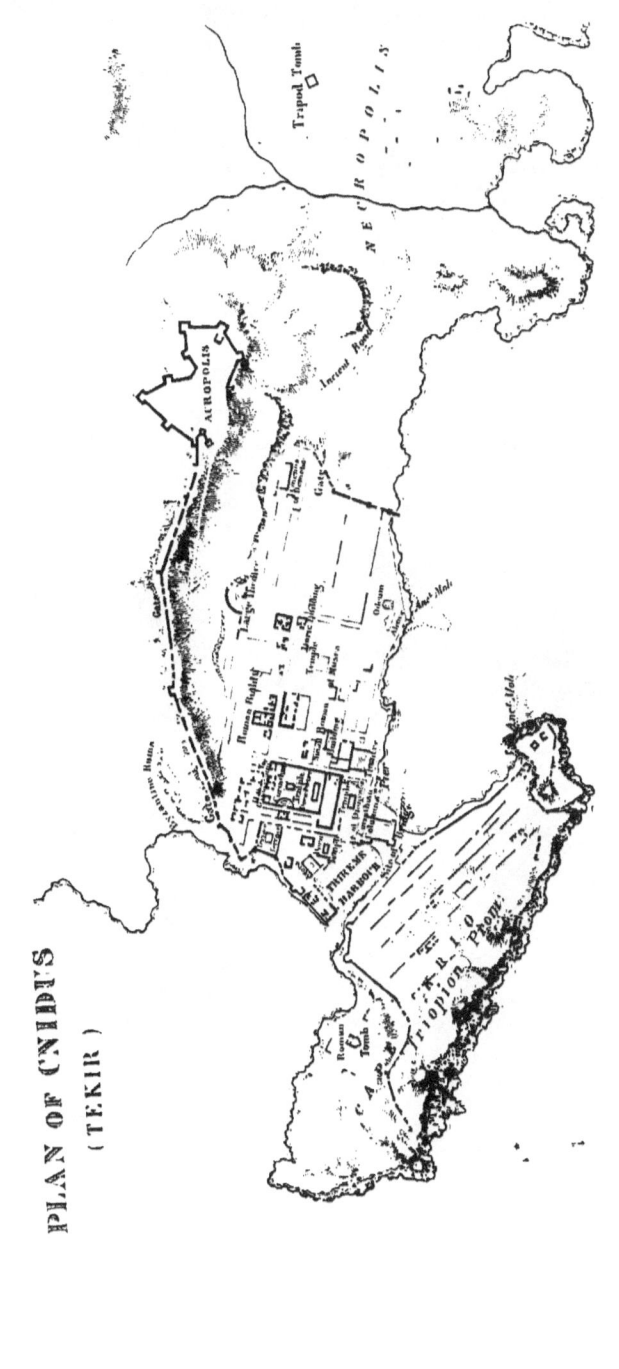

PLAN OF CNIDUS
(TEKIR)

on its inner side by a gradual slope down to
the still water now divided by the isthmus. The
natural shelter thus afforded was converted by the
Greeks into two harbours, protected by moles. In
the largest of these two harbours one of the moles
by which it was shut in from the south-east may still
be seen in a nearly perfect state; some of the blocks
of stone of which it is constructed must weigh
fifty tons, and as its foundations have been laid in
nearly 100 feet of water, it must have been a work of
great cost. The smaller harbour opens to the north-
west, and is nearly closed by a broad quay jutting
out from the mainland. This is evidently the
λιμὴν κλειστός mentioned by Strabo, the mouth of
which must have been defended in antiquity by a
chain.

To the north-east these harbours are shut in by
the mainland, which rises by a gradual slope to the
foot of a steep ridge of limestone.

The slope of the mainland confronts the opposite
slope of the peninsula, forming a kind of natural
counterpart; and it was on these two opposed slopes
that the ancient city was built, rising on a succession
of natural terraces from the water's edge.

It is probable that here, as at Halicarnassus, the
peninsula, being more easily defensible, was first occupied, and that the settlers gradually extended their city
over the opposite part of the mainland. Its ultimate
limits are clearly marked out by the walls, which are
in nearly as perfect a state here as at Halicarnassus.
On the Triopian peninsula they inclose about two-
thirds of the ancient island, commencing at its

eastern extremity, outside the great mole. The line of defence is carried along the summit of the mountain ridge on the south, and thence down to the mouth of the smaller harbour, which is defended by a semicircular tower, remarkable for the solidity and preservation of its masonry. On the continent the limestone ridge, ascending gradually from the shore of the smaller harbour, shuts in the city on the north, separating it from a steep ravine, which may be considered as the fosse of this natural line of defence. The wall of the city, commencing from the mouth of the smaller harbour, is carried along this line to the point where the ridge terminates on the east in a kind of natural bastion defended by sheer precipices.

This position has been converted into an Acropolis of great strength, which juts out from the main line of circumvallation, defending the north-east angle of the city.

On the south this Acropolis terminates in a sheer precipice, below which the ground falls in a steep slope to the sea. The wall may be traced from the foot of this precipice to the water's edge about 300 yards to the east of the mole. Here it meets a sea wall, which is continued from this point along the northern shore of both harbours to the western extremity of the land wall.

In the year 1812, when Cnidus was visited by a mission from the Dilettanti Society, the ruins were probably much more extensive than at present. From the accessibility of its harbours, this site has been much resorted to by Turks and Greeks as a quarry for building purposes. About twenty years ago, several shiploads of marble were removed from Cnidus by order of Mehemet Ali, Pasha of Egypt, who employed them in the construction of a new palace. Notwithstanding this extensive spoliation, the ruins cover a large area, and the general plan of the city can be easily made out. It rose from the opposite shores of the harbours in a succession of terraces, at right angles to which are streets and flights of steps, still very clearly to be traced out. These terraces are continued up to the very foot of the limestone range, above which line the steepness of the slope and the absence of soil would hardly have admitted of their formation. The most conspicuous feature in the whole topography is a platform in the western part of the city, marked " Corinthian Temple " in the Plan. This has been bounded on the south by a Doric portico, the ruins of which are lying *in situ*, and which must have been of very noble proportions.

In the centre of the platform are the ruins of a small Corinthian temple, on the west an Odeum, and on the shore below the *peribolos* of a larger temple intermixed with those of a Byzantine church. Immediately to the east of this *peribolos* is a theatre still tolerably perfect, and to the west a long street leading straight up from the isthmus to a gate in the northern wall.

To the west of this street are the ruins of a small Doric temple on the shore of the small harbour, and beyond this on the same shore a square area inclosed with a colonnade, which was probably the *Agora*.

On the quay at the head of the small harbour are foundations of some large building.

In proceeding northward along the street already noticed, which leads from the isthmus to the city gate, nothing but Byzantine ruins meet the eye. The ground is covered with dense brushwood, amid which appear at intervals the fragments of many vaulted roofs built of concrete and rubble, which have fallen in solid masses.

On the north a street, intersecting at right angles the street already described, appears to have traversed the whole length of the city about midway between the harbour and the fortified heights above, leading to a gate in the eastern wall.

To the north of this street is the site of the largest theatre in Cnidus, now nearly stripped of its masonry, and east of this theatre a road leading by a zigzag ascent to the Acropolis. The eastern part of the city abounds less in ruins than the western part, and from its great steepness could have been little built on.

Passing across the isthmus by some foundations which probably mark the site of an ancient bridge, we come to the peninsula, once an island. Here are scarcely any architectural remains above the surface, except a succession of parallel terrace walls connected at intervals by flights of steps.

The promontory at the eastern extremity of this peninsula bends round, forming a small bay or recess in the harbour.

This part of the port is well sheltered from the south, and, when the mole was perfect, must have

afforded safe and convenient anchorage close into
shore. Hence the rock has been levelled here, so
as to form a broad quay for the disembarkation of
merchandise.

The greater part of the ruins still visible on
the site of Cnidus seem to be of a late period, for
Cnidus, like most cities on the west coast of Asia
Minor, seems to have unhappily been "repaired and
beautified" under Roman administration.

I began by making a small excavation in a
theatre near the southern port, a plan and section
of which is given in the Ionian Antiquities published by the Dilettanti Society.[65] Commencing

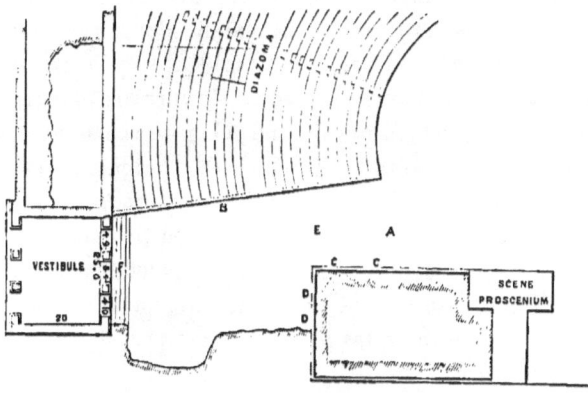

inside the Scene near its western extremity, I continued the cutting in a westerly direction, so as to
lay bare the end wall of the *carea*, B, which here,
as was usually the case in Asiatic theatres, runs
obliquely to the scene. The accompanying cut shows
the result of the excavation.

At E was a stone with a socket for the hinge of a gate, and opposite to it, in the end wall of the *cavea*, a hole cut in the face of one of the stones, into which the bolt of the gate must have passed. Near this spot was a rough-hewn stone chair and the base of a statue inscribed with a dedication by the Cnidian people to one Julia Epianassa. In front of the Scene, and parallel to it, I found two rubble walls, C C, of late Roman or Byzantine construction. These appeared to be part of the basement of some building erected on the site of the Scene at a late period, the ground floor of which was approached by a flight of steps, D D, leading up from the level of the orchestra. Continuing westward from this point along the end wall of the *cavea*, I came to a flight of steps marked F in the plan, which led to a Corinthian portico, the ruins of which were found lying on the steps in the position, probably, in which they originally fell. This portico was evidently of a late period. I also opened the vomitory of the theatre on this side.

As this excavation did not yield much, except a few Greek inscriptions of slight interest and some lamps and terra-cottas of the Roman period, I soon abandoned it.

Examining the Admiralty Chart of Cnidus, I observed that a particular spot under the Acropolis is noted as containing statues.

I have already noticed that the approach to the Acropolis from the south is by a zigzag road, to the east of the great theatre.

Immediately to the east of this road the southern

face of the Acropolis terminates abruptly in a sheer precipice, at the foot of which an artificial platform, rather more than 85 paces in length, and supported on three sides by a wall of massive polygonal masonry, juts out like a pier from the side of the mountain. The spot marked "statues" in the Admiralty Chart is near the eastern boundary of this platform.

The precipice which bounds this platform on the north may be described as a natural wall of limestone rock, from 50 to 70 feet high, and running nearly east and west for about 320 feet. This wall slopes at an angle of 79° with such regularity as to suggest the idea that it has been scarped by the hand of man. This impression is confirmed by the fact that in the steep face of the rock three niches are cut for the reception of statues.

More exact examination of this site, however, has proved that this escarp was a natural formation.

The first object which caught my eye on exploring this ground, was a small Greek *stelé* inscribed with a dedication, lying near the eastern wall of the platform.

Close to this was the statue noticed in the Ionian Antiquities, a draped female figure, seated in a chair, headless, and nearly covered with earth.

I commenced an excavation near the *stelé*, and in the course of half an hour came upon a small statuette, lying only a few inches below the surface of the soil, and perfect, all but the head, which I found broken off close by. It represents a draped female figure, wearing the tall cylindrical head-dress, which, from its resemblance to a corn-measure, is called *modius*, and holding in her right hand a pomegranate flower. A smile plays over the features, which are very like those of Aphrodite.

These symbols, and the peculiar composition of the drapery, at once enabled me to recognize in this figure the type of Proserpine.[66]

All round this statuette were a number of lamps of black glazed ware. Digging on and continuing to find lamps, I laid bare a number of rough foundation-walls intersecting each other at right angles, so as to form a group of small cells or compartments. Some of these had been lined with stucco. Throughout these enclosures I found black lamps intermixed with small terra-cotta figures, representing young girls bearing pitchers of water on their heads, *hydrophoroi;* and with these remains were several unbroken ridge-tiles.

The walls of these enclosures were built in the roughest manner without cement. The material was mostly rubble: squared blocks of tertiary limestone, evidently, from some previous building, were occasionally used in the courses. Some of these blocks were faced with stucco.

Continuing the excavation westward from this group of cells, I came to a limestone base intended for the reception of a statue. On it was an inscription in elegiac verse, recording the dedication of a temple, οἶκος, and a statue, ἄγαλμα, to Demeter and Persephone by Chrysina, wife of Hippokrates and mother of Chrysogone.

It is further stated that this dedication was made

in obedience to the god Hermes, who, appearing in a dream, declared to Chrysina that she should be the priestess of these goddesses at a place called Tathne.

On reading this inscription, I entertained no doubt that it related to the site which I was exploring. On the very platform on which I then stood had once been a temple, dedicated to Demeter and Persephone, surrounded by its *peribolos*, or sacred precinct; and there can hardly be a doubt that the name of this site was the Tathne mentioned in the inscription.

Chance having thus as it were put the key of this ancient sanctuary in my hand, I was encouraged to proceed further in exploring the site.

Close to this base I found a group of fragments of sculpture in white marble, among which were a beautiful head, probably of Persephone, rather under life-size; a hand and arm of a young girl; a terminal figure, from which the head had been broken off; and a veiled female head, which to my great satisfaction I fitted on to the neck of the seated figure which had been my first discovery.

The addition of the head made it certain that this figure represents Demeter. The features have the matured and perfect beauty which befits the mother of Proserpine; a divine calm is diffused over the features, such as we may conceive the goddess to have worn on receiving back from Hades her long-lost daughter.

The back of this statue is left flat, a proof that it must have been placed in a niche. When seen on the level of the eye, the body exhibits certain deviations from the usual standard of proportions; but these deviations may be accounted for by the position of the statue in a niche far above the spectator. The height of this statue is rather more than five feet. Close to the head I found another base, inscribed with a dedication to Demeter and Persephone by a lady named Plathainis. The objects dedicated are called thank-offerings and atonements.

Near these marbles I found in several places portions of thin sheets of lead, broken and doubled up. On being unrolled, these sheets proved to be tablets, inscribed with imprecations in the name of Demeter, Persephone, Pluto, and other Infernal Deities. In each inscription are specified the name of the person on whose head the imprecation is invoked, and the cause of offence which had drawn it forth. Most of these tablets appear to have been dedicated by Cnidian women. The grievous offences which called forth such tremendous comminations are of several kinds.

One lady denounces the person who had stolen her bracelet, and adds, by way of postscript, an imprecation on any one who may have defrauded her with false weights.

The non-restoration of garments lost or left in deposit is made the subject of another imprecation.

Other accusations are of a more serious nature.

A certain Nakon, husband of a lady called Prosodion, seems to have been seduced from his domestic allegiance by some Cnidian Laïs, who is duly devoted to the Infernal Deities in consequence. Another injured matron invokes a curse on the head of the person who has accused her of administering poison to her husband. The non-restitution of a deposit forms the subject of two other inscriptions.

In all these inscriptions a deprecatory clause is inserted, by which it is intended to exempt the author of the curse from all liability to be involved in its consequences.

In the character in which these inscriptions are written there is an approximation to the more cursive form of the Greek papyri of the Ptolemaic period. The language contains many errors, both in grammar and orthography, such as a regular lapidary would not have committed. This is also the case in the papyri of the Ptolemaic period. I am inclined to think that the date of these tablets falls somewhere between B.C. 200 and B.C. 100. They may, however, be of the Roman period.

Such maledictory inscriptions, called *defixiones* or *κατάδεσμοι*, formed part of the system of ancient magic, and were probably in use among the Greeks from an early period, as there is allusion to them in two passages of Plato. A curious and well-known instance of the use of such magical devices is recorded by Tacitus in his Annals. In describing the last illness and death of Germanicus, he states that there were found concealed in the walls and floor of his house remains of human bodies, with certain poems and imprecations, *carmina et devotiones*, and the name of Germanicus inscribed on leaden tablets. It was thought that these magical instruments were employed by Piso to compass the death of his enemy.

Several tablets similar to those found in the *temenos* have been discovered at Athens, Alexandria, and Cuma. All these, probably, had been deposited in tombs; those found by me at Cnidus are, I believe, the only ones known to have been obtained from the site of an ancient temple.[67]

Continuing my excavations westward along the foot of the scarp, I came to a mass of squared stones and rubble, on removing which the walls of a small chamber became visible, nearly on a level with the surface of the ground. This chamber was of an elliptical form, and built of tertiary limestone blocks without mortar. The joints of the masonry were all more or less disturbed, as if by an earthquake; and hence I am inclined to think that the original form of the chamber, before it was so disturbed, was circular, not elliptical. The dimensions of the interior were nine feet in the longest diameter. The mass of stones and rubble with which it was blocked up appeared to be the ruins of the roof, which was probably an example of Egyptian vaulting.

On clearing away this superincumbent mass, I came to a quantity of fragments of sculpture, marble bases, and other antiquities, filling up the chamber to the depth of seven feet.

The most remarkable of these objects were two marble pigs, mounted on bases, one of which was inscribed with a dedication to Persephone by Pla-thainis, a lady whose name occurs in several other inscriptions from this site. These pigs were about two feet long; there were also found two smaller pigs, about half the size.

In the worship of Persephone and Demeter the pig was a symbol of special import.

When my Turkish workmen had dug out these marble representations of the unclean animal, they exchanged knowing glances one with another. It was tacitly agreed that these objects must on no account be recognized as pigs, especially in the presence of the Giaour; so they insisted on calling them marble bears, a pious and convenient euphemism in which I was quite ready to acquiesce. With these pigs were found two calves, several dedications by priestesses and other women, a term surmounted by a rude head representing Proserpine, a female head and several fragments of statues, a votive model of her mystic *calathus*, and fourteen pairs of female breasts, all sculptured in marble. These last objects were very peculiar in form. Each pair of breasts was connected by a handle, mounted on a plinth.

It is well known that the custom of dedicating models of any part of the body which had been affected by disease has been retained from pagan antiquity, both by the Greek and Roman churches (see *ante*, I. p. 31). Votive breasts, sculptured in marble, may be seen in the British and other museums; but the form of those found in the *temenos* is peculiar, and suggests the idea that they were anciently used as weights. This supposition is confirmed by the fact that they are of various sizes, the plinths ranging in length from $6\frac{3}{4}$ inches to $1\frac{1}{2}$ inch. I have not, however, been able to discover any ancient standard to which they can be adjusted.

After clearing out all this mass of marble, and

getting nearly to the bottom of the chamber, we came
to a layer of smaller and more fragile objects. Here
were small saucers and vases of red ware, lying intermixed with ivory hair-pins and bodkins, and with a
number of fragments of small rods of transparent
glass, twisted and inlaid with spiral threads of opaque
glass. In the same stratum were a number of small
tablets of white marble, from two inches to four
inches long, and about one-eighth of an inch thick.
Each of them was pierced for attachment to a wall,
or to some object. Their surfaces had been polished,
and bore traces of colour. These, doubtless, had
been used as labels, on which the forms of dedication
had, in the case of the smaller objects, been inscribed.
At the very bottom of all was a stratum of fine sand,
in which lay some hundreds of small glass bottles
packed in rows. I succeeded in obtaining 44 unbroken specimens. These bottles ranged in length
from seven to three inches. They had long narrow
necks; some few were bulbous in form.

The material was transparent glass, rather green in
hue, and not of a very fine quality. As these bottles
were packed in regular layers, it is evident that they

must at some time or other have been deposited at the bottom of the chamber where I found them ; but how they escaped unbroken, with so great a mass of marble and rubble lying over them, is difficult to explain. I can only suppose that the more fragile objects at the bottom of the chamber became completely covered with sand before the superincumbent mass fell, or was thrown in above them.

The bones found with the bottles proved on examination to be those of the hog, a small kind of ox, the goat, and birds about the size of the common fowl or dove. These animals were probably sacrificed to Demeter and Persephone.

The manner in which the glass and more fragile objects were packed in layers at the bottom of the chamber reminded me of the discoveries in the field of Chiaoux at Budrum. On that site, where it is probable that a temple of Demeter once stood, layers of small terra-cotta figures and of lamps were found lying in a clay bed between lines of foundations, over which were lying fragments, probably, from vaulting.

I have already pointed out, *ante*, p. 72, that within the precincts of ancient temples were vaulted chambers, *favissæ*, built for the reception of votive objects. The fact that both at Cnidus and Halicarnassus I found objects packed in layers, inclines me to think that in both cases the building where they were found was such a magazine or *favissa*.

Continuing our excavations westward, we came to another group of rough foundations, running 40 feet from north to south, and forming three cells' or chambers. The walls were built of the rudest

masonry. In one of these chambers was the base
of a small statue, and a hand and arm, which had
probably belonged to the same figure. The other
two compartments were full of lamps, mostly lying
in the soil at the depth of about three feet, but some

placed in the crevices of the walls. The finest of
these lamps were of glazed black ware. The forms
were well designed, and seemed copied from works
in bronze. Some of them have as many mouths as
eight or ten.

At the sides they were generally ornamented with masks or ivy-leaves. The other lamps were of very ordinary form and fabric, and of the late Roman period. Several hundreds of them were found. In the same soil were found a number of terra-cotta figures, mostly representing draped female figures. Some of these were of extreme beauty.[68]

In this part of the platform we were enabled to carry our excavations quite to the foot of the escarp which bounds the site on the north. On this line, nearly under the niches, we found an interesting statue, rather more than six feet high, representing a draped female figure.[69] The head, which had originally been fitted into a socket at the base of the neck, was found lying close to the body. Immediately in front of this statue was a base, inscribed with a dedication to Demeter, Persephone, and the gods associated with them, by Nikokleia, wife of Apollophanes. If this base belongs to the statue, as would seem from the relative positions in which they were found, the figure would represent Demeter. The type is peculiar. The features and form are those of an elderly woman wasted with sorrow, and do not exhibit that matronly comeliness and maturity of form which usually characterize Demeter in ancient art.

If we suppose this figure to be Demeter, the deviation from her usual type can only be explained by supposing that she is here represented as the *Mater Dolorosa* of Hellenic mythology, disconsolate for the loss of her daughter. In the Homeric hymn to Demeter it is stated that the goddess, while wander-

ing in search of her lost Persephone, assumed the
form and garb of an old woman, and traversed the
earth for many days without tasting food. Her
appearance is likened to that of an aged nurse or
housekeeper in a regal house.

This description accords very well with the statue
discovered in the *temenos*. It may be observed that,
contrary to the usual practice in ancient statuary,
the eyes are represented looking up. It is possible
that the artist of this statue may have intended to
represent Demeter looking up to the god Helios,
and imploring him to aid her in her search. It
may be objected, on the other hand, that the type
of the features and form are hardly in character
with ideal representation ; and that the statue
must, therefore, be a portrait. In that case it
probably represents a priestess of the *temenos*. We
learn from Pausanias[70] that in the sacred precinct of
the Chthonic Demeter at Hermione, near Trœzen,
were statues of her priestesses.

Near this figure we found an interesting terra-cotta
lamp, modelled in the form of Hekate attired like
Artemis. Instead of a torch in each hand, she holds
up one of the spouts of the lamp, which was supplied
with oil through a hole at the back of the figure.
Her left arm rests on a small figure standing at
her side, apparently the Aphrodite Persephone,
the statuette of which has been already noticed.[71]

Advancing further to the west, I found another
group of cells formed by rough walls, built at right
angles. Within and about these cells were several
hundred lamps of the kind already described, and

a number of fragments of sculpture in Parian marble, principally hands and feet of female figures on various scales. Marks of red colour appear on several of the fragments. On one of the feet the thick sole of the sandal has two red bands, and has been painted red under the foot. All these objects were found strangely intermixed with masses of broken rock which had fallen from the heights to the north. In one place I found a piece of drapery embedded, like a fossil in a mass of rock. The edges of the fractured sculptures were very fresh; from which it may be inferred that they are lying where they originally fell.

The discovery of these remains induced me to explore further the ground where they were lying. This, however, was no easy matter; for at this point, distant about 50 feet from the western boundary of the *temenos*, the escarp is completely broken away; and large masses of rock have, consequently, been projected forward into the inclosures, and throwing them out of the perpendicular.

After the lower part of this mass of rock and *de- tritus* had been removed, the work was constantly impeded by the necessity of dislodging detached fragments, which, being undermined as we advanced, overhung the excavations, threatening to overwhelm us. By the application of a steady continuous strain of tackles, we succeeded in bringing down the largest of these masses, weighing probably about 50 tons. This obstacle was afterwards disposed of by blasting, and the ground below cleared down to the ancient surface of the platform. The excavation

was then continued northward as far as the line of
the escarp, beyond which all further progress was
barred by great masses of rock which had fallen into
the breach in the escarp, and which form the but-
tresses of the sloping mountain-side behind them.

The western boundary-wall of the *temenos*, and
the rude foundations already noticed, continued to
run on under the rubble up to the point where the
masses of rock arrested our further progress, beyond which there was no trace of remains of any
kind. Within the chambers formed by these rude
walls were lamps and fragments of terra-cotta, and
in the rubble a little below the surface was a marble
base, seventeen inches long, inscribed with a dedication to Demeter, Persephone, Pluto Epimachos,
and Hermes. This base is of fine Parian marble,
and of elegant proportions. The letters are
beautifully cut, and in many of them traces of
red colour still remained on the first discovery of
this marble.

From this dedication we learn that Pluto or Hades,
Demeter, Persephone, and Hermes, were associated
in a common worship in this *temenos*. The discovery
of a dedication to the Dioscuri and a terra-cotta
figure of Hekate on the same site, makes it probable
that these deities were also worshipped here. Thus
the whole *temenos* would be dedicated to the divinities of the nether world.

When cognate divinities were thus combined in a
common worship, they were called by the Greeks
Θεοὶ σύμβωμοι or σύνναοι. The epithet ἐπίμαχος applied to Pluto in this dedication, may refer to some

local legend, like that recorded by Pausanias in
reference to the people of Elis, who are said to have
worshipped this deity with special honour, in ac-
knowledgment of the aid rendered by him in a
certain war.   On the handle of a terra-cotta lamp
found near this inscription, was the head of Pluto
in relief; and a fragment of another terra-cotta
probably represents him seated on his throne.[72]

We had now explored all the northern half
of the platform, from its eastern to its western
boundary, carrying the excavations as near the
foot of the escarp as the rock allowed.   We
next proceeded to explore the southern half of
the *temenos*.   In this part of the platform scarcely
any remains of sculpture or pottery were found; but
at the distance of 21 feet to the north of the southern
boundary-wall was the lowest course of a line of
wall which appeared to have been reconstructed out
of more ancient Hellenic materials.   This line ran
nearly parallel with the southern boundary of the
temenos during the greater part of its length.   At
the distance of 33 feet to the north of this line were
two large blocks, which must have served to receive
a gate.   The door in an ancient building swung on
a pivot revolving in an upper and lower socket: a
hinge of this kind is still used in Turkish houses at
Budrum.   The blocks found in the *temenos* were
evidently fitted to receive a metallic socket in which
a pivot played.   Nearly on the same line with these
blocks were the foundations of a second inner wall,
running through the *temenos* from east to west,
built of polygonal limestone blocks, roughly jointed.

From the position of the two blocks and the jamb, it seems probable that the gateway to which they belonged stood somewhere about the centre of this wall.

Thinking it possible that portions of sculpture had rolled over the southern boundary-wall, I dug the ground along its foot for a length of about 77 feet in the centre of the *temenos*, and 40 feet at the south-western angle.

Nothing was found in this excavation except a large stone spout, which had evidently served to conduct water from the summit of the terrace wall, and which is represented in the accompanying cut.

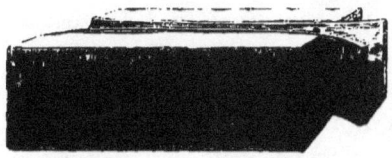

Spout, 4 feet 4 inches long.

It would seem from its position when found, that this stone had fallen from the summit of the southern boundary-wall, as, on the platform immediately above, a surface-drain, 12 inches wide, was discovered running between this wall and the inner isodomous wall.

On the hill-side, at some distance below the foot of the platform, I found a base dedicated to Demeter, which once probably stood on the platform, whence it has been rolled down.

I had now explored the whole platform through its length and breadth.

The result may be thus briefly stated :—

All the sculptures and other antiquities were found in a line running east and west through the northern part of the platform, and at a distance seldom exceeding 70 feet south of the escarp. Those remains sometimes cropped up to the surface, but were generally found at a depth of about three feet. Nearly all the objects discovered lay either within or very near inclosures of chambers of the rudest masonry.

By reference to the Plan it will be seen that these inclosures form three principal groups, situated respectively at the eastern and western extremities of the *temenos* and a little east of the centre.

It may be assumed, from the evidence of the dedication by Chrysina (*ante*, p. 177), that a temple or οἶκος once stood on this platform. The only architectural remains, however, which I discovered were part of a Doric capital in limestone, 9¾ inches in diameter; a fragment of Doric cornice in tertiary limestone, covered with a fine stucco, painted in red, and in depth 5 inches; three drums of a plain cylindrical column, of which the respective diameters ranged from 1 foot 9 inches to 1 foot 5 inches; and a portion of a fluted column 9 inches in diameter. Both these columns have been composed of tertiary limestone covered with stucco.

The insignificance of these remains, and the absence of regular foundations throughout the site, lead me to suppose that the temple here was very small, and was probably consecrated by Chrysina to the worship of the Infernal Deities in her own freehold. This is to be inferred from the fact that the

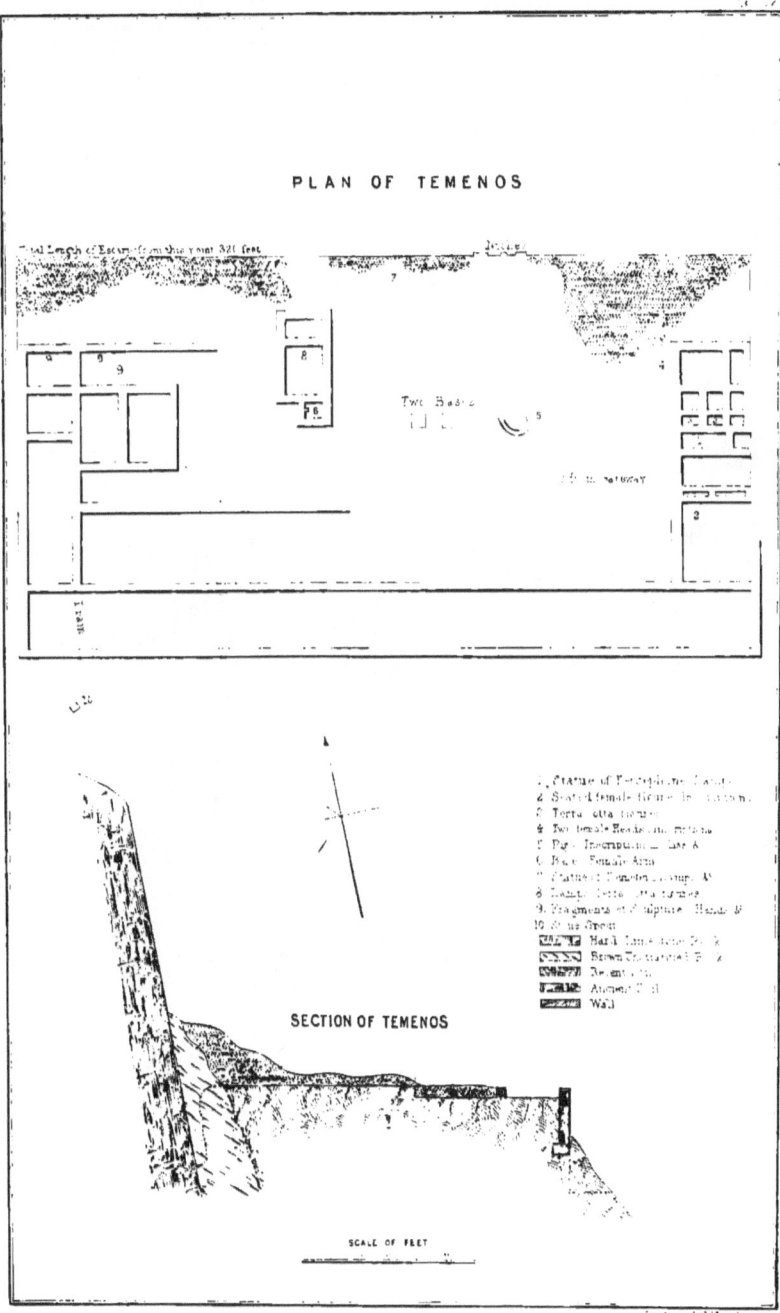

PLAN OF TEMENOS

PLAN OF TEMENOS OF DEMETER.
CNIDUS

numerous dedications found *in situ* are all made by priestesses of Demeter and Persephone, or private individuals, and none by the Senate and people of Cnidus.

If we assume that the *temenos* was private ground, the *οἶκος* dedicated by Chrysina would be a kind of chapel, like those mentioned in a curious inscription published by Böckh, called the Will of Epicteta; and from the analogy of that and other ancient documents of the same class, it is probable that the priestess of the Infernal Deities was to be appointed for ever from among the descendants of Chrysina, and that the cost of keeping in repair the sacred buildings was charged on land held in trust for that purpose.

It is obvious that an edifice thus dedicated and endowed would not have rivalled in scale and sumptuousness the public temples of Cnidus ; nor would it have had the same chance of being renewed and repaired as often as it fell into decay, inasmuch as its maintenance must have depended on the piety or fortunes of a single family, and not on the State.

The date of the dedication of the temple was probably about B.C. 350. This may be inferred from the form of the letters in the dedication by Chrysina, and also from the general character of the dedicatory inscriptions, which, with the exception of the leaden tablets, and of one or two others, may, I think, be assigned to the half-century between B.C. 350 and 300.

If we can thus determine by palæography the date of the dedicatory inscriptions, it is to be presumed

that the statues, on the bases of which these dedications were inscribed, were of the same date—a
conclusion which is corroborated by the style of the
sculptures discovered on the site. The artists by
whom these works were produced would thus be
either contemporaries of Praxiteles, or belong to the
generation immediately succeeding him. Considering the great beauty of the head of Demeter, and of
some of the fragments found in the *temenos*, it does
not seem an unwarrantable conjecture to suppose
that the statues there dedicated may have been executed under the influence of the great artist whose
Venus was for many centuries the chief glory of
Cnidus.

The fragments from the *temenos*, when compared
with the sculptures from the Mausoleum, exhibit
more tenderness and refinement of expression, and
greater richness of line ; while, at the same time,
they are less grand and monumental in character, as
indeed might have been expected if, as I suppose,
the Cnidian statues were dedicated severally by private persons.

Most of the statues and other votive monuments
in the *temenos* probably stood in the open air on
bases, in the line in which I found their remains, or
in the niches cut in the face of the rock. It would
appear from the evidence of the excavations, that, at
some time or other in antiquity, the temple and
statues were thrown down and scattered about,
either by an earthquake or the hand of man ; but
the ground continued to be accounted sacred, and the
rough inclosures were built for the reception of votive

objects. The quantity of lamps of a late period found in the soil proves that the dedication of such offerings must have been continued till the 2nd or 3rd century A.D.

The ground at the foot of this escarp consisted of detached masses of partially decomposed breccia.

These masses had one plane surface, lying over against the escarp in a direction nearly parallel to its plane. Sometimes the plane of the breccia had been forced into such close contact with the plane of the limestone escarp as to adhere to it; but more generally the two planes were separated by a space of two or more inches, which, to any one unacquainted with the real formation of the ground, appeared like a deep groove cut in the native rock.

On removing a portion of the overlying masses by blasting, I found the escarp behind them descending at the same angle, 79°, and presenting the same regular slope. Continuing the blasting to a depth of 28 feet below the surface, I found no change in the inclination or character of the rock. The entire height, from the top of the escarp to the point reached by blasting was 127 feet. (*See* Plate 22.)

When I first examined the escarp, the extreme regularity of its slope, the general smoothness of the surface, and the occurrence of the niches, led me to suppose that the rock had been wrought by the hand of man; an opinion which the authors of the Dilettanti volume, and other travellers, have expressed. As, however, it has been now clearly shown by blasting that the rock descends to a great

depth inclined at the same angle and with the same
level surface, it cannot be the work of human hands,
and must be considered as an upheaved limestone
stratum, overlaid at its base by broken strata of
breccia, which lean against it in the manner already
described. The singular configuration of the ground
may have been caused by volcanic action, of which
the crater in the island of Nisyros would probably
be the centre, as this island is only twelve miles
distant from Cnidus.

The dedication of the *temenos* to Hades and Persephone makes it *à priori* probable that this site
was thus selected on account of some physical
peculiarity, which, in the eyes of the Greek, was
associated with the worship of the Infernal Deities.

Thus, Pausanias tells us that at Hermione in the
Peloponnese, near the Temples of Demeter and
Pluto, was an inclosure dedicated to Pluto, in which
was a fissure in the earth, through which it was supposed that Herakles had brought Cerberus from the
nether world. At Hierapolis, Nysa, and Thymbria, in
Asia Minor, were caves exhaling mephitic vapours,
called Plutonia and Charonia; and, in like manner,
Poseidon and other Cosmic deities were worshipped
in those places where their supposed influence was
directly felt in earthquakes and other portents.

In the case of the Cnidian *temenos*, the scarp-like
regularity in the surface of the rock must have struck
the Greeks as a phenomenon such as they would con-
nect with supernatural agency, and may have been
the original cause why this spot was dedicated to
Pluto and Persephone. To the eye of the Greek the

form of the ground might have suggested the idea that
a chasm in the earth had opened here ; and thus local
tradition would claim this spot as the scene of the
rape of Persephone.

Such a site inclosed by its *peribolos* Pausanias
saw near Lerna, in Argolis. " Here," he remarks,
" it is said that Pluto, on carrying off Persephone,
descended into the infernal regions." If the *temenos*
was consecrated as the supposed scene of this myth,
the two statues described *ante*, p. 177 and p. 187,
may represent two distinct aspects of Demeter.

I have already suggested that the standing figure
may be the Demeter Achæa (the Mater Dolorosa of
the ancient world) wandering disconsolately in search
of her daughter ; while the seated figure may represent the same goddess rejoicing, at a subsequent
period of the myth, in the return of Persephone.
With these must be taken in connection the terra-
cotta lamp, representing the light-bearing Hekate; for
it was that goddess who, torch in hand, accompanied
Demeter in her search for Proserpine. The marble
pigs, again, may be connected with the same myth,
for, according to a legend preserved by Clemens
Alexandrinus, the chasm down which Persephone
was carried off, swallowed up at the same time the
pigs of a certain Eubuleus ; while another tradition
declared that these unclean animals were sacrificed to
Demeter, because they foiled the goddess in her pursuit of her daughter's ravisher, by obliterating with
their snouts the tracks of his chariot-wheels.

The small terra-cotta figures bearing water-pitchers
on their heads may represent the daughters of

Keleos, king of Eleusis. The local legend, as
recorded in the Homeric hymn, describes these
damsels as coming to draw water from the well at
which Demeter rested when her wanderings had
brought her into Attica.

The statuette of Persephone described *ante*, p. 176,
has no mark of having ever been attached to a base;
it was, therefore, possibly carried about as an idol in
religious rites. The type of the goddess is peculiar,
and though not earlier than the other sculptures,
evidently embodies an archaic mode of representing
Persephone. Many repetitions of this statuette exist
in European museums, generally forming groups with
a larger female figure. Professor Gerhard, who was
the first to note all the extant examples of this type,
recognizes it as the representation of the Aphrodite
Persephone, corresponding to the Venus Libitina
of Roman mythology. In this blending of the attributes of these two antagonist goddesses in one type,
we may trace the same idea which runs through the
whole myth of Persephone; namely, that out of death
comes regeneration.

In examining the objects found in the *temenos*, the
inquiry naturally presents itself, whether, from the
evidence before us, we can determine the particular
form of worship which may have prevailed on this
site. Among the objects discovered may be recognized certain emblems, such as the *calathus*, the *cista*,
the pig, which are known to have been used in the
Eleusinian mysteries, but which probably were not
peculiar to these Attic rites, but connected with the
worship of Demeter and Persephone generally.

Again we do not find among the objects discovered in the *temenos* any trace of the myth of Triptolemos, or any evidence of the association of Dionysos with Demeter, as was the case in Attica. We may consider, therefore, that it is rather as an Infernal or Chthonic than as an Agrarian Deity that Demeter was worshipped in this *temenos*.

The connection of this goddess with Cnidus may be traced back to the period of the mythic founder of the city, Triopas. It was he, according to the legend, who, flying from Dotion in Thessaly, when he had incurred the wrath of Demeter by cutting down her sacred grove, landed at Cnidus with a band of followers, and there established rites called Triopian, after his name. These were the same *Triopia sacra* which Telines, the ancestor of the first Gelon, transported from Telos to Sicily; and such, according to Herodotus, was the mysterious nature of these rites, that their Hierophant, Telines, owed to them his remarkable political ascendancy at Gela.

Herodotus also states that the tradition of these rites was handed down through the lineal descendants of Telines, who continued to officiate as Hierophants after they were established as a dynasty at Syracuse.

It seems at first sight natural to suppose that if the worship of Demeter and Persephone at Cnidus was originally called Triopian, the seat of that worship would have been the Hieron Triopion, which was dedicated to Apollo, Poseidon, and the Nymphs. There seems, however, no positive evidence to show that such was the case, nor is there any difficulty in assuming that the name of the mythic founder of

Cnidus may have been given to two distinct temples. On the other hand, if the *Triopia sacra* were established on the first colonization of Cnidus, it seems difficult to believe that the original seat of this worship would have been the *temenos* discovered by me; for in that case some relic of archaic art would have been found in the *débris*; whereas I have already pointed out that none of the inscriptions or other remains were earlier than the time of Phidias.

Upon the whole, therefore, I am disposed to think it probable that in the *temenos* dedicated by Chrysina, the *Triopia sacra* formed the basis of the mystic worship, but that the original seat of this worship must be looked for in some other part of Cnidus, perhaps in the Peninsula.[73]

XLV.

BUDRUM, *May* 30, 1858.

IT is time to give an account of our operations on the site of the Mausoleum which have been carried on for several months under the superintendence of Lieut. Smith, and which are now brought to a close. At the date of my last letter (see *ante*, p. 137), we had advanced beyond the northern wall of the *peribolos* as far as the road marked in the Plan. The excavations have now been extended to the east, west, and south of the quadrangular area first explored, and carried in places to a depth of 23 feet; the northern

wall of the *peribolos* has been traced for 337 feet
from the north-east angle, and the eastern wall for
265 feet from the same angle; and many hundred
feet of subterranean galleries have been explored.

The results of these operations may be thus
summarily stated.

First, as regards the limits of the *peribolos* itself.
Observing that on the east the platform on which
the Mausoleum stood terminates abruptly in a
ridge running north and south, below which the
present level of the land sinks abruptly about eight
feet, I drove galleries through this ridge, and continuing them till a few feet beyond it to the east,
I encountered the eastern *peribolos* wall.

The part nearest the north-east angle could only
be traced by its foundation courses, or by the bed
cut in the rock to receive them; but further to the
south, the wall was composed of two and sometimes
of three courses of white marble, beautifully chiselled
and jointed. The foundations of this wall were on
a lower level than those of the northern wall, and
in its lower courses it must have served as a *revête-
ment* to the artificial platform.

On one of the upper courses we found
a very small elephant cut in ivory, probably votive.

After tracing this wall by mining for 265 feet, we
lost all trace of it, nor was I able to discover the
southern limit of the *peribolos*. I think it probable,
however, that its line is marked by a ridge a little
south of the point to which I was able to advance
by driving galleries. Following the northern *peri-*

bolos to the west, we lost all trace of it at the
distance of 337 feet from the north-east angle. Now,
according to Hyginus, the entire circuit of the *peribolos* was 1,340 feet.

One-fourth of this sum would be 335 feet, which,
supposing Hyginus to have used the Greek foot,
would in round numbers equal 339 English feet.

This length so nearly corresponds with the length
of north wall actually traced, that the four sides
of the *peribolos* probably formed a square. The
Mausoleum would thus stand but a few feet in
advance of the northern wall of the *peribolos*, and
half-way between the eastern and western walls.
Why it was thus placed, rather than in the centre of
the *peribolos*, will presently be shown.

Assuming that the precinct round the tomb was
a square of about 339 feet each way, the greater
part of this space of ground has now been dug
over.

From the east side of the quadrangle the
ground has been dug nearly as far as the eastern
wall of the *peribolos*, and on the south side we
have advanced for about 90 feet.

Our further progress in this direction has been
arrested by the obstinacy of two old Turks, who
absolutely refuse to sell us their houses and land on
any terms. On the west we have advanced for
about 70 feet from the side of the Quadrangle
to the boundary of a field planted with figs, which
we are not allowed to invade. Both on the eastern
and southern sides we found a black vegetable soil
for a depth varying from four to eight feet. Below

this was either the native rock or a lower stratum composed of a mass of rubble intermixed with large blocks of stone, all apparently formed of the decomposed rock of the platform. This mass of rubble is of various depths. In some places it extends to 35 feet below the upper surface.

Whenever we have dug to the bottom of it, the native rock has been found cut in ledges and angles, as would be the case in an ancient quarry. In several places, on removing the black superficial soil, we came to a layer of chippings of marble and green stone, intermixed with fragments of native rock, by the decomposition of which the whole had been amalgamated into a compact mass. Lying on this layer were many fragments of pottery, among which were several small terra-cotta figures, exquisitely modelled, and probably of the period of Scopas. It should be noticed that though we continued to find fragments of sculpture or architecture in the black upper soil all round the Quadrangle, nothing was found in the lower soil which could be identified as coming from the Mausoleum.

In some places on the eastern side the lower soil was composed of zigzag strata of rubble and chippings of green stone, such as would be formed by casting in rubble from opposite directions.

All these facts may be explained if we assume that, wherever the rock failed from having been quarried away, the platform of the *peribolos* was artificially prolonged, by shooting into the deeper parts the rubble which accumulated in the course of cutting the beds for the foundations, and

dressing the stone for the Mausoleum.   On the
south side of the Quadrangle are two chambers cut
in the rock, which must have been sepulchral, and
near the south-east corner a large rectangular
cutting, at the bottom of which, 23 feet below the
surface of the field, I came to a stone coffin about
seven feet long, empty and without a lid.   At the side
of this coffin I found an iron dagger and a terra-
cotta vase in the form of a female head.

It may be inferred from the *modius* on the head
that this terra-cotta represents Persephone.   The
style of the modelling is archaic, and I should
imagine that this terra-cotta was of a date consider-
ably anterior to the Mausoleum.

It would seem from the discovery of these
remains that the quarry on which the platform of
the Mausoleum was formed was used as a cemetery in times long antecedent to the time of
Artemisia.

Those who have explored the sites of ancient
cities know that such a combination of quarry and
cemetery was very common wherever the Greeks
found a stratum of free-stone suitable for building
purposes. The cemetery of Damos at Calymnos,
described *ante*, I. p. 285, is a case in point. We may
now see why the foundations of the Mausoleum
were placed so near the north wall of the *peribolos*
instead of in its centre. It was because the rocky
platform afforded sufficient area for the foundations,
which rest, in fact, on a step cut in the base of the
conical hill to the north.

This hill is of volcanic origin ; the rock of which
its base is composed is a calcareous tufa, in which
volcanic materials are cemented together. To the
north of the *peribolos* the original features of the
quarry are quite distinct. The rocky slopes of the
hill nearly to its summit are cut down vertically
with monolithic chambers and graves at intervals,
the position of which is marked in Plate 1. This
hill was probably the Necropolis of the early settlers,
before Mausolus enlarged the city by the incorpora-
tion of several neighbouring towns. It is interesting
to observe that when the people of Halicarnassus
competed with other cities of Asia Minor for the
honour of erecting a temple to the emperor Tiberius,
they alleged in support of their claim that their

city had not experienced the shock of an earthquake for 1,200 years, and their temples were built
on the native rock [74]—the truth of which latter
statement has been proved by excavations on the
sites of the Temple of Mars and the Mausoleum.

On the west side of the Quadrangle the soil was not
above three feet in depth over the native rock, which
is here cut irregularly into shallow beds and steps.
Very few fragments of sculpture and architecture were
found in the soil either here or on the east side. At
the south-west corner of the Quadrangle was a small
house, which I removed, and which was chiefly composed of fragments of steps from the pyramid,
similar to those which were found beyond the
northern wall of the *peribolos*. A little to the south-
east of this spot we came to some fragments of the
chariot-wheel and the hough joint of one of the
colossal horses. The position of these fragments
relatively to the more massive marbles from the
pyramid discovered on the north, would indicate that
if the Mausoleum was thrown down by an earthquake, the rocking motion must have been from
north-east to south-west.

A draped female torso, a youthful heroic head, and
a male head, life size, wearing the Phrygian cap, were
also discovered on the south side, at the distance of
32 feet from the edge of the Quadrangle.

The subterraneous galleries by which the platform
of the Mausoleum is pierced are on two different
levels, and may therefore be distinguished as the
Upper and Lower Galleries. It will be perceived
on reference to the Plan, Plate 2, that the lower

gallery runs all round the Quadrangle of the Mausoleum, having no outlet except on the eastern side, near the south-eastern angle.

This gallery evidently served for the drainage of the building. On the eastern side a drain issuing from under the foundations of the basement flowed into the eastern gallery, and on the western side another passed out of the building under the great stone (see *ante*, p. 98), emptying itself into the gallery through a bronze grating inserted in the covering slab of pavement. (*See* the cut.)

Ten shafts occur in this series of galleries, of which four are placed at the four corners of the

Quadrangle. On reference to the Plan, it will be seen that this lower gallery, though it surrounds the Quadrangle, does not run parallel to its lines, making many deflections, especially in its southern branch. It is probable, therefore, that parts of this gallery were cut at a period anterior to the building of the Mausoleum, and that its architects adapted these earlier passages to the plan of their building, connecting them together so as to form one duct.

The external drainage of the building was probably conducted into the shafts. One of the shafts on the eastern side which receives the contribution of a small drain from the interior may be considered as the *terminus*, or point of junction to which the branches of the lower gallery tend. From this shaft a main duct leads in a south-eastern direction to within 45 feet of the eastern *peribolos* wall. Here we lost all trace of it; but it was probably continued as a built gallery, on account of the great depth of soil over the rock, which is here 25 feet below the surface. In a field below the eastern side of the platform is a large reservoir cut out of the native rock, which probably received the drainage of this gallery.

The upper gallery, which runs at an average level of seven feet above the bed of the lower gallery, has been traced for 160 feet beyond the road north of the Mausoleum, where it was still tending upward to the north-west in the direction of a deep shaft in the theatre. Entering the *peribolos* somewhere about its north-west angle, this gallery runs on in a straight line to the south-east as far as a shaft in the Vakouf field.

Here it divides into two branches, one of which, after being interrupted by the south-west corner of the Quadrangle, is resumed beyond it, running on to the south-west, and being lost at the same point as the lower gallery.

It is probable that they both converged in a large reservoir cut in the rock outside the eastern *peribolos* wall. It is evident that this branch could have had no connection with the original plan of the Mausoleum, for at the point where it opens into the west side of the Quadrangle, its mouth was nearly closed by the foundation courses of the basement, which we found still in position. It must therefore have been of an earlier date; and in preparing the bed of the foundations in this place, the portion of gallery lying within the Quadrangle must have been cut away.

The other branch of the upper gallery, after proceeding in a south-eastern direction for about 100 feet, makes a singular elbow, after which it turns nearly due south for another 100 feet, and then making a right angle, runs on till it finally disappears on the line of the eastern *peribolos* wall. That this gallery served as an aqueduct is proved by the fact that in one place it is closed by two party walls, twelve feet apart, and each pierced by four pipes at different heights. The remains of a similar barrier were to be traced at the commencement of this branch in the Vakouf field. The object of these walls was evidently to check the too sudden rush of water from the hill. It seems probable that when the other branch of the upper gallery was intercepted by cutting the Quadrangle, this was substituted for it as a main aqueduct, to prevent the water from the hill from lodging anywhere within the *peribolos* and loosening the artificial platform.

The lower gallery nearly throughout its length is cut in the solid rock, with a height of from six to eight feet. The upper gallery is largest in the part to the north of the road, where in places its height exceeded eight feet, with a width of about three feet. Where the rock failed, this gallery was built of massive blocks, the roof being formed either of two stones leaning against each other, or of horizontal slabs. Along the sides shallow niches were cut in the rock at intervals, in which, doubtless, lamps were placed during the excavation of the galleries. In proportion to the great length of galleries excavated, very few antiquities of interest were found in them. Numbers of handles of *diotæ*, inscribed with the names of magistrates of Rhodes, Cnidus, and other ancient cities, were obtained from the lower gallery; and in the upper gallery to the west of the Quadrangle was found a sardonyx cut in the form of a disk, and pierced diametrically with a small hole for attachment as an ornament. This stone is a fine specimen of a very rare kind of sardonyx. It was probably brought down from the high ground to the northwest.

We have now explored the site of the Mausoleum as far as present circumstances permit.

To complete the examination of the *peribolos*, it would be necessary to obtain possession of the four houses on the south, which up to this time their

owners have pertinaciously refused to sell. This
negotiation must be left to time. At some future
day, the two old gentlemen who hold the houses
may repent of their obstinacy and accept with
thankfulness the extravagant price which they have
so often refused.

After this long account of our diggings, it may
amuse you to read the enclosed letter, which was
picked up in the streets of Budrum and handed
over to me. It bears no signature ; but the writer
is evidently one of the sailors of the Supply.

"Dear father and moter, with gods help i now
take up my pen to right these few lines to you
hopeing to find you in good health & sperits as
thank god it leaves me at present. Dear father of
all the drill that a seaman was put to i think the
Supply's company have got the worst, for here we
are at Boderumm a useing the peke madock &
shovel. nevur was there such a change from a sea
man to a navy; yes by George we are all turned
naveys sumetimes a diging it up & sometimes a
draging it down to the waters edge & then imbarking
it. Dear father this is the finest mable that ever
i saw ; we get on so very slow that i fear we shall
be hear a long time; the city of Ninevea as been
sunk such a long time that we find nothing but
mable ; every thing els is compleatley roted away.
what is most to be seen is the crockery ware that
they used in those days ; their is upwards of a hundred turks & Greeks mixt together ; they have dug
up to lions, but they are very much broken about
from lying so long in the ground or by the shok of

the earthquake when the place was destroyed.
Dear father we have pleanty of frute one sorte
and another, we have almons figs grapes pome-
granets & melons, but i doant know whether melons
are counted frute or vegetable, we eat them raw
& so do every one els here. We have them in
great plenty, they are by far the best frute that we can
get here; i have one now on my right hand has big
has a peck, or measure; the best of it is we cannot
manage to eat more than half a dozen at the time but
they are the best thing a man can eat when he is
thirsty. Dear father we have had one male since we
have bean here; i am a frade that the answers to my
letters are lost, if so it was my fault—send me word
of Eliza, the first chance i was sadley disopainted, i
hoped to get intelegence of eliza. Dear father i
will write every male from here, send me Georges
and Charlotte adressis; give my kind love to her &
tell her i have got a keepsake for her & saley;
rember me to Jessy tell him i hope to have a
turkish curicau for him. i think i shall bring him a
gravestone they are very romantiet and hansom;
mind give my kind love to mother. god bless you
direct to Boderumm malta or elswhere Mediteriaien."

While I have been writing this letter, the last of
our stores have been embarked; the great sheers
which so long stood on the pier in the harbour for
hoisting heavy cases have been struck, and in a few
minutes we shall be under weigh for Cnidus. Our
last act before abandoning the ground where we
have so long laboured, was to make a small mound
within the Quadrangle, which will be marked on the

Plan to enable future travellers to identify the site where once stood one of the Seven Wonders of the ancient world. Much as has been accomplished by the exploration of this site, I cannot abandon Budrum without a feeling of deep regret that so much still remains to be done to complete these researches. It is certain that the Castle of St. Peter is built in a great measure out of the ruins of the Mausoleum. What remains of architecture and sculpture its massive walls and ramparts contain, could only be known by the same work of thorough demolition which led to the discovery of the ruins of the Temple of Victory in a Turkish bastion on the Acropolis at Athens.

The fortress at Budrum, though interesting as an intact specimen of mediæval architecture, contributes so little to the defence of the Turkish empire that it will probably be allowed to fall into decay. On the other hand, the harbour at Budrum might be made an excellent one if the ancient moles at its entrance were restored. The demolition of the Castle would furnish excellent materials for their reconstruction; and the cost of such a work would be amply compensated, if we could determine the problem of the structure of the Mausoleum by the evidence of the architectural marbles which would be thus recovered.

XLVI.

AFTER the monotonous record of our last operations at Budrum, it is pleasant to be able to announce the remarkable discovery which we have recently made here.

One day last year when I was digging at Budrum, an intelligent Greek, called Nicholas Galloni, whom I had known at Calymnos, paid me a visit. Looking at the lions from the Mausoleum as they lay in the courtyard of the konak, he observed that he knew of a much bigger lion, which he had seen on a promontory a little south of Cnidus.

I took a note of the fact, and as soon as we were established here, inquired of all the natives whether they had ever heard of such a lion. I got no answer to my inquiries but a shrug of the shoulders and a *kim billir*—"who knows?"

During the early spring the north wind blew so hard, that I deferred exploring the exposed ridges of the coast till more genial weather. One morning in May, Mr. Pullan started on a roving commission to look for the lion. At the distance of about three miles south of Cnidus the coast throws out a bold headland, lying opposite Cape Crio, and distant from it about three miles. On the summit of a cliff which forms part of this headland, Mr. Pullan observed the ruins of an ancient tomb. On the bare rock below this tomb lay the long-sought lion.

He is truly a magnificent beast, measuring ten feet in length and six feet in height, and cut out of one block of Pentelic marble. He lay on his side, his nose buried in the ground. His forepaws and lower jaw have been broken off, probably when he fell. The side which has been exposed to the weather is much worn, and has assimilated so much in colour to the surrounding rock, that when I showed him to the inhabitants of the district and asked why they had never pointed out to me where he lay, they told me that they had often seen a great rock lying there, but had never perceived that it represented a lion till I told them so. On examining the ruins of the tomb, I find that it has been a square basement, surrounded by a Doric peristyle with engaged columns, and surmounted by a pyramid.

To the east of this tomb the ground slopes gradually. The upper part of the declivity is strewn with architectural ruins. The lion lies a little below these. It is evident from its position relatively to the tomb, that it must have originally surmounted the pyramid. It may have been thrown down by an earthquake, and must have fallen in one solid mass, probably pitching forward on the forepaws, which have been united to the body by a joint, and all trace of which has now disappeared.

On making this great discovery, I proceeded at once to pitch my tent on the spot, and to transport from Cnidus sheers, ropes, blocks, timber, and all necessary means and appliances for raising, packing, and embarking our colossal prize. The sheers having been carefully adjusted over him, he was turned over without any difficulty, mounting slowly and majestically in the air, as if a Michael Angelo had said to him, "Arise!"

While he had been lying grovelling on the earth we had never seen his face at all; so that, when we had set him on his base, and our eyes met for the first time his calm, majestic gaze, it seemed as if we had suddenly roused him from his sleep of ages. I should mention that he has no eyeballs, only deeply-cut sockets, of which the solemn chiaroscuro, contrasting with the broad sunlight around, produces the effect of real eyes so completely as to suggest the notion that the artist here, as in many instances in ancient sculpture, preferred representation by *equivalents* to the more direct imitation of nature. But, on the other hand, we have abundant evidence to show that coloured eyes, composed of vitreous pastes, were sometimes combined with marble in ancient statuary.

There is a curious anecdote in Pliny of a lion with emerald eyes which surmounted the tomb of a certain petty prince in Cyprus. This lion overlooked the sea, and the dazzling rays of his emerald eyes, if we may venture to believe Pliny, used to scare the tunny-fish on that coast! [75]

The contemplation of the Cnidian lion in the bright and delicate atmosphere for which he was originally designed, taught me much as to the causes why modern artists fail so generally when they attempt public monuments on a colossal scale.

Their work is designed, executed, and criticised in progress, in small studios, where they can form no true judgment as to distant open-air effects. Hence, much is elaborately wrought which contributes little to the ultimate result, and the true elements of grandeur are altogether missed. When I stood very near the lion, many things in the treatment appeared harsh and singular; but on retiring to the distance of about thirty yards, all that seemed exaggerated blended into one harmonious whole, which, lit up by an Asiatic sun, exhibited a breadth of chiaroscuro such as I have never seen in sculpture; nor was the effect of this colossal production of human genius at all impaired by the bold forms and desolate grandeur of the surrounding landscape. The lion seemed made for the scenery, and the scenery for the lion.

The genial climate in which the Greek artists lived must have enabled them to finish their colossal sculptures in the open air, and on the very site for which they were designed: hence the perfect harmony between man's work and nature which is so eminently the characteristic of Greek art in its best time.

After raising the lion by the sheers, we lowered him into a case suitable to his dimension, which was bolted together with iron rods.

Once in the case, he was blocked up and secured in every possible way, so as to prevent all movement

or friction. Nobody can pack a heavy mass of
sculpture better than a ship's carpenter. We then
threw a pall of old hammocks over the body, and
nailed him down in his coffin with a *resurgam*.
The next thing was to drag him down a newly-
made road, which we had cut zigzag down
the mountain-side to the sea. The case was
placed on a sledge made of the strongest materials,
and hauled for about three days by a hundred
Turks, in the course of which operation sundry coils
of new rope were expended, and several of my
workmen knocked down by flying blocks which
gave way under the great strain. At last we got
the lion down to the edge of the cliff, whence he
was to be hoisted on to a raft by a pair of sheers.
This proved to be a very difficult operation ; for as
the sheers could only be fixed on a narrow ledge of
rock some feet above the sea, and as, from the depth
of the water here, we had no means of construct-
ing a pier, it was impossible to bring the case in the
first instance perpendicularly under the sheerhead.
We attempted, therefore, after hauling it to the
extreme edge of the rock, to launch it into the air,
easing its descent gradually by a number of check-
tackles attached to it behind. The strain of this
immense weight, as it inclined forward over the
cliff, broke off a large rock to which one of the
check-tackles had been fastened; the case then
lurched forward in a slanting direction, and, most
fortunately, was brought up against one of the sheer-
legs, into which one corner embedded itself. On
the giving way of the check-tackle, the poor Turk

in charge of it was carried along with the rock
which broke away, and two of his ribs were
fractured. My hundred Turkish workmen set up
a dismal shout, losing all nerve and presence of
mind, as they always do in any great emergency.
Fortunately, Mr. Edgeworth, the doctor of the
Supply, was at hand, and I was glad to be assured
by him that the Turk had sustained no dangerous
injury. If, instead of lodging where it did, the case
had in its fall upset the sheers, snapping the heavy
chains by which they were hung, the accident might
have been much more serious. Corporal Jenkins,
grimly smoking his pipe after the catastrophe,
observed that I was very lucky not to have had
what he called, in soldier's language, a heavy
butcher's bill to settle.

Having got the case jammed against the sheer-leg
in this uncomfortable manner, we had now to consider how to extricate it. The problem was not an
easy one. The weight of the lion in his case was
about eleven tons; and this unwieldy mass was
hanging over the edge of the cliff in such a position
that no mechanical means at our command could
move it more than a few inches, either backwards or
forwards. Everybody was in despair except a Greek
from whom I had hired two caiques on which to
place a raft, and who was of course delighted at the
prospect of a claim for demurrage. After trying
several ineffectual experiments, we finally succeeded
in our object by the following method :—The case
was first secured from slipping further forward by
bending a new hawser round it, which was then

strained tight ; and also by supporting the sides and
end next the sea with shores, such as are placed
round a ship in dock. An inclined plane was then
formed under the case by planks laid on the rough
surface of the rock so as to fill up all inequalities.
After these precautions had been taken, one of the
purchases which held the case to the sheerhead was
slackened, and, on this strain being removed, the
leg of the sheer was cleared from the corner embedded in it. The sheers were then altered so as to
give plenty of room for the passage of the case
through them ; and, the shores being removed, it
was launched forward into the air till it hung plumb
with the sheerhead, when it was lowered on the raft,
thence to be transferred to the hold of the Supply.

Even this last operation was not unattended with
anxiety ; for the lion, in his case, weighed about
eleven tons, and the ship's ordinary hoisting power
could not deal with more than seven tons. Additional strength was, however, provided by some of
those ingenious makeshifts which sailors know so
well how to invent ; and, to my infinite relief, I saw
the lion at length lowered into his final resting-
place, the hold of the ship. The work of embarkation, in consequence of these difficulties, occupied
one month.

Now that we have secured this great prize, it is
curious to reflect that I might never have known of
it at all, had it not been for the accident of a ship-
wreck off Mytilene about a year ago.

The connection between this event and the discovery of the lion was in this wise :—The ship

wrecked was an English steamer: I was Lloyd's
agent for Mytilene; and my friend, the Calymniote
Galloni, who first gave me information about the
lion, was a sponge-diver, anxious to be employed in
recovering cargo from the wreck. Hence his visit
to Budrum, when, to ingratiate himself with me, he
communicated this valuable intelligence, which,
probably, without some such special motive, he
might have kept to himself.

XLVII.

CNIDUS. *Aug.* 25. 1858.

AFTER having accomplished the embarkation of the
lion, we proceeded to explore thoroughly the ruins of
the Doric tomb from which he had fallen, each of
the architectural marbles being carefully drawn
and measured by Mr. Pullan as we proceeded. The
result of our examination of the remains *in situ* is
as follows.

The tomb, as I stated in my previous letter,
is a square basement, surrounded by a Doric peristyle with engaged columns, and surmounted by a
pyramid. The marble which had formed the facing
of the sides still remained in the lower courses of the
basement, above which were courses of petrified
beach forming the core of the masonry.

Although the peristyle was thrown down, sufficient
materials existed for its restoration. Portions of the

lower step of the basement still remained in position on all the four sides of the tomb, being most perfect on the west side.

The basement, measured from angle to angle of this step, formed a square of 39 feet $2\frac{3}{4}$ inches each way.

The columns and their capitals were formed of drums engaged in the marble wall behind them in such a manner that each drum, instead of being circular, had a projection at the back, by which it was toothed into the masonry. This mode of construction must have given great strength to the wall. The drums of the columns were, for the most part, only blocked out; some few, however, are fluted. As from the destruction of the upper part of the stylobate, none of the bases of the columns were found in position, their height had to be calculated from the general proportions of the order.

Much of the architectural detail was only roughly blocked out; but the execution, wherever it had been completed, was marked by that simplicity and decision of line which characterizes the best period of Doric architecture.

Between the cornice of the basement and its lower step a course of marble slabs still remained, toothed into the coarser masonry behind them. This course shows the manner in which the two materials were bonded together.

A great number of the steps forming the external pyramid were discovered in the ruins. Most of these had an average width of $14\frac{3}{4}$ inches for the tread.

On an angle step, however, one tread measured

Plate 23

SOUTH ELEVATION

WEST ELEVATION

LION TOMB CNIDUS.

1 $\frac{3}{4}$ inches, the other 10 inches; and this smaller dimension occurred in several other steps not belonging to the angles. The depth of the face of the step averaged 13 inches.

It may be inferred from the difference in the width of the tread, that the area of the Pyramid, like that of the Mausoleum, was oblong. This form would certainly be most suitable, if, as can hardly be doubted, the apex of the' Pyramid served as the pedestal for the lion. (*See* the restoration of this monument, Plate 23.)

In one place a hole large enough to admit a man's body had been made in the wall of the basement. On entering at this aperture, I found a circular chamber within, blocked up with the ruins of its roof, which, as in the case of the well-known treasury of Atreus at Mycenæ and other Greek buildings, had been formed by a dome vaulted in the Egyptian manner, that is to say, with concentric horizontal courses, overhanging each other so as gradually to converge to an apex.

On clearing out this chamber, I found that it was 17 feet 3 inches in diameter, and in form like a bee-hive. The apex of the vault has been bridged over by an immense circular stone, shaped like a bung, and which was employed as a kind of keystone. In his account of the treasury of Minyas, at Orchomenos, Pausanias describes such a structure of roof: [76]—

"It is built of marble, and is of a circular form; the apex of the vault is not brought to a very sharp point, but the crowning stone is called the keystone, ἁρμονία, to the rest of the structure."

The tomb is entered by a doorway in the centre of the north side ; the jambs and lintel of this doorway have been shattered, and their appearance shows that this entrance has, at some time, been forced. The pavement of the chamber was laid on the native rock, the surface of which had been cut away in places to receive it. The joints of the stones were polygonal, as in Cyclopean masonry. A large portion of them had been taken up, doubtless for the purpose of ascertaining whether any treasure was concealed below.

The lower part of the chamber is, as I have already stated, built of marble blocks, and is pierced with openings, which radiate like embrasures from the centre of the chamber to the outside of the basement. There can be no doubt that these passages were intended as receptacles for bodies. Such an arrangement of cells, or θῆκαι, branching out from a principal chamber, may be seen in Hellenic tombs at Budrum, and at Pyli in the island of Cos. I have never, however, before met with the circular arrangement adopted here.

There are eleven of these cells, three on each side of the tomb, except to the north, where the doorway occupies the middle place. All of them were choked with rubbish, but no trace of sepulchral remains was obtained from them, except some human bones.

No bones, pottery, or other antiquities, were found in the chamber itself; but, on one side of the doorway outside, was a *lekythos* $3\frac{4}{10}$ inches high, which had originally been covered with black varnish (*see* the cut). Near it were found some fragments of painted vases.

The whole of the ruins, which, except on the side facing the sea, extended to a distance of 40 feet all round the basement, were examined stone by stone, and the ground underneath them dug down to the native rock, but no fragment either of sculpture or inscriptions rewarded our search.

We are, therefore, left without any evidence as to the date of this tomb, except such as is afforded by the style of the sculpture and architecture.

When compared with the sculptures of the Mausoleum, this lion appears to be the work of an earlier school; the style is rather more severe, and less rich and flowing. If this impression be correct, we may take the half-century between B.C. 350 and B.C. 400 as the probable date of this tomb. It would, therefore, be a work of the Republican period, when it is not likely that so sumptuous a monument would have been erected by any private individual for his own family. It is more probable that the tomb was of the class called by the Greeks *Polyandrion*,—such as were dedicated to the memory of those slain in battle for their country.

Among the ruins on the western side was discovered part of a large slab, on which was sculptured
in relief a circular shield.   This was evidently
too large to have formed part of the architrave,
but may possibly have been inserted over the
doorway.

If the tomb was a public monument, the unfinished shield was probably intended to receive an
inscription recording the names and services of the
persons commemorated.

The completion of the work may have been
arrested by political events ; and most probably by
one of those revolutions so common in the republics
of antiquity, by which a dominant party was suddenly
expelled from power, and all their acts annulled.

If we suppose this tomb to have been erected
between B.C. 350 and B.C. 400, it is not improbable
that it commemorates the defeat of the Lacedæmonians by the Athenian commander Conon, in the
great naval action which took place off Cnidus B.C.
394.   The site of the Lion tomb is one well suited
for such a monument.   It stands on the edge of an
abrupt precipice, cut sheer down to the sea ; and
the summit of the pyramid commands an extensive
panoramic view over the Archipelago.

The fact that this monument was crowned by a
lion as its *epithema* corroborates the supposition that
the persons whom it commemorates had been slain
in battle.   It is clear from the evidence of ancient
literature, that when the lion was placed on the
tomb of heroes, it was selected as an emblem of
valour and force.   On the battle-field of Thermopylæ

stood a marble lion, under which was inscribed the well-known epigram by Simonides in honour of Leonidas.

At a later period the Thebans, after their defeat by Philip of Macedon at Chæronæia, commemorated their slain countrymen by a monument surmounted by a marble lion, the fragments of which still remain to mark the site " fatal to liberty." [77]

The Chæronæian lion is represented in a sitting position, and his countenance has an expression of angry defiance which would well accord with a monument designed in memory of a defeat: on the other hand, the majestic repose of the Cnidian lion seems the fit expression of the calm and conscious strength of victory. If this monument be really what I suppose it to be, a memorial of the great naval action in which Conon defeated the Lacedæmonians, no nobler trophy could have been chosen than this lion, planted on his lofty pedestal as a conspicuous seamark, to remind the passing mariners for centuries to come of the supremacy of Athens on the sea.

Since we have been engaged in removing the lion, a curious incident has occurred which shows that expeditions like ours can hardly be carried on in safety on this coast without the protection of a ship of war.

While I was at Budrum, having been authorized by the Embassy to draw for a large amount on the Pasha of the district, I had no difficulty in getting my bills cashed by the Mudir of Budrum. Since I have been here, my friend Mehemet Ali, who

collects the tribute of the peninsula over which
he rules, proposed in like manner to be my banker,
as, by cashing my bills, he would be enabled to
remit the tribute to the Pasha at Mughla in paper
instead of in specie. Accordingly, I applied to him
for a remittance of £700, and, not thinking it desirable to have charge of so large a sum on shore,
specially directed him not to send it before a certain
day, when I knew that the Supply would come in
from Budrum. Mehemet Ali forthwith proceeded
to call in the tribute from all the villages round
him, which was duly paid up in copper piastres
and half-piastres. Six mules having been laden
with this treasure, were then despatched to Cnidus
in charge of some cavasses, who were so proud of
their mission that they proclaimed it at every village
where they halted on their way, taking care to
magnify the sum with that noble contempt for
exactness in figures which distinguishes the Oriental
mind.

The fame of this treasure destined for "the mad
English Consul who was digging holes in the
ground at Cape Crio" of course spread far and
wide; and, by some singular accident, the cavasses
contrived to arrive at Cnidus *just one day sooner
than the time I had fixed.* My perplexity was great
when I saw the rows of great camel's-hair sacks
piled up on the floor of my hut. As £700 cashed
in piastres and half-piastres amounted to about
80,000 pieces of money, I knew that the mere
counting over such a sum would take hours; and
then the money was so bulky that I had no place to

stow it in, except an empty cask. While I was
debating whether I should order the cavasses to
take it all back to Mehemet Ali, and what I should
do if they refused, the sentinel, to my infinite
relief, sang out that the Supply was coming round
the Cape. By another singular accident, she too
arrived one day before her appointed time. In
another half-hour my sacks were all safe on board
ship; and, with the assistance of my trusty Mehemet
Chiaoux, who, like most inhabitants of the Levant,
takes especial delight in the handling and counting of
money, I covered the quarter-deck all over with little
piles of copper coins, divided into decades and centuries, and arranged rank and file to facilitate the
counting, which we accomplished just in time to save
the daylight.

The next morning, my Turkish workmen announced
to me that a strange looking vessel had been seen
hovering on the coast. As she had thirty men on
board—a number much exceeding the crew required
to navigate her—the natives here at once suspected
that she was a pirate; and this suspicion became a
certainty when she suddenly made a swoop on the
coast, and, landing an armed party, carried off a
bullock before the very eyes of an old peasant who
was too frightened to offer the slightest resistance.
The night after this raid, Corporal Jenkins happened
to be keeping watch at our camp at the Lion tomb,
all alone, his Turkish workmen having deserted him
to celebrate the Bairam in a neighbouring village.
In the middle of the night he was roused by the
sound of oars, and saw the piratical boat pulling

into the little secluded bay below the promontory where his tent was pitched. Carbine in hand, he challenged them, and, getting no satisfactory answer, thought it as well to let them know that he was ready to give them a warm reception, and so fired just over their heads. Not liking the whistling of an English bullet, they at once put out to sea again, and we have seen no more of them; but, looking at the curious coincidence of their apparition just at the moment when the money, according to all reasonable calculation, would have been in my hut instead of on board the Supply, I cannot help believing that their visit was pre-arranged, possibly at the instigation of the cavasses themselves. I reported the circumstance to my friend Mr. Campbell at Rhodes, who, like all Consuls, was delighted at the chance of reporting a case of piracy to the Admiral, in the hope of eliciting in return a visit from a ship of war.

This anecdote will give you some idea of the difficulties under which commerce is carried on in this part of the Archipelago. Such is the insecurity of the sea, that bills of exchange can only be negotiated in those few islands where there is a regular service of mail steamers. In other places, money is smuggled in as stealthily as if it were contraband; and those who hold it are afraid to turn it to any proper account, for the reputation of being rich has cost many a man his life in these islands. Thus commercial enterprise will remain undeveloped till some modern Minos arises to put down piracy with a strong hand.

XLVIII.

RUINS OF CNIDUS, *Sept.* 30, 1858.

AFTER my visit to Branchidæ last year, I represented to Lord Clarendon that the statues on the Sacred Way, from their remote antiquity and historical associations connected with the site, would be a most interesting acquisition for the British Museum, and that, if left in their present position, they were liable to further mutilation and ultimately to destruction.

In consequence of this report, a firman authorizing the removal of those statues was obtained from the Porte by Sir Henry Bulwer; furnished with which I proceeded to Geronta in the Supply on the 26th of last month.

I took with me Corporal Jenkins, sixty Turkish workmen from Cnidus, tents, and all the tools and tackle necessary. Encamping on the Sacred Way, we lost no time in transporting to the shore at Karaköi the ten seated figures, with the lion and sphinx. The distance is about three miles, the road an easy incline, and, as we were provided with excellent four-wheeled trucks, we accomplished the work of transport at the rate of one statue *per diem*. After accomplishing this principal object of our expedition, I made some excavations along the line of the Sacred Way. Behind the row of statues was a continuous line of wall, marking the edge of the ridge, which runs to the north-west, along the side of the Way.

Beginning from the south-east I laid bare this wall for 73 feet, when I found its line interrupted by a concrete foundation of an oblong form, in which was a large block of a kind of limestone, about 7 feet long by 2 feet 8 inches thick. On one face of this block was an inscription in archaic Greek characters, containing a dedication by the sons of Anaximander, of some work of art executed by an artist called Terpsikles. This inscription was repeated on the opposite face of the stone. From the form of the letters I should suppose that this dedication was of the same age as that on the lion, described *ante*, p. 76; namely, about B.C. 560.[78]

As the base is narrow in proportion to its length, and as the inscription is repeated on the opposite face, the work of Terpsikles may have been a group sculptured in the round.

This stone had evidently been removed from its original position, as the concrete foundation in which it was embedded seemed to be Byzantine. I continued to trace this wall to the north-west for about 300 feet from the point where we commenced digging. Its masonry was regular, but did not seem to be Hellenic, except for about 16 feet in the latter part of the line, where we came to a wall of very massive masonry, one stone of which was nearly 12 feet long. This may have been the side of the basement of an ancient tomb. While tracing this line of wall, I explored the Way itself, of which I found the southern kerbstones still in position.

They consisted of a single course of rough blocks well jointed together, with headers at intervals laid on the native rock. One of these blocks measured 4 feet 4 inches by 1 foot by 14 inches.

We traced this line of kerbstones for 133 feet to the north-west. No other part of the original pavement remained in position. It was probably composed of polygonal blocks nicely adjusted, as in Cyclopean masonry. The width of the roadway was probably about 20 feet.

Along the side of the Way were two basements of tombs, which appeared to be Hellenic, and which had an external casing of four slabs fitted together like a box, and resting on a moulded plinth. Within this casing was solid masonry. In the centre of one of these tombs was an oblong slab pierced in the middle with a round hole, and laid on the earth. Two skulls and part of a skeleton were found in this tomb, and in the other two fragments of a small draped terra-cotta figure of a good period.

To the north-west, beyond the point to which we traced the line of kerbstones, were foundations of several other basements of tombs. One of these was built of massive blocks, the largest of which measured 10 feet in length. The courses, 3 feet 4 inches in width, enclosed an oblong area without pavement, in the centre of which was a slab pierced in the middle with a circular hole, as in the tomb already noticed. The masonry of this basement was not good, and it may have been constructed out of the materials of an earlier tomb to mark some sacred site.

These operations occupied me from the 26th of August to the latter part of September, when we returned to Cnidus.

I could have wished to have more completely explored the Sacred Way, where other archaic statues and inscriptions would probably be found if the whole site were dug over. But the appearance of dysentery among my workmen warned me that the unhealthy season had commenced, and that my little camp would soon become a hospital, and as the provisions of the Supply were running short, and her departure for Malta could not be long delayed, I thought it better to bring the Branchidæ expedition to a close, while we could avail ourselves of her services.

Before leaving Geronta, I spent a day at Palatia, the ancient Miletus, distant about two hours to the north. I was glad to hear during my visit that Prince Ghika, the Caimacam of Samos, had been making excavations near Palatia. He is a man with enlightened views, who has done, perhaps, more for the civilization of his island than has been attempted by any of its rulers since the days of Polykrates. He has a taste for archæology, which has led to some interesting discoveries at Samos. When I met him at Constantinople two years ago, he told me a curious anecdote of the people of Nicaria. This island, lying a little to the west of Samos, is so barren and so destitute of harbours that the inhabitants are forced to maintain themselves by charcoal-burning on the mainland opposite.

Their poverty is extreme, and they are considered the most barbarous of all the islanders in the Turkish Archipelago. Once upon a time, a Nicariote who had resided at Smyrna long enough to imbibe a taste for civilization, on returning to his native country, ventured to set up a four-post bedstead. His fellow countrymen resented the innovation as warmly as if he had set up his carriage. Breaking open the door of the unhappy Sybarite when he was comfortably asleep, they tore the bed from under him, and made a bonfire of it in the market-place; and since that day no Nicariote has ever ventured to deviate from the Spartan simplicity of life which has been handed down for many generations in this quaint little island.

The Supply left us on the 28th, bound for Malta and England. She took with her the big lion and upwards of 100 cases of sculpture and other antiquities, and will return to this place next spring. During her absence, Admiral Fanshawe promises to send a ship of war here about once a month to replenish our provisions and see how we are getting on.

Our little English colony here is now reduced to ten persons. Smith has gone home in the Supply on six months' leave of absence. Mr. Pullan and the two photographic sappers have also left us, and the departure of the Supply deprives me of the services of Mr. Hughes, her carpenter, who, during the most of the time since we have been established at Cnidus, has been with me on shore, and whose services have been of very great value. I have still,

however, my trusty Corporal Jenkins at my right
hand, and two steady sappers, one a smith and the
other a carpenter; and with their assistance I hope
to keep the rest of the party in a fair state of
discipline.

XLIX.

IF Halicarnassus could boast of its Mausoleum,
and Rhodes of its bronze Colossus, the little state of
Cnidus could point with just pride to its statue of
Aphrodite, the masterpiece of Praxiteles, in exchange
for which Nicomedes, king of Bithynia, offered to
redeem the whole public debt of the city, and which,
under the Roman Empire, attained so great a
celebrity that the *dilettanti* of all countries were
attracted to Cnidus solely for the sake of seeing this
famous work.

In the dialogue called "Amores," Lucian gives
an account of one of these pleasant pilgrimages, and
discourses upon the matchless beauties of the statue
in language so lively and forcible that we can hardly
suppose so glowing a description to have been made
up from accounts of other travellers, still less to
have been a mere figment of the imagination.

If, then, Lucian actually visited Cnidus, there is
no reason to doubt the accuracy of his statement
that the temple in which the statue of Venus was
enshrined was very small, with an entrance at either
end, and that around it was a spacious *temenos*,

planted with shady trees, and affording an agreeable place of resort to the people of Cnidus.

But in what part of the ancient city was this *temenos?*

When we survey the entire site contained within the ancient walls, the eye singles out a conspicuous platform which overlooks our encampment, and in the centre of which are the ruins of a small Corinthian temple. This platform, as has been already noticed, has been bounded on the south by a Doric colonnade overlooking the harbour, and on the west by an Odeum. The extent of this platform, its commanding and conspicuous position, and the small scale of the temple, led Colonel Leake to consider this the site of the celebrated Temple of Venus.[79] But if Lucian's description of the *temenos* is not a mere rhetorical invention, it suggests to us a site very different in character from the platform surrounding the Corinthian temple. The *temenos* of Lucian's Aphrodisium abounded in trees and ornamental shrubs, which afforded a grateful shade to the citizens. The platform, on the contrary, is much exposed in winter to the north wind, which sweeps over the city with extraordinary fury. The soil is at present of the most arid kind, and contains no springs. Doubtless it may have been artificially fertilized by irrigation from conduits, but it is difficult to imagine how a grove planted there could have had that sheltered and retired character which formed the chief charm of Lucian's *temenos*. His description would rather lead us to look for the site of the *temenos* somewhere in the environs of the city, on

ground broken by ravines and sheltered by mountains.

The ruins of the Corinthian temple are of the
Roman period, and are probably at least as late as
the time of the Antonines.

We made an excavation here in two places, but
found nothing to encourage us to continue. We
met with neither inscriptions nor architectural fragments of an earlier and purer period, such as might
have been expected, had this temple been built, as
Colonel Leake supposes, on the site of the earlier
Aphrodisium for which the work of Praxiteles was
originally designed.

I next examined a mass of ruins lying on the
north side of this platform, among which I noticed
an inscription first published by Mr. W. J. Hamilton,
in which the people of Cnidus decree divine honours
to some public benefactor, who is described as priest
of Artemis Iakynthotrophos."⁰ The honours to be
paid to him are crowns of gold and olive, statues in
bronze, in marble, and in gold; proclamations, and
the most honourable seats in all the public games;
maintenance for himself and his descendants at the
expense of the State; a public funeral on his death,
and a monument to be placed in the most conspicuous part of the Gymnasium; a golden statue
to be placed in the temple of Artemis' Iakynthotrophos; an altar, sacrifices, a procession, and a
quinquennial gymnastic contest. As these games
were to be called the *Artemidoreia*, there can hardly
be a doubt that the citizen thus honoured was
Artemidoros, probably the very man who gave

Julius Cæsar warning on the day of his assassination, and whom Plutarch describes as a teacher of rhetoric, resident at Rome, but a native of Cnidus.

This Artemidoros had a son, Theopompos, whom Strabo mentions as a person of great influence, and a friend of Augustus, and who, as we learn from another Cnidian inscription, was called Caius Julius, evidently in honour of the Emperor, of whom his father was so devoted an adherent. Both father and son were men of the same class as their contemporaries at Lesbos—Theophanes, Lesbonax, and Potamo (see *ante*, I. pp. 66-8),—shrewd courtiers, who turned their influence with the reigning Emperor to good account for the benefit of their native city, and whose patriotism was rewarded with the most extravagant honours.

A little to the north of the spot where this inscription was lying, is a street running east and west through the ancient city, and bounding the platform on the north. At the point where this street is intersected by another coming from the south, I noticed two lines of Hellenic wall meeting at right angles, and rising about one course above the surface of the ground. On digging within this angle, I found the foundations of these walls at the depth of about seven feet. The masonry may be described as a plinth surmounted by a course of broad slabs, set back to back, above.which was a string-course, the whole of limestone. Above this limestone base had been a wall built of tufa, covered with painted stucco. Following these lines, I uncovered an area extending 58 feet by 51 feet.

The interior was divided into three nearly equal
spaces by party walls running from north to south,
these being again subdivided into smaller chambers
by cross-walls from east to west, which appear to be
of a late period. In the south-east angle was a
mosaic pavement, with a simple pattern worked in
black on a white ground. Near this pavement I
found a limestone base, the inscription on which
showed that it had formed the plinth of a term of
Hermes. In this inscription, which is partly in
Iambic and partly in Trochaic verse, Hermes himself
addresses the reader, and speaks of his own arrival
as if he had been newly imported into Cnidus.
Within this same building I found a base with a
dedication to the same Artemis Iakynthotrophos
who is mentioned in the inscription relating to
Artemidoros.[81]

We also dug up here some fragments of Ionic
capitals and architraves, cut out of a calcareous
tufa covered with stucco. Many small fragments of
this stucco were found in the soil, on which the ornaments with which it had been painted were still quite
fresh. Red, yellow, black, and occasionally green,
were the colours employed. At the depth of 4 feet
below the surface was a layer of potsherds, extending
over the greater part of the site; among which were
many grotesque figures in relief from lamps and
small vases.

The general plan of the building which occupies
this site suggests the notion that it may have
formed part of a *Gymnasium*; and this conjecture is
confirmed by the discovery of the base of a terminal

statue of Hermes, the patron of the *palæstra*, and by the mention of a *Gymnasium* in the inscription relating to Artemidoros, already referred to, which was found near this place. A third inscription found on this site contained a dedication to πεισινοῦς, "the persuader of the mind," an epithet which probably designates Hermes as the god of eloquence.[2] If we suppose that a Gymnasium extended over this site, it probably occupied much of the extensive platform to the south; and the discovery of two dedications to Artemis Iakynthotrophos so near the small Corinthian temple, makes it probable that it was dedicated to that deity rather than to Aphrodite, as Leake supposed.

I have already noticed that the south side of the great platform has been bounded by a Doric colonnade. It has been supposed by Colonel Leake that this may have been the *pensilis ambulatio*, or terrace supported on columns built by Sostratos, the architect of the celebrated Pharos at Alexandria, and a native of Cnidus. Among the ruins, however, of this portico, I noticed a piece of architrave inscribed with the name of Theopompos in majuscule characters.[3]

This was probably the Theopompos, son of Artemidoros, whom I have mentioned; and the occurrence of his name on the architrave would lead to the conclusion that the *stoa* was a work of the Augustan age.

On the shore below this portico is the site of a large temple, within the *peribolos* of which our encampment is placed. This was probably dedicated to Dionysos, as immediately to the east of it is the theatre which has been already noticed (*ante*, p. 173). To the east of this theatre a broad terrace runs along the shore of the great harbour, above its sea wall.

About half-way between the theatre and the eastern wall of the city is an alcove built against the side of the hill and facing the sea. Near the edge of the terrace below was a pedestal of white marble inscribed with a dedication to Serapis and Isis, in gratitude for the cure of some disease. Lieutenant Smith made an excavation here on a line of foundations a little to the east of the alcove, and discovered a small theatre facing the south, which, from the smallness of its scale, was evidently an Odeum where musical contests must have taken place. The chord of its arc measured 23 feet 3 inches.[84]

Instead of a *scena*, it had a platform formed of a single row of large blocks, which must have supported a screen of metallic railings, with a gate at each end, as is shown by the sockets cut at intervals in the pavement. The substitution of this screen of metal for the usual solid masonry of the *scena* may be accounted for by the fact that in so small a *cavea* no boundary wall on this side would have been required to condense the sound. In front of the platform was a pedestal occupying the centre of the space usually assigned in the ancient Greek theatre to the orchestra. The present height of this pedestal is 1 foot 8 inches; its length 6 feet. A step led up to it on the west. On this base, called by the Greeks *thymele*, the performer must have stood, as we see by the pictures on several vases, on which musical contests are represented.

On digging to the south of the alcove, a concentric semicircular foundation immediately in front of it was laid bare, below which were a series of steps and landing-places leading down to the terrace below. These steps were of good masonry, and had been veneered with marble.[5] The proximity of the alcove to the Odeum, and its apsidal form, suggest to me the idea that it was a tribune where the judges sat, by whom prizes were awarded to the victors in the musical contests.

About 200 yards to the north-east of this alcove was a small platform covered with Byzantine ruins, and bounded on the south by a wall, the beautiful masonry of which showed that it was of a good period of art. Clearing away the ruins on the surface, which evidently belonged to a Byzantine church, I came to the foundations of a small Doric temple, 65 feet long by 49 wide, with four columns in the southern front. The interior is divided into two nearly equal compartments by a wall running east and west, and the northernmost of these compartments is again subdivided into two chambers. In front of the colonnade, on the south, is a small court bounded by the wall which first attracted my attention on this site, and which forms the external boundary or *peribolos*.[6] The temple stands on a platform cut like a step out of the side of the hill, and bounded on the north and east sides by a deep cutting in the native rock. A deep drain running round these sides carries off the water from the hill.

R 2

On the stylobate was a Byzantine wall, into which were built many fragments of the columns, architrave, and frieze. The diameter of the columns, taken at 4 feet 6 inches above the stylobate, was 1 foot 11 inches. The bases of three of the columns being found in position on the stylobate, showed that the intercolumniation equalled two and a half diameters.

The Order and the upper part of the walls of the temple were built of tufa, which had been covered with fine stucco. Below this tufa, the walls of the chambers were built of grey marble, the structure being the same as that of the supposed Gymnasium (see *ante*); viz., two slabs placed back to back on a plinth, and surrounded by a string-course, at the height of 4 feet 2 inches from the foundations. The interior surface of these slabs was finely polished, and the joints adjusted with a nicety hardly to be surpassed in the finest cabinetmaker's work. This mode of combining marble and tufa in architecture was evidently much in use at Cnidus, Rhodes, and Halicarnassus, in buildings which did not require very massive walls. I have already remarked, in the description of Rhodes (*ante*, p. 178), that where such a mode of building prevailed, there must necessarily be fewer vestiges of Greek architecture than where marble has been more generally employed.

In the course of the excavations, we dug up portions of six statuettes, which appear to represent Muses, an opinion which is confirmed by the evidence of two inscriptions discovered on this site.

One of these is a dedication to the Muses of a statue of a certain Glykinna, of which Epikrates is named as the sculptor.[7]

The other is a circular altar inscribed with a dedication to Apollo Pythios by Kephisodoros, chief magistrate (*Demiourgos*) of Cnidus.[8]

The evidence of these two dedications gives reasonable ground for supposing that the temple was dedicated to Apollo Pythios and the Muses; and this is confirmed by the discovery of so many statuettes, the types of which correspond so nearly with those under which the Muses are usually represented. These statuettes have been about two feet high, and were probably placed in niches in the walls of the chambers, as at regular intervals in the marble string-courses ledges are cut, suitable to receive the bases of such small figures.

Near the site marked *Agora* in the Plan, I found a block of marble inscribed with a dedication of some work of art to Athene Nikephoros and Hestia Boulaia. The dedicator is one Hagias, secretary of the Senate (*Boulé*), the name of the artist, Zenodotos, son of Menippos, a Cnidian.[9] In Athens, and probably in Greek cities generally, a statue of Hestia was set up in the *Prytaneion*, a building where public guests were fed at the expense of the State, and which at Cnidus, as we learn from another inscription (see *ante*, p. 238), was called Demiourgion. The Senate probably met in this building, which may have stood somewhere near the presumed site of the *Agora*.

L.

Cnidus, *March* 15, 1859.

I HAVE already noticed in the general description of Cnidus (*ante*, p. 168), the rocky promontory called Triopion, which forms the bulwark of its harbours, and which was probably occupied by the first Greek settlers, before they established themselves on the mainland opposite. On this Triopian headland stood a temple dedicated to Apollo, where the members of a league of maritime states, originally called the Dorian Hexapolis, met, and where games in honour of Apollo, Poseidon, and the Nymphs were celebrated. The six states composing this confederation were the three Rhodian cities Lindus, Camirus, Ialysus, together with Cnidus, Cos, and Halicarnassus.

How early this league was established we do not know; but some time before the Persian war, the people of Halicarnassus were excluded from it, in consequence, as we are told by Herodotus, of the act of one of their citizens, Agasikles, who, after a tripod had been adjudged to him as a prize in the Triopian festival, took it away to his own house, instead of dedicating it to Apollo. Thenceforth the league was called the Doric Pentapolis. It is probable that the increasing predominance of the Carian element in the population of Halicarnassus contributed to its exclusion from the league. How much longer after this event the confederacy lasted we are not informed; but it is not likely to have survived the foundation of Rhodes, B.C. 408, by which the political importance of the three Rhodian members of the Pentapolis must have been annihilated.

I was in hope that some trace of the ancient Temple of Apollo might still be met with on Cape Crio; but my search has been quite unavailing. The ground is in most places so steep, that it would be difficult to find an area large enough for a temple; but the ancient terraces which supported the soil seem to have been very generally replaced here by walls of inferior masonry; the site of the temple may therefore have been swept away by torrents, which, if not intercepted by ducts and cisterns, would here carry everything before them.

The only ruins of interest which I could find on the peninsula were those of a Roman tomb, situated on rocky ground outside the western wall of the city (see Plate 21). It was discovered by Corporal Spackman, who, penetrating into the middle of some brushwood, stumbled on part of a female statue in white marble. On clearing away the bushes and removing a quantity of soil and rubble, I laid bare the foundations of a tomb, resembling in plan some of the early Christian churches. It consists of a chamber, with a vestibule on the north and an apse or alcove on the south. In each side wall is a smaller apse or alcove.[90]

In front of each alcove was a sarcophagus of white marble, nine feet long. The alcove on the west had contained the marble statue, the discovery of which in the brushwood had originally induced me to explore this tomb.

The body of this figure, from the waist downwards, I found in its original position, on a marble pavement within the alcove, and in good condition.

From the fragments which remain, the figure may be restored, all but the arms; but from the head to the waist the surface is completely destroyed. In the left hand this figure holds the well-known attributes of Ceres, the poppy-head and ears of corn. The head-dress seems to be that in use in the time of Domitian, when Roman ladies took delight in building up head-dresses composed of parallel rows of curls.[91]

As the statue is certainly of the Roman period, it may represent some empress in the character of Ceres. The drapery is rather heavy, though not ill composed.

At the feet of this statue we found numbers of small lamps of coarse red unglazed ware, of the Roman period. These were doubtless votive offerings. Two of the sarcophagi were richly decorated with festoons suspended at the angles from Satyrs' heads, and sustained by naked boys standing on pilasters. Above these festoons are two Gorgons' heads, in relief; and, on one of the sarcophagi the bust of a draped male figure, doubtless the portrait of the person interred within.[92]

In the earth near the base of the statue, and in one of the alcoves, were several fragments of thin marble slabs on which decrees of the Senate and people of Cnidus have been inscribed. These have

been sawn at the backs, and may have been let into
the walls of the tomb. The only one of these fragments of which the subject can be clearly made out,
contains a decree relating to a certain Lykæthios or
Lykæthion, son of Aristokleides, whom the Senate
and people of Cnidus honoured with a crown and a
statue for public services. A commissioner is named
in the decree, who is to receive from the president of the Senate 3,500 drachmæ, equal to about
£109. 7s. 6d., for the expense of setting up the statue.
It is curious that in this inscription we find the word
ἀφεστήρ, which we know from Plutarch to have been
the title by which the office of president of the
Senate was designated at Cnidus. I am not aware
that this word occurs in any ancient author except
in the single passage where it is referred to by Plutarch. The decree was ratified by open vote, both
in the Senate and the assembly of the people, and
carried in both bodies unanimously. The inscription
has recorded the number of votes given on this occasion; but an unlucky fracture of the marble in
this place has deprived us of an interesting piece of
information.[93]

We learn from the Politics of Aristotle that the
Senate of Cnidus originally consisted of sixty members, called ἀμνήμονες. No son was eligible to be
a senator during his father's lifetime, and, among
brothers, only the first-born. The revolution by
which this constitution was abolished at Cnidus was
brought about by the people, under the leadership
of the excluded members of the oligarchical families.
These changes must have taken place some time

before the date of the Politics of Aristotle, in which
they are recorded, and were probably connected
with the code of laws introduced by the Cnidian
astronomer Eudoxos in his native city about the
time of Mausolos.

Lucian, in his description of the Temple of Venus,
speaks of the ἀστικοί at Cnidus as distinguished
from the πολιτικὸς ὄχλος. These ἀστικοί were
probably the descendants of the old oligarchical
families, who, even as late as the time of Lucian,
may have retained some of their original privileges,
and lived apart from the rest of the citizens, in the
ἄστυ, or older quarter of the city.[91]

The chief magistrate at Cnidus was called *Demiourgos*, a name in use in other Doric states.

The other fragments of inscriptions also appear
to form part of honorary decrees. The age of these
inscriptions appears to be the same as that of the
statue; but it is not certain that they were ever set
up in the tomb, though, on the whole, this seems not
improbable. In this latter case the tomb may have
been erected at the expense of the State. The walls of
the alcoves have been lined with a wainscoting of
white marble, veneered in thin slices, above which I
found stucco, ornamented with vertical crimson
stripes. In the rubble I found a number of slices
of coloured marbles, cut into geometrical forms,
which must also have been used in the decoration of
the walls. I dug the ground all round this tomb in
the hope of finding graves; but no trace of sepulchral remains turned up.

LI.

AFTER examining this tomb, I transferred my workmen to the Necropolis, lying immediately to the east of the city, on the mainland (*see* Plate 21). The ancient road which issues from the city on this side is easily traced by the row of tombs on each side.

This road, after skirting the steep side of a mountain spur, runs to the edge of a deep ravine, which must have been anciently bridged over. From this point it may be traced at intervals for about six miles, as far as Yasi-köi. The tombs are generally square basements, covered with a flat roof, which forms a platform, on which have stood round altars or *cippi*. Many of them are built against sloping ground, and therefore consist of only three walls. Inside these basements are chambers, sometimes rectangular, sometimes arched over with a barrel vault, and lined with stucco.

In many cases a *peribolos* wall surrounds two or more adjacent tombs : the space thus enclosed may be considered the *Hieron* or sacred precinct round the tomb. The *cippi* are almost always circular, and have stood on square plinths. They are generally ornamented with a snake coiled round in relief, and sometimes with festoons suspended from bulls' heads. When I first began exploring this Necropolis, the ground was so overgrown with brushwood, that it was very difficult to make out anything. One day, crawling on my hands through the bushes, with the vague hope of stumbling on the tomb of the Cnidian astronomer Eudoxos, as Cicero found that of Archimedes amid the *dumeta* of the Necropolis at Syracuse, I came suddenly on a block of marble, on which was engraved in fine characters a Greek inscription in elegiac verse.[95] In this inscription the traveller, before entering the city, is invited to turn a little out of his road to visit the *temenos* of the hero Antigonos, who was probably some mythical or semi-historical personage honoured with a sacred precinct round his tomb.

Within this *temenos*, the inscription proceeds to tell the traveller, were a temple and an altar, *thymele*, where poets might recite their compositions; a *stadium* and *palæstra*; baths, and a statue of Pan playing on the *syrinx*. The whole precinct must therefore be regarded as a *gymnasium*, which was probably bequeathed for that purpose by the hero Antigonos, just as the gardens called Akademia, at Athens, were said to have been given originally by the hero Akademos.

From a comparison of the commencement of the inscription with the two last lines, it may be inferred that the statue of Hermes, as *temenouros*, or guardian of the *temenos*, stood at the entrance, and that the god himself is supposed to address the traveller.

From the opening lines, it is clear that the *temenos* stood near the public road, and at a short distance from the city.

The inscription describes the temple as situated in a ravine, ἄγκος, apparently on the left-hand side of the road. Between the spot where I found the inscription and the city gate are several ravines, but no level ground suitable for a *palæstra* and *stadium* ; earthquakes, however, and aqueous deposit from the mountains may have greatly changed the aspect of this district. As the inscription mentions baths, the site was probably near some natural fountain, of which there are several along this road. I should mention that the stone, being of small dimensions, may easily have been transported from a distance to the spot where I found it.

The association of athletic exercises with the worship of the Muses, and with poetical and musical contests, was very general in the ancient *gymnasia*.

Such an union was, in fact, to the Greek mind only the expression of the general idea that the highest training, mental and bodily, should be rhythmical.

Very near the spot where this inscription was lying, I noticed a row of short thick columns in a dense mass of brushwood, clearing away which, I laid bare the foundations of an early Christian church, of which the east end terminates in an apse.

I made an excavation here, and about two feet below the surface came upon the pavement of the church. This was chiefly composed of slabs, bearing Greek sepulchral inscriptions, which had evidently been stripped from neighbouring tombs in this Necropolis.

The larger of these slabs had been the sides of *sarcophagi ;* the smaller ones were generally *stelæ* or upright tombstones. Others were on square plinths, on which short sepulchral columns or *cippi* had stood. In these the inscription generally commences with the words ὁ δᾶμος, and the deceased person is styled Ἥρως. Nearly all the inscriptions were of the Roman period, and most of them probably belong to the second and third centuries A.D.

The only ones of much interest were the epitaph of a lady named Atthis, in elegiac verse, dedicated by her husband, and a list of the subscriptions contributed by the members of a *thiasus*.[96] These *thiasi* were religious societies or clubs, which assembled periodically to perform sacrifices in honour of some particular deity.

It is evident from the examination of this little church that the early Christian inhabitants of Cnidus must have rifled an immense number of tombs, and it is probable that in this and other ancient cities the amount of treasure found with the dead was very large, and may have formed a considerable item in the revenue of the monasteries, which we so constantly find planted in the midst of Greek ruins.

It is evident that during the latter days of Paganism this kind of sacrilege grew more and more frequent; hence, in the later sepulchral inscriptions, the imprecations constantly invoked on the head of the tomb-burglar, and backed by menaces of heavy fines. When, however, under the influence of Christianity, the sepulchres of Pagan ancestors ceased to be regarded as sacred, and the vengeance of their Manes was despised, an universal raid was made against

the tombs ; and thus we find in Italy an edict of the
Gothic king Theodoric, setting forth, that whereas
so much valuable treasure was locked up in tombs,
it was the duty of all men to set it free by desecra-
ting the dead.[97]

On an eminence a little to the east of the ancient
church is a very remarkable tomb, which has
attracted the notice of Texier, Hamilton, and other
travellers.

It consists of two square basements, placed in the
centre of a precinct or *peribolos*, which is surrounded
by a wall 125 feet square. This wall, except on the
north side, is in a very perfect state. The entrance
is at the south-east angle. The basements are each
about 20 feet square. Upon them have stood small
pillars, composed of hexagonal blocks placed one on
another, each course consisting of a single block. It
is probable, as several travellers have supposed, that
these structures were surmounted by bronze tripods,
for Texier found one with four sockets sunk in the
upper surface, which is engraved in his "Asie
Mineure," and which he considers the uppermost
hexagon. These blocks are now all thrown down,
and lie about the basement.

We cut trenches in various parts of the *peribolos*,
and dug all round the basements, of which the one
nearest to the west had on each side small square-
headed cells. In these I found three small stone
cists, and a fragment of a fourth inscribed with the
name "Kourotrophos," an epithet of the Chthonic
deity, Demeter or Gaia.[98]

No other sepulchral remains were found in these

cells, except three very coarse unpainted vases;
and it was evident from the position of the cists
that they had been opened and disturbed. The
excavation, however, clearly proved that the whole
site was sepulchral; the extensive enclosure round
the tomb was probably a *temenos*, or precinct dedicated to some deity or hero.

While we were exploring this tomb, I detached a
set of pioneers with felling-axes to clear away the
brushwood between this site and the city. They
had made considerable progress in this work when
I received a despatch from Lord Malmesbury, in-
structing me to bring the expedition to a close;
and with much reluctance I abandoned the Necropolis, of which I had as yet explored only a small
portion.

Before leaving this ground I made several excavations on the slopes near the architectural tombs, with
a view of ascertaining whether there were any graves
in the soil, as at Budrum and Calymnos.

I found no trace of such graves, but the extent
of ground covered by the Necropolis was so great
that no such casual examination of it can be considered conclusive. Graves are best discovered by
peasants in the ordinary course of tillage, after a
district has been cleared.

LII.

CNIDUS, *May* 25, 1859.

SINCE I have received the order to cease all excavations, we have been occupied in packing up all our stores, so as to be ready to embark as soon as the Supply arrives, which will I hope be in a few days.

The Coquette, which visited us a few weeks ago, brought back my old messmate Lieut. Smith, who returned much refreshed by his six months' furlough. It was a great satisfaction to me to see him here again, for I have had rather too much on my hands lately. Corporal Jenkins, who, in the absence of any officer of higher rank, has been in command of the small detachment of sappers and marines all the winter, was suddenly laid low by a dangerous fever, which brought on congestion of the brain, and which I cured by the desperate remedy of severe bleeding. Our little colony has been looked after by Admiral Fanshaw all the winter, and according to his promise, a ship of war has called regularly every month since the Supply left, till lately, when an interval of two months occurred before the Coquette came in. Their non-arrival put me into a curious difficulty; remembering the mysterious visit of a pirate last summer, I thought it as well not to let anybody suspect that I kept a large sum in my hut for the payment of my Turkish

workmen. So after the Supply left us last autumn
I discontinued my usual weekly payments and
announced that the workmen would in future be
paid once a month, after the arrival of the ship of
war, which was to call periodically. My Turks
naturally inferred from this that each successive
ship brought me a fresh supply of money; and this
fiction was kept up till, after waiting two months
with no tidings from the Admiral, we began to fear
he had forgotten us altogether. It was impossible
to delay paying the men the long arrears now due to
them, and at the same time I did not care to awaken
speculations as to the amount of money I had in my
hut. In this emergency I took my old trusty friend
Mehemet Chiaoux into my confidence, and disclosing
to him the fiction we had been carrying on so long,
sent him over to Budrum with instructions to ne-
gotiate there an imaginary bill of exchange, the
proceeds of which he was forthwith to bring back
to me, taking care to let everybody know, on his
return to Cnidus, that in consequence of the non-
arrival of the ship of war, he had been sent to
Budrum to get money to pay my workmen. The
stratagem succeeded admirably. My trusty messenger made haste on his way, and returning in three
days, presented himself to me in presence of all my
workmen, ostentatiously brandishing before their
eager eyes a well-filled canvas bag, at the sight of
which they set up a shout of joy, little suspecting
that it contained, not money, but *lemons!*

Since our diggings have ceased and our packing
has been completed, I have employed a few days in

exploring the peninsula at the extremity of which
Cnidus is situated. In these excursions I have
been accompanied by Lieut. Smith. Our first object
was to follow the traces of the ancient Way, which,
as I have already mentioned (*ante*, p. 251), passes
this, the Eastern Necropolis of Cnidus, in the direction of the village of Yasiköi, distant about six
miles. The modern road to that village follows the
line of the Way very closely, being marked by a
succession of remains of tombs on each side. These
ruins are all square or circular basements, which
have probably been surmounted by pyramidal structures, like that of the Lion tomb. One of these
basements, distant about half an hour from Yasiköi,
is circular, and 72 feet in diameter. It has been
broken open from the top. As we approached
Yasiköi, we skirted on our right a small stream,
along the right bank of which was a long line of
Hellenic wall, beautifully fitted with polygonal
masonry and evidently built to protect the bank
from the violent action of the stream. On our
right beyond this embankment was an isolated
steep hill, on scaling which we found on the summit
the remains of a mediæval castle, called Assar
Kalessi, consisting of rough walls built with mortar.
This hill commands a fine sea-view towards Rhodes,
and was therefore probably fortified in antiquity.
From Yasiköi we went to an adjacent village called
Chesmaköi, situated a little to the south-east of it. In
a plain three-quarters of an hour to the east of Chesmaköi, we fell in with an ancient road running east
and west, which we identified as the Way which we

s 2

had traced from Cnidus to Yasiköi. Following this
piece of road, we came to the remains of an ancient
bridge, formed by horizontal courses of stone approaching each other gradually, and converging at
the apex into an acute angle, instead of a curvili-
near arch. The roadway over this bridge is 24 feet
wide. It is built of blocks of blue limestone of
moderate size, and the masonry is certainly Hellenic.
This bridge has evidently been protected by a fortress on a rocky eminence about a mile to the south,
called Koumya Kalessi, and which overlooks the sea
towards Rhodes and Syme. The massive walls of
this fortress still stand ; the masonry is polygonal.
On the south side is a very perfect gateway, and
inside the fortress several buildings of the Byzantine
period. To the south a fertile valley stretches down
to the sea, planted with vallonea and almond trees.
At the foot of a range of hills on the east side of
this valley is part of the concrete basement of a
tomb, and below it a broken marble sarcophagus of
the late Roman period, with grotesque masks at the
angles. On the shore are some Byzantine ruins
marked in the Admiralty Chart. Eastward of
Chesmaköi, on the road from Cnidus to Datscha,
and at the distance of four hours and a half from
the latter place, is a ravine called Dum Galli. Here
we found an isolated mass of limestone weighing probably about 200 tons. A portion of the face of this
rock, about five feet square, is wrought nearly smooth,
and on it in letters nine inches long is inscribed the
word HPΩIOY, above which a rude circle is incised.
This inscription probably extended further to the

left, where the rock is broken away. From the form of the Ω its date may not be later than the reign of Alexander the Great.

East of Dum Galli I did not explore the peninsula, but Smith has paid several visits to Datscha, the residence of the Aga. Near this village the valleys are fertile and well-cultivated, producing good crops of figs, olives, and vallonca. In a bay to the south of Datscha is a good harbour for caiques, called Datscha Scala, and on the shore a little to the east of this harbour is an ancient sea-wall built of large isodomous blocks, and still about 12 feet high, which probably marks the site of the ancient Acanthos. Between this point and Marmarice is a mountainous neck of land which has been visited by the officers of our Hydrographical Survey, but which is so little known that I hope some future traveller will explore it carefully.

The scenery between Datscha and Cnidus is very varied and picturesque. On the north a high ridge of mountains running east and west through the peninsula descends in sheer precipices down to the Gulf of Cos, sloping less abruptly towards the southern coast, on approaching which the ravines expand into fertile valleys. In the wild mountain range which overlooks the Gulf of Cos, the leopard or Caplan, as the Turks call him, is still to be met with, and from time to time makes a descent into the valleys to carry off a sheep. Mehemet Ali has given me the skin of a fine specimen of one of these beasts, which has been lately caught in a trap. In the fertile valleys which occur at intervals on the

southern coast, the fig, almond, and olive trees
flourish, and in particular districts the vallonea oak,
which is the principal article of export from the
peninsula. In antiquity the Cnidian territory was
celebrated for the excellence of its wines; but as
most of the owners of the soil are Mussulmans, the
vine is no longer cultivated here. The population
is sparse, the peasants, cut off from the civilizing
influence of commerce and navigation, are mere
boors, very different from the active and intelligent population of Budrum. It is said that many
of my present workmen had never possessed money
till I employed them at Cape Crio; and that out of
fifty inhabitants of this peninsula whom I took with
me to Branchidæ last autumn, many had never
before quitted their native peninsula, Mehemet Ali
having contrived to keep them there like serfs, on
the pretext of their perpetual liability to be drawn
as conscripts, but in reality to prevent their emi-
grating in quest of higher wages than he chooses to
give. In these rambles through the Doric peninsula, my old Budrum ally Mehemet Chiaoux has
been our chosen companion, beguiling the way with
many a quaint sententious remark or curious anecdote. It is only after long study of the Turkish
mind that an European begins to discover how
much of poetry and tenderness of feeling lies hid
under that mask of stolid apathy which the Oriental
puts on when first brought into contact with the
Giaour. The more intelligent of the Turkish peasants are remarkable for their genuine unaffected
love of nature and interest in created things. If

you ask a Turkish peasant the name of a wild
bird, he does not answer you with a contemptuous
shrug of the shoulders as a Greek is apt to do, but
he will immediately begin to tell you all manner of
curious facts about the habits of the bird; and sometimes these elements of natural history are intermixed with strange scraps of old legend, which have
been handed down, like many Turkish customs, from
the time of the Greeks.

The other day we heard a bird uttering a plain-
tive note, to which another bird responded. When
Mehemet Chiaoux heard this note, he told us with
simple earnestness, that once upon a time a brother
and sister tended their flocks together. The sheep
strayed, the shepherdess wandered on in search
of them, till at last, exhausted by fatigue and sorrow,
she and her brother were changed into a pair of
birds, who go repeating the same sad notes. The
female bird says, "Quzumlari gheurdunmu,"—"Have
you seen my sheep?" to which her mate replies:
"Gheurmedum,"—"I have not seen them."

When Mehemet Chiaoux told me this myth, I did
not know that a nearly similar legend is to be found
in the curious Greek novel Daphnis and Chloe, by
Longus.[99]

LIII.

AFTER nearly three years of rough life on the coast of Asia Minor, I find myself once more within the pale of European civilization, rejoicing in the prospect of a few months' leave of absence in England before I proceed to my new post, the Consulship at Rome. We left Cnidus on the 8th inst. Our last few days there were very pleasantly spent. About three weeks ago we had a visit from the Euryalus, on board which H.R.H. Prince Alfred is now serving as midshipman under Captain Tarleton. After staying a day at Cnidus, the Euryalus went over to Budrum, where I had the honour of showing the Prince the site of the Mausoleum, now a desolate-looking spot, of which the idea is finer than the reality.

I took my last farewell of my old friend Mehemet Chiaoux on the deck of the Euryalus. Prince Alfred having expressed a wish to buy some Turkish embroidery, Mehemet Chiaoux at my request brought some specimens on board. Ninety-nine inhabitants of the Levant out of a hundred would have taken advantage of such an occasion to ask an exorbitant price. Mehemet Chiaoux was content to charge H.R.H. no more than the real value of such articles. In seven years of weary sojourning in the Levant, I have known no such honest truthful man as this poor Mussulman.

On our way back to Cnidus, the Euryalus called at Cos. We found the Caimacan under a cloud, a Commissioner having been sent from the Porte to overhaul his conduct. But on the present of a pair of silver-mounted pistols from the Prince, he became suddenly elated. "What do I care for that man from Stamboul," he said, "now that I can show this token of the friendship of an English Prince?" When the Euryalus was at Tunis the other day, the Bey, after receiving a visit from Prince Alfred, said, "Now that I am the friend of the Queen of England's son, may all my enemies burst;" whom he intended to include in this anathema he did not say.

Soon after the Euryalus left us, the Supply returned from Malta, and we forthwith set about the welcome task of embarking all our cases and stores. I had just completed my share of this work, and for the first time for many months began to feel at a loss for some occupation, when a beautiful English yacht sailed into our silent harbour. I was agreeably surprised to find on board Lord Dufferin and his mother, and their friend Capt. Hamilton. They came from Egypt, where Lord Dufferin has lately excavated a small temple near Thebes, and were glad to find themselves in a cooler latitude. They passed several days with us, during which we wandered about the picturesque valleys of the peninsula, the uncouth inhabitants of which were much surprised at the strange apparition of the Frank

lady on horseback, whom they persisted in regarding
as Lord Dufferin's wife. On the last of these pleasant days we had a farewell picnic on the broad
terrace which overlooks our encampment, and the
next morning at daybreak the yacht and the
Supply got under weigh together. Lord Dufferin
went northwards to Patmos and Samos, and we to
Rhodes. My object in going there on my way to
Malta was to examine a number of most curious
antiquities recently discovered by Messrs. Biliotti
and Salzmann, in a necropolis near Kalavarda,
which I have already noticed in a previous letter.
(See *ante*, I. p. 236.) In the course of the last
three months those two gentlemen have succeeded
in the discovery of a most interesting series of
tombs, which evidently belong to a very early
period of Greek civilization in Rhodes. They
have found quantities of painted fictile vases with
birds and grotesque animals and flowers, on a drab
ground, small figures and vases of porcelain, some of
which are inscribed with hieroglyphics resembling
those found in Egypt; small bottles of variegated
glass, and earrings and other jewels of gold and
electrum, ornamented with figures and flowers em-
bossed and in filagree. Some of the objects may be
of true Egyptian fabric, but the greater part are
probably imitations, the hieroglyphics being evidently
copied by persons ignorant of their true meaning,
just as Chinese characters are copied on porcelain of
European fabric. Amongst the gold ornaments are
a pair of earrings, having as pendants winged bulls,

resembling those found by Mr. Layard in Assyria. It is probable that many of these antiquities were imported into Rhodes by the Phœnicians, who, according to Hellenic tradition, had already settlements in Rhodes when the Greeks first established themselves there, and who, trading in objects of Egyptian fabric, probably increased their profits by manufacturing imitations of these articles. The necropolis from which these interesting remains have been obtained is of great extent, and in its neighbourhood we must look for the site of Kamiros, one of the three ancient cities of Rhodes which Homer mentions, and of which the political extinction was brought about by the founding of the metropolis, B.C. 408.

I had the satisfaction of securing this collection of antiquities for the British Museum, on reasonable terms. Messrs. Biliotti and Salzmann are so encouraged by this first success that they now propose carrying on their enterprise on a larger scale. I left them as a legacy one of our Cnidus huts, a revolver, and the remainder of our stock of pale ale and preserved meats. As we had no time to pack the newly-purchased antiquities before we left Rhodes, this had to be done during our voyage to Malta. Luckily the weather was so fine that we were able to work uninterruptedly at this task on the quarter-deck until we entered the harbour at Malta.

As we came to an anchor and I heard the welcome voice of Admiral Codrington hailing us from his

barge alongside, the carpenter drove the last nail
into the last case, making the three hundred and
eighty-fourth which I have sent home since the
commencement of the expedition, and my long task
was ended.

NOTES.

---

[1] This group of villages may be compared with that in the district of Iiera. (See *post*, note 11.)

[2] See *ante*, vol. i. p. 31, and the passage in Lucian, cited note 81, ibid.

[3] Böckh, C. I. No. 8729. It appears from this inscription that the bridge was built by the monastery of St. Michael, A.D. 1115.

[4] On the Artemis of Thermæ, see Böckh, C. I. No. 2172.

[5] Archæologia of Soc. Ant. London, xxxi. p. 502.

[6] Stephanus Byzantius, Βρῖσα. Etym. Mag. Βρισαῖος. Böckh, C. I. No. 2042.

[7] See *ante*, i. p. 213.

[8] See *ante*, note 96, vol. i.

[9] Etym. Mag. v. Αἰώρα. Panofka, Griechinnen und Griechen, Eng. trans., London, 1849, p. 9.

[10] Plin. N.H. v. 31, § 39.

[11] M. Boutan in his Memoir on Mytilene, Archives des Missions Scientifiques, Paris, 1856, v. p. 298, remarks, that the seven villages which the district of Iiera contains, are all governed by one Turkish Aga, and that this arrangement has probably been handed down since these villages formed one ancient community. The same observation applies to the group of villages called Calloni. See *ante*, note 1 of this volume.

[12] The calves' heads on this coin of Eresus also occur on the silver coins of Antissa in Lesbos.

[13] Aristoph. Equit. 313.

[14] For two other specimens of the dodekadrachm, see Vaux, Numismatic Chronicle, London, 1864, new series, vol. i. p. 101, pl. 6, fig. 1; for the octodrachm of Geta, see Millingen, Sylloge of Ancient unedited Coins, p. 35, pl. I. 15, 16.

[15] Dethier und Mordtmann. Epigraphik von Constantinopolis. in the Denkschrift. d. Philos. Hist. classe d. k. Akad. d. Wissensch.

Wien, 1864, p. 330. Frick, in Jahrbücher für Classische Philologie, Leipsig, 1859, iii. Supp. Bd. Heft 4, p. 554.

[16] Dethier, Epigraphik, p. 5. See pl. 2 of the same work.

[17] Dethier, p. 32.

[18] Dethier, pl. 2.

[19] Frick. (See *ante*, note 15.)

[20] See my History of Discoveries, &c., ii. p. 673.

[21] Dethier, p. 5.

[22] Procop. De Bello Goth. i. 15. Chronic. Alexandr. ed. Roder. 1615, p. 664.

[23] Ross, Hellenika, Halle, 1846, i. p. 67. Kiepert, Memoir über die Karte von Kleinasien, p. 77.

[24] Marked Warbut-köi in Kiepert's Map. See Prokesch von Osten, Denkwürdigkeiten aus dem Orient. iii. p. 444.

[25] See Prokesch von Osten, Denkwürd. iii. p. 444.

[26] In my History of Discoveries, &c., ii. p. 558, the width is stated to be 59 feet 5 inches. This dimension gives the width as measured from the edge of the upper *torus* of the bases of the columns on each side. The dimension 59 feet $10\frac{3}{4}$ inches in the text is measured from the edge of the plinth of the same bases.

[27] See my History of Discoveries, &c., ii. pp. 566-7.

[28] The ruins at Lagina were visited by L. Ross in 1844. See his Kleinasien u. Deutschland, pp. 91 and 104.

[29] Museum Marbles, x. pl. 41, fig. 1.

[30] Böckh, C. I. Nos. 2693, 2715.

[31] Steph. Byz. *s.v.* Λάγινα. See ibid. *s.v.* Ἑκατήσια.

[32] See my History of Discoveries, &c., ii. p. 609, note *j*.

[33] Ibid. p. 337, note *c*.

[34] Ibid. p. 694, No. 4, pl. 86.

[35] Ibid. p. 694, No. 5, pl. 86.

[36] Engraved, Museum of Classical Antiquities, i. p. 186.

[37] Compare an inscription. Böckh, C. I. No. 8889.

[38] Ross, Reisen, iv. pp. 30—41.

[39] In Mr. Fergusson's Mausoleum of Halicarnassus restored, he remarks, p. 27, that, in my letter of April 3, 1857 (Papers respecting Excavations at Budrum, p. 11), I give this dimension as 110 feet; that Lieut. Smith in his letter (ibid. p. 20) calls it 107 feet, and that in the text of my history it is 108 feet. This last measurement I took from Lieut. Smith's plan, which was completed subsequently to both the letters referred to, and is therefore more likely to be correct. With regard to the discrepancy in the

---

previous measurements, I would observe that such errors are easily accounted for, when it is considered that the ground was only explored by small instalments as we could obtain it, and that the measurement first given, viz. 110 feet, was probably taken with the tape across garden-walls and various obstructions, whereas the final measurement, 108 feet, was taken with the chain along a clear line.

[40] In my History of Discoveries this dimension is stated to be 127 feet, not 126 feet. In my letter (Papers respecting Excavations at Budrum, p. 11), and in Lieut. Smith's letter (ibid. p. 20), the latter measurement is given. Since the text of the present work has been printed, I have remeasured this distance on the original plan, and find that the north side of the quadrangle measures 127, and the south 126 feet. Mr. Fergusson, p. 24, thinks it ought to be 127 feet 6¾ inches exactly; but if he had seen the rough way in which the rock was cut, he would not, I think, have attached so much importance to this dimension.

[41] Ionian Antiquities, published by Dilettanti Society, pt. 1, pp. 11—28. pll. 1—17.

[42] Herod. ii. 121.

[43] See Mr. Birch's Memoir in my History of Discoveries, &c., ii. p. 667.

[44] In plate 9 the hair is restored by the evidence of this fragment.

[45] Lucian, Infer. Dialog. xxiv.

[46] Pausan. x. 15.

[47] See my History of Discoveries, &c., ii. p. 249.

[48] Brunn, Geschichte der bildenden Künstler, i. p. 283, ii. p. 377.

[49] I have followed Mr. Pullan in this measurement, which is taken from the back of the steps. Lieut. Smith measuring them on the front, makes their height 11¾ inches.

[50] Fergusson, the Mausoleum of Halicarnassus restored, London, 1862, p. 28.

[51] See ante, i. p. 333.

[52] Mr. Westmacott, in the passage referred to, suggests that I may have mistaken mere stains in the marble for pigments, and seems to think it strange that colours which were so clearly visible at Budrum, should be no longer visible when he examined the Mausoleum sculptures after their arrival in England. I therefore here print three letters on this subject, written by gentlemen who have been specially trained to the study of ancient art, and who

are therefore not likely to have mistaken the evidence of their senses.

No. 1, from G. F. Watts, Esq.

Little Holland House, Jan. 8, 1865.

MY DEAR NEWTON,—There is no doubt in my mind that the tints visible on the drapery of some of the fragments of sculpture when first exhumed at Halicarnassus are to be attributed to artistic application of colour; certainly the blue and red so distinct on many of the slabs of the frieze, and the red in the mouth of the lion, could not possibly be regarded as accidental stains. Mr. West-macott cannot understand that colour, which had been preserved for two thousand years, should have entirely disappeared in the few months occupied in the transmission of the sculptures from Asia-Minor to England; but I can state from positive experience that colour on some of the fragments, which, when the sculpture was first taken out of the ground, was as perfect as if painted but a few weeks, entirely disappeared in the course of two or three hours. Yours most sincerely,

G. F. WATTS.

No. 2, from Dr. S. Birch, Keeper of the Egyptian and Oriental Antiquities, British Museum.

British Museum, Jan. 25, 1865.

MY DEAR NEWTON,—In reply to your inquiries, I have the clearest recollection of the presence of colour on the Budrum marbles. I particularly recollect a faint and delicate red colour inside the mouth, and on the tongue of one of the lions.

Believe me, yours truly,

S. BIRCH.

No. 3, from W. S. W. Vaux, Esq., Keeper of the Coins and Medals, British Museum.

British Museum, Nov. 4, 1864.

MY DEAR NEWTON,—In reply to your query, I beg leave to state that I was present when nearly all your antiquities from Halicarnassus were unpacked in 1857 and 1858, and that I distinctly remember observing colour on—1. The tongue of one of the lions, which was red. 2. On (I think) part of the thigh of another lion, which was reddish-brown, or tawny. 3. On folds of the drapery of the large mutilated seated figure (Zeus?), which was of a purple hue. I believe there were other instances, which, like these, are now almost wholly lost. That the above were visible *when they arrived in this country* I can swear.

Ever sincerely yours,

W. S. W. VAUX.

Mr. Westmacott further remarks that it is not a little singular that the colour observed by me on the architectural marbles on their first discovery should be still visible, while that on the sculptures should have so completely disappeared. This is an unfortunate argument, for, as it happens, one of the most perfect specimens of blue colour was to be seen on the soffit of the lacunar stone engraved in my History of Discoveries, &c. pl. xxvii. fig. 8, when it was first disinterred. Not a vestige of colour now remains on this marble, and nearly on all the larger architectural marbles the colour once visible has equally disappeared.

It is true that on some of the small mouldings blue and red pigments may still be seen; but these have been preserved only because they have been protected from the atmosphere by being kept in a glass case since their arrival at the Museum, instead of being openly exhibited, as the sculptures have been.

By the aid of a solution of wax, alcohol, and turpentine, I have succeeded in partially preserving the colours on some of the sculptures from Cyrene. Time will show whether this preparation will continue to resist the influence of the London atmosphere. I take this opportunity of pointing out another error in the same work of Professor Westmacott, for which, as it stands in his text, I appear to be responsible. He states, p. 104, that the name of the sculptor Terpsikles occurs on one of the seated figures from Branchidæ, citing my History of Discoveries, &c., as his authority, but without giving the page. Had he referred to the work which he thus loosely quotes, he would have seen that the name Terpsikles does not occur on one of the seated figures, but on a stone, of which all that can be affirmed is that it is the base of a work of art of some kind. See my History of Discoveries, ii. p. 538 and p. 782.

[53] See my History of Discoveries, &c. ii. p. 55.

[54] Ibid. ii. p. 52 and p. 271.

[55] Ross, Reisen, iv. p. 37, places the fountain Salmacis a little to the west of the konak of Salik Bey. (See his plan of Budrum, ibid. p. 39.) Admitting that a fountain exists there, though I

certainly failed to discover it, it is obviously too far from the right
horn of the city to be the fountain meant by Vitruvius.

[55] History of Discoveries, ii. p. 11 and pp. 675-6.

[57] Ibid. i. pl. 73.

[58] Ibid. ii. p. 784.

[59] Ibid. ii. pp. 785-6.

[60] Ibid. pp. 550-1.

[61] Ibid. pp. 547-8. Cf. A. Kirchhoff, Studien zur Geschichte
d. Griech. Alphabets, in the Abhandl. d. k. Akad. d. Wissensch.
zu Berlin, 1863, p. 133.

[62] See my History of Discoveries, ii. p. 775.

[63] K. H. Brunn, Geschichte d. Griech. Künstler, ii. p. 383.

[64] Strabo, xiv. p. 634. K. F. Hermann, Lehrbuch d. Gottes d.
Alterthümer, § 19, 18. So in the monasteries of Zambika and
Kremastò, in Rhodes, lodgings are provided for those who attend
the *panegyris*. (See *ante*, i. p. 184.)

[65] Antiquities of Ionia, pt. iii. pll. 22-3.

[66] See my History of Discoveries, i. pl. 57.

[67] Ibid. ii. 719-45.

[68] Ibid. i. pll. 59-60.

[69] Ibid. i. pl. 56.

[70] Pausanias, ii. 35, § 4.

[71] History of Discoveries, i. pl. 84, fig. 5.

[72] Ibid. i. pl. 84, figg. 2, 4, ii. p. 714.

[73] Ibid. ii. pp. 414-26.

[74] Tacitus, Ann. iv. 55.

[75] Pliny, N.H. xxxvii. 5, § 17.

[76] History of Discoveries, ii. p. 487.

[77] Casts of the head and hind-quarter of this lion are now in the
British Museum.

[78] See my Hist. of Discoveries, &c. ii. p. 781.

[79] Antiquities of Ionia, published by Dilett. Soc. iii. p. 22.

[80] See my Hist. of Discoveries, ii. p. 766.

[81] Ibid. p. 745.

[82] Ibid. p. 749.

[83] Ibid. p. 771.

[84] Ibid. i. pll. 54 and 72.

[85] Ibid. pl. 72.

[86] Ibid. i. pl. 68.

[87] Ibid. ii. p. 757.

[88] See my Hist. of Discoveries, ii. p. 765.

[89] Ibid. p. 771.

[90] Ibid. i. pl. 70.

[91] Juvenal, vi. 501.

[92] See my Hist. of Discoveries, i. pll. 69–71.

[93] Ibid. ii. pp. 758–65.

[94] Ibid. pp. 354, 360.

[95] Ibid. p. 747.

[96] Ibid. p. 756 and 768.

[97] Dennis, Cities of Etruria, i. p. 85.

[98] See my Hist. of Discoveries, ii. p. 769.

[99] Longus, Pastoral. i. 13.

THE END.

COX AND WYMAN, PRINTERS, GREAT QUEEN STREET, LONDON, W.C.

www.ingramcontent.com/pod-product-compliance
Lightning Source LLC
Chambersburg PA
CBHW031338070726
47496CB00017B/1272